Louette Harding

Louette Harding is a journalist as well as a writer. She is married and lives with her husband and their daughter in a 17th century thatched cottage in Cambridgeshire. Her previous novel, TWO INTO ONE, is also available from Coronet.

Also by Louette Harding

Two Into One

Women Like Us

Louette Harding

CORONET BOOKS
Hodder and Stoughton

First published in 1997 by Hodder and Stoughton
A division of Hodder Headline PLC
A Coronet paperback

10 9 8 7 6 5 4 3 2 1

A CIP catalogue record for this title is available from
the British Library.

ISBN 0 340 65448 1

Printed and bound in Great Britain by
Mackays of Chatham PLC, Chatham, Kent

Hodder and Stoughton
A division of Hodder Headline PLC
338 Euston Road
London NW1 3BH

For my family

Acknowledgements

I would like to thank all at Willers Mill Wildlife Park in Shepreth, Cambs., for their expert advice; Geoff Wilkinson, who took my jacket photograph; Alexander Carter-Silk, who advised on certain legal queries; and Frank Townsend of Savills.

Chapter One

Shortly after my fortieth birthday last year, I made a resolution. I would stop living in a childish world of daydreams and flights of fancy. I would engage more with the real world. I would be more . . . *pro-active* . . . that was the word. I would grow up.

I had worn my hair on my shoulders for some years, it had retreated to that length from the long fall of my youth, but I had never before summoned the courage to cut it short. But now I went to see Maçon – Maçon of the crew cut and three gold earrings – at the black-and-silver painted salon.

'Chop it off,' I ordered breezily. 'Do what you like.'

You would have thought it a hairdresser's dream command, but he stood, holding aloft a hank, grinning nervously at my reflection. 'Are you sure?' he said.

'Go for it.'

An hour and a half later, a brisk, efficient Eleanor, with a modish crop, stared coolly at me from the mirror; I was a new woman.

This new Eleanor Banyer, PR executive, a woman who was going to replace her hatchback with one of those slinky-backed sports cars any week now, this Eleanor needed some new clothes, so she stopped at the classy boutique on the way home. Here, she tried on and bought a navy pin-striped trouser suit and a white cotton body, which was wonderful quality apart from the press studs being inconveniently sewn nearer to the back than the front. Oh, well, on balance I could get by, str-etch the back flap when I was fastening it so that it popped together properly.

At home, I rushed up to the bedroom and tried the outfit on once more. My husband, Michael, arrived home from a game of squash. I saw him, still in shorts, extricate his rangy legs from my car, which he had borrowed.

'Michael, Michael! Wait there!' I shouted down to his key-jangling, post-sorting presence in the hall. 'What do you think?'

I emerged, with a showgirl's flourish, at the head of the stairs.

'Oh, my good Gawd!' he said. Sweat stained the front of his T-shirt and gleamed on his cheekbones. 'You've cut your hair. Er, it looks all right. When you get used to it . . .' He pulled his lips into a straight line, which was supposed to be of approval, and nodded.

I went back to our bedroom and regarded my shorn head in the mirror. The little cushion which had appeared below my chin was cruelly undisguised. Oh! to have a chin like Audrey Hepburn's. Oh! to own a ballerina neck.

Five minutes later, when my daughter, Miriam, appeared in the doorway, she found me, in tights and white body only, bourrée-ing across the carpet in front of the closet mirrors, arms flapping like a swan's.

'Mum?' she said. She launched herself from the door and hurled herself upon the bed which soughed woefully. 'Who're you being now?' she said, voice muffled in the pillow. 'Darcey Bussell?'

'Huh! Not even in my dreams. I was thinking more . . . Margot Fonteyn.'

'She's dead,' said the voice growing clearer as she rolled onto her back.

'I know.' And at that moment the poppers on the body burst open, so that a tail flap swung, inelegantly, from my bum.

My boss Nicola says that the world is divided into two types of women; those who put their children first, and those who put their husbands first. It was only some months after she declared her theory to me that I realised that her planet, apparently, contains no women who put themselves first.

According to Nicola, if the house went up in flames the average woman would rush to rescue her children, but leave her husband to shift for himself, to burn to a crisp if he didn't wake in time. Well, of course, I thought, and as I did so I found myself identifying Michael on the mortuary slab, skin turned to soot, reminding me of . . . of the burgers he insisted on cooking on the barbeque in summer, blackened crust of an exoskeleton encasing a raw core that leaked fluid and blood . . .

'El,' said Nicola, and snapped her fingers sharply by my eye.

I jumped. 'How do you do that?' I said. 'I can never do that.'

It was an ordinary day, sulky and indolent as a teenager, and, feeling in need of external gaiety, I had persuaded my colleagues to go to the Italian for a girly lunch. The four of us manoeuvred our coats and bags onto the backs of the bentwood chairs, wrestled with the laminated menu cards – unwieldy things, the size of tea trays – and anticipated our ninety minutes of expenses-paid leisure. We were proficient women, each of us holding a senior position in the public relations company for which we work, but together we were capable of being monumentally silly. We looked forward to the opportunity, the chance to shed our outer efficiency. Exfoliate. Exfoliate. Slough off the tired cells of execu-woman.

'Right,' Nicola had said. 'The truth game. The house is on fire, you can rescue just one person or object from the conflagration. El. You first.'

And I had been swept away. And I had chosen Miriam, my daughter. And thereby I had exposed something I did not want to think about just then, namely, the state of my eighteen-year-old marriage. That morning, somewhere between Archway and Kentish Town on the tube, I had decided to divorce Michael. I was fed up with being taken for granted.

Outside, the traffic nosed grumpily past the zebra crossing, negotiating the one-way system. The sky was as heavy as a forty-year-old woman's spirits. The city's coating of damp grit dulled the plate glass of the restaurant front, smeared the

3

asphalt, fell silently, unnoticed, onto the white collars of the workers hurrying by. A little girl in a shocking pink anorak, hood up against the wind, skipped past, her mother or her nanny tailing her. Alone of all the people in the street scene framed by the window, she looked happy. She was six? Five or six? The best age – not to be, but to live with. Miriam at six was perhaps the most fun she'd ever been . . .

'Most women feel like El.'

'I don't.'

'Oh, you do. Don't pretend. You're an earth mother. You're like one of those ancient goddesses with multiple boobs.'

'Are you having wine?'

'I shouldn't. I've got a heavy afternoon.'

'Multiple boobs! Call yourself a friend?'

'It's better than multiple chins, believe me. White or red?'

'I've discovered this amazing new jaw exercise. Look. You go like this . . . Don't make me laugh . . .'

It wasn't new. It was that one where you try to touch your nose with the tip of your tongue. In my mind's eye, I was young and pretty once more, a teenager walking down a Surrey high street. It was the day that that group of passing lads had ogled me, their heads swivelling, whispering comments, not rudely, but almost reverentially, and one of them, intent on me, had walked into a lamp post. I loved that memory . . .

The others had picked up the threads of their conversation once more. I can't remember who said what, I can only tell you who was there; Nicola, Catherine, Anthea and I, a selection of fortyish women whose attempts to subdue the inclement years owed something to acquired style and, it has to be admitted, a great deal more to material outlay. And although I looked younger than my age – depending on the light – it had been many years since even the most oleaginous waiters had quietly decided, as if by herd instinct, that I was now a 'madam', no longer a 'miss'.

I had looked in the staff loo mirror, under the neon strip, mid-morning.

Catherine was embarking on a rather predictable rationale for Princess Di's and Fergie's relative popularity as explained by their perceived maternal urges. I tried to imagine someone not feeling about their child as I feel about mine. The notion seemed preposterous. From my first inkling of Miriam's existence, the magic had infected me. I had crept back to the bathroom at intervals, before the required half hour was up, as if I could hurry happiness, or will it into being. It seemed bizarre, in a way, that my future could be changed, molecules shifting as in alchemy, by a test tube balanced in the plastic packaging of a pregnancy kit.

A dark ring meant positive. A round O. A bare symbol to up-end my life. I saw it forming. *It is, it is . . . No, it's not . . . Yes, it is. It is.* I rang Michael. I was a mother.

'I'm a Dad,' he whooped, as he waltzed down the hospital corridor on the night, almost fifteen years ago, when she was born. I saw him as he was then, a tall man, with an abundance of dark hair, wearing threadbare cords from which were leaking the clutch of 10p coins he'd stored for 'phoning the families. He got through to my mother and lo! she materialised by my hospital bed two days later, wearing a pale coral moue of irritation: she was a grandmother.

'Do you think I need an eye lift?' she asked, retouching her lipstick in the mirror of an Estée Lauder compact. 'Naughty crow's feet?' she queried.

I regarded her; her hair an improbable ash-blonde, blow-dried upon her shoulders, brown eye shadow ringing blue irises, the powder collecting in the fine lines, as you might expect of a woman of her age. She was then in her early fifties but was – there is no other phrase for it – well preserved. She was going to have the eye lift anyway, but she wanted me to say no.

'Yes,' I said. 'I think it's a good idea.'

Most friends and relatives who visited in those early days realised how momentous this birth was. Relatives from the provinces sent floral arrangements in cutesy pink teddy bear vases; London friends brought fashion-victim baby-gros. But Phyllida, Michael's eldest sister, came bearing books, deposited a burdensome pile of them in my lap. They had titles like *You*

Can Make Your Baby Brighter. The You was outsized compared to the rest of the type, just in case you missed the message. I browsed through them, between the routine of feeds and nappy changes and hospital meal-times (why is having a baby such a mushy process? Your food, their food, their yellow nappies?). It was made absolutely plain to me that if Miriam was going to enjoy 'a head start in life', a lot depended on her mother.

Phyllida's books were like Phyllida: selflessly busy-bodying. I closed the covers and packed them at the bottom of my case. When I went home, I debated what to do but I guessed that if I threw them out, Sod's law was that Phyllida would want them back – perhaps to lend to some other expectant mother she was taking in hand. So they nosed their way onto my shelves, like an unwelcome guest – like Phyllida herself

A few months after the birth, a neighbour from my antenatal class came for coffee, bringing her baby and her toddler. She cast her eye around the room, at the Heal's sofa (an arm-and-a-leg job), at the kelim, at Michael's collection of striking modern art and sculpture.

'Don't you have safety caps for your electrical sockets?' she said.

Well, I had some, but not enough, it seemed. I did not have a lock on the cupboard under the sink where we kept the household cleaners either. I had a baby gate on the stairs, though, and the medicines were stored out of reach. Miriam was only four months, she could barely sit up without subsiding, five minutes later, like an amorphous blob from a sci-fi movie.

'Tut, tut, tut,' said neighbour-mother's thoughts, which mysteriously had become visible. 'You're not up to much as a mother, are you?'

I asked the health visitor about it when I went to the clinic for one or other of the tests. 'Well, it would be sensible but you shouldn't be made to feel guilty,' she replied, smoothly. 'I had a mother last year whose child drank some household fluid,' she added.

Household fluid! I was racked with guilt. At home, I dived

into one of Phyllida's tomes entitled *The Wise Mother*. I learned of unimagined dangers, of a host of missed opportunities which trailed me, like a sad-eyed chorus, around the house for the next few hours. Already I had let Miriam down. I should have conveyed information to her *in utero*, playing songs and talking to my bump, which would have provided early instruction in 'verbal communication'. My diet during pregnancy, so imperative to her future health, had probably been lacking in potassium. My moods had affected her future temperament. I remembered hurling the cast-iron cauldron at Michael the night he had insisted on making me a cottage cheese salad for dinner, when what I had craved was a hamburger and chips. There was still a deep crack in the ceramic tiles of the kitchen floor, commemorating my hormones.

I was not too late, the magazine informed me. I should stick postcards of the old masters around her crib. (Which ones? Rembrandt, perhaps. Monet would be too predictable. And imagine the psychological effects of exposure to Bosch from the cradle.) When I jiggled her on my knee I should count each bounce aloud – ah-one an' two an' three an' four – and in this way she would gain her first experience of rudimentary arithmetic.

Neighbour-mother took several weeks to invite us for the return coffee. She showed us through to the kitchen. A card was stuck to the door by two strips of Sellotape; 'door', it said, the letters clear and simple in black felt pen. There was another on the stripped pine rocking chair on which I sat; 'chair'. Indeed, a whole flotilla floated over the cupboards – 'cupboard', – onto the table – 'table', and through into the sitting room – 'drawing room'.

This, I gathered, was the latest advance in teaching your toddler to read.

I was so amazed I tried to tell Michael about it that night, when he came home late, climbed into bed and began to fondle my left breast. He was intent on his conjugal rights. The bed rocked. The mattress pulsed.

'Ah-one an' two an' three an' four,' said the voice in my head.

7

* * *

Throughout the years, there were plenty of those horrid, free-fall, lurching moments when it felt as if every other woman was headed down a different path and I, stubborn, or merely lackadaisical, was not taking my maternal obligations seriously. There had been a little boy at Miriam's primary school; William was his name. He was rumoured to be a genius. It was said that the headmaster played chess with him every Friday lunch hour, until he tired of being beaten by a five year old. I turned to look at the prodigy one afternoon, when I had escaped work early to meet Miriam at the school gates – such a treat that was to me.

Jocasta Roberts saw me looking. 'He was hot-housed, you know,' she said, her voice pitched low with scorn. 'He's just a manufactured intelligence.'

It was the ultimate insult. But Jocasta was one to speak. Her two were already being taught the 'cello and the flute by a special far Eastern – or was it mid-European? – method. Their birthday party invitations were actually printed with the legend: 'Books and educational toys only'. When I took Miriam to one party, Jocasta met me at the gate, hurriedly informing me, 'We've only got good old-fashioned games. The old ones are the best. Did you know that pin the tail on the donkey improves hand-eye coordination?'

It was Jocasta and Theo, come to think of it, who had been so competitive at the PTA quiz night, that time. Smiling amiably, the parents had shuffled into the hall, tossing self-effacing comments across the tables. Ah, but you should have seen the gleam of combat in certain eyes when the competition began, heads bent over scraps of paper, digging out general knowledge from the dustiest recesses of memory. Jocasta and Theo had been cock-a-hoop when they'd won. There were sour mutterings from beaten parents about them taking it rather seriously. I heard someone say that their two were swots but not intrinsically bright at all.

And as for us, well, I think we were faintly disgruntled at trailing in a poor sixth in that quiz. It was as if we were publicly exposed as owning a lower IQ than we had assumed;

for if we were mediocre, what did that say for Miriam?

A gale of laughter plonked me down in the present day. I seemed to have missed a twist to the conversation, a not uncommon occurrence. Why was it that my colleagues did not seem to be afflicted with minds that wandered, that swooped off on private trajectories and dumped them down, several minutes later, at a later stage in a discussion? Their eyes always seemed to be in focus; their minds in gear. I am sure Nicola, for one, put my absences down to a kind of gormlessness. But not Anthea, of course. She and I had known each other for donkey's years, since the mutual first day of our first jobs in London. After eighteen months, we had gone our separate ways, but, years later, I had engineered her current post at NML. I had been a guest at her wedding and held her hand throughout her protracted and bloody divorce. In fact, it was of Sean that she was speaking now. I tried to tune back in, unobtrusively.

Nicola had ordered a large plate of *pasta primavera* which she was not eating as competently as you might expect of someone in an off-white Jil Sander jacket. She pushed her rocket salad towards me and nodded, hastily scooping a strand of spaghetti from her chin.

'It seems incongruous to me,' Anthea was saying. 'Anthea Booth-Perry. Maybe I should just go back to being Booth? Plain Anthea Booth. Sean's gone back to being Sean Perry. He never suited a hyphen, it just didn't go with him, like some men don't go with suits, or others don't look right in jeans. But I seem to be lumbered with the double-barrel, because that's what the children are called, of course. It's a shame they don't arrange all this for you when you divorce. Imagine if I married again! I could end up with three surnames. Anthea Booth-Perry-Smith! Or what if my husband had welded his ex-wife's name to his, as well. I'd have four surnames! Anthea Booth-Perry-Smith-Mumbo-Jumbo!' she snickered and blew at the blonde corkscrews of her fringe. 'Oh, I just don't know what to do!'

'What happened at Mayerling?' I asked her. The idea of

remarriage had surfaced recently, because she was lonely, and had therefore begun to reconstruct a metropolitan social life.

'Ben took me. He's an old friend,' she explained to the others.

'Friend-friend?'

'Uh huh. Totally platonic. But I was prepared to overlook it. It's been fourteen months, two days, three hours and twenty-two minutes since I last got laid. But he wouldn't stay. Beetled off into the dark night, the sod. Now, that wouldn't have happened ten years ago, would it? It set me thinking: whatever happened to the friendly fuck?'

We exploded. Nicola had a coughing fit from mixing her nasal snigger with red wine. I applied my napkin, dipped in mineral water, to the Jil Sander jacket. Crouched forward, one knee on the chair seat, I heard a ricocheting noise as my poppers burst open once more.

I had forgotten about divorcing Michael by the time I got home, plodding up the street and round the bend, the identical Victorian terraces now clothing themselves in their distinguishing greenery, Jocasta's wisteria and *fatsia japonica*, the Wilsons' variegated ivy, our rowan tree,

Michael was already sitting at the kitchen table, had been there for some time, judging by the nearly empty bottle of cheapish Californian red in front of him.

'Pig of a day,' he said.

'Mmm hmm.' I treated his statement as a question.

I opened the fridge door and noted half a loaf of sliced white, a packet of garlic sausage that was just past its sell-by date, and a pack of crudités. There were chops in the chill compartment and three baking potatoes in the basket, wrinkled, the topmost with a pair of soft white shoots sprouting, like two obscene grubs. I sliced them off with my thumbnail and they fell onto the counter, dead.

'They laid off Jim and Barbara.'

I placed the chops on the grill pan, opened the crudité packet, slid it towards him, all this before I registered what he'd told me. I felt bad about that, though I knew he forgave me on the drawing of a breath, his irritation inhaled and exhaled, because after all these years he had acquired this husbandly attribute. He did not expect so much of me any more; I was permitted my daily, my hourly, failures.

'You thought they would.'

'Mystic Michael and his accurate predictions,' he said with a melancholy smile. There were light grey streaks amid his dark hair, soft lines pencilled around weary eyes. He looked what he was, a kind and decent person, frayed after forty-one years of everyday living, eighteen of them spent married to me, who proposed to him on a train station in central London. Those were the days when we coupled like rabbits . . . I pushed the mind pictures away.

Miriam walked in. 'Hi-ya,' she said. She peered through the oven door at the chops, wrinkling her nose and muttering 'Blug!' – but quietly – switched the kettle on without checking the water level, and pounced on a celery stick.

'I had a brilliant day,' she announced, lounging with her back against the kitchen units. 'We had dance and drama and there's going to be a *Stars In Their Eyes*-style competition. Oh, and you know my history of art project? I got A plus.'

She paused for our congratulations.

'Oh, well done,' I said, diving for the kettle which was sending out asthmatic distress signals. I tried to fill it without the finicky business of taking off the lid but the stream of tap water caught on the spout and planed outwards, spraying everything within a three-foot radius, including Miriam.

'Mum!' She examined her denim back dubiously. She looked faintly put out – and not just at my clumsiness. Normally, when she made her entry in the evenings she was greeted by the full beam of parental concentration. There was no triumph so small that it did not deserve praise, no disappointment so trivial it escaped condolence. This little figure, small, bony, with imp's features beneath layers of dark, wayward hair, incongruously dressed in man-sized sweatshirts, tight leggings and galumphing, aggressive boots, cheered us by her presence.

'Jim and Barbara have been made redundant,' Michael explained, also perceiving her faint indignation.

'Oh.' She was tongue-tied, of course. She picked up another stick of celery and methodically peeled the veins from its back, two by two. 'Poor them. Are you upset?'

'Well, I am a bit. I've worked with them for a long time.'

'But you're not for the chop, are you, Dad?'

'I don't think so.'

'Oh, good, I need dual income parents to maintain me in the necessary style.' She ruffled his hair and clomped out.

I pulled up a kitchen chair and sat down opposite him. We were both smiling a little now.

'What it is to be young,' I said, pouring myself some wine, though I didn't really fancy it. A heaviness had settled in my temples and stomach after the lunchtime glass. 'You aren't worried, are you?' I wanted reassurance, too.

'No, not at the moment.' He stretched his hand out for the bottle and emptied the corky dregs into his glass. Drinking so heavily was most unlike him. We both knew there was a 'but' that followed his answer.

Jim and Barbara, alongside whom he had worked for the better part of a decade at the food technology laboratories, were older, sleepier, unwilling to adapt to the working practices of the moment. Barbara wore voluminous frocks in floral-sprigged cotton and her fading hair in a coiled plait. Her hobby was needlepoint. It was as if, despite her scientific background, she was unable to cope with the brashness of life in the final years of the twentieth century. She left at 5.30 promptly every evening, as did Jim, to catch the train. Michael watched them while he oversaw the team's research, which was into the effects on animal physiology of accumulating residues of antibiotics, fertilisers and insecticides.

Michael was not so remote from reality. We had discussed it at home. We had even adopted the jargon. The department, we knew, was ripe for 'downsizing'. Those who survived would be particularly talented, hard working, or cheap. He had taken Jim and Barbara aside and tried to warn them,

'I'm not going to change the habits of a lifetime now,' Jim told him.

And Barbara had added, 'But Mikey, they won't sack me. I've

been here too long. Part of the fixtures and fittings.'

Kay, who normally worked at the bench between the two of them, had been especially unsettled today. She'd said it felt as though the angel of death had passed over Egypt and she'd just discovered she was an Israelite.

They were all scanning the skies now. They felt they must justify the mercy shown them, and they would do this by working harder still, covering for the personnel who had caught the 6.15 for the last time that evening.

Michael blew a stream of air across the neck of the wine bottle, which reverberated to a mournful note. The mortgage and the school fees and all the accumulating residues of middle-class life seemed hard bought to him tonight; of that I was sure.

That evening there was a drug awareness lecture at Miriam's school. I had pencilled a tick on the box on the photocopied slip she had brought home, so I was committed. They were the sort of school which marked off the names of attending parents as they arrived. I was a few minutes late and slipped into a seat at the back, one of those hard wooden seats with a bar that pressed against a nodule in the centre of my spine.

There was an amazing array of mundane household substances arranged on the dais at the front, which an eager man in a sludgy pullover and faded jeans talked us through. There seemed no end to the liquids an inane child might sniff or drink.

The pullover had moved to a large white board. 'Let's chalk up the names of some drugs,' he said. It was going to be one of those audience participation lectures.

A hand went up. 'Alcohol,' said a woman whom I recognised as the mother of a girl in Miriam's class. The pullover wrote it up.

'Nicotine,' said a male voice. Another squeak of the felt tip. Plainly, we were going to pussyfoot around naming the legal stimulants first, as if we were too innocent to have even registered the names of narcotics. Where had we all been in our youth? Seemingly none of the room had inhaled.

13

'Grass,' said a bold male voice at the front. It was the chap I'd always thought must be an advertising executive, for no better reason than that he wore lurid bow ties, and his grey hair in a ponytail.

Cocaine, Crack, Heroin, E, LSD; the names were coming thick and fast now. People had stopped pretending they knew nothing about the subject. Someone asked how you differentiated between the symptoms of drug use and the normal symptoms of adolescence. I slid out of my row. I was tired. I'd just collect some pamphlets and go.

At the back of the hall, I paused and looked around at all the greying heads so earnestly focused in one direction, guessing at their private thoughts. When I got home I slotted the pamphlets into our household files, under miscellaneous. I felt so virtuous for having attended.

On my return I sat in front of the television blindly, conjuring up fancies in my mind like flickering scene changes. I won the lottery, of course, not the jackpot, nothing too improbable, but fifty, no, eighty thousand, enough to make a difference. I saw myself collect the cheque. I had suddenly acquired a flat stomach. Had I had liposuction? Nah, too painful, according to my mother's account. I had exercised. I had joined the gym around the corner from work; I rose at 6.00 every morning to get there in plenty of time before the working day. The me of my dream had a full fridge. The me of my dream acquired telekinetic powers with which to tackle chores, and thereafter she used them to blow away the schoolfriends who had been sarcastic to Miriam last week.

She was slouching in the chair in the corner, cackling at some tacky programme.

'Have you done your homework?' I asked her. Sometimes I feel like her walking check list. 'Have you practised your violin?'

She tsked and even in the flickering half-light I could see her exaggerated sigh.

'Lighten up, Mum.'

Michael yawned and stretched. 'Give her a break, El.'

I looked at her.

'I've done it, OK?' She meant the homework. I knew full well she hadn't played the violin in a fortnight.

On screen, the compère said, 'And if there's one thing that REALLY annoys you about him . . .' The contestant bent double in a stuttering giggle and the audience, sensing an intimate disclosure, began to shriek.

'GO ON! GO ON!' prompted the compère.

The contestant, a blonde girl with hair a bit like Anthea's, was near crying with laughter now. 'It's the way he clamps himself against my leg in the morning,' she gulped. 'He's like a DOG!'

The audience erupted. Miriam snorted, little guffaws of laughter. 'Grim!' she said. In the half-light she flashed a look at me. We were not yet beyond her going pink at references to sex that took place in front of me. And Michael shifted behind his newspaper.

'Hmmm,' I said loftily. But the corner of my mouth was crinkled upwards. Had Miriam not been there, I'd have made a wry remark to Michael. But I was also wondering if I should wield the remote control and remind Miriam about the violin. I didn't want to cast myself as the killjoy but we did shell out £120 a term for her music lessons. At that point the compère said, 'Be right back now,' and his face was replaced by a coffee commercial.

Miriam jumped up. 'Tea?' she said and bowed extravagantly before blundering past my chair to the kitchen, upsetting the magazine balanced on the arm. She reappeared in the doorway a minute later, watching for the second half of the programme while the kettle boiled. There was a shuffling and clapping as she launched into her imitation of the Irish dance show that had swept the West End. Although she had never been taught a step in her life, it was a witty pastiche and looked surprisingly accurate, all shuffling feet and high-stepping knees, that gradually got higher and more abandoned from reckless to galumphing.

'The demented marionette version of *Riverdance*!' Miriam yodelled.

At the end of this display, she stamped a heel forward, held her palms out. 'Yo!' she cried.

There was a staccato puffing of amusement from Michael in his corner.

I smiled too, but all at once I felt sad.

I adored her. The bursts of spontaneous tomfoolery that punctuated her teenaged dignity were so endearing. So why was it that I wanted her to be ever so slightly better than the figure slumped by the television or capering in the hall? All the women like us, like me and Anthea and our ilk: how had we managed to take it all so *seriously*? When had the word 'mother', become a job description?

It was as if a woman's satisfaction lay in the prospect of remaking what she loved. My brother used to take apart the clock or the transistor radio and put it back together again, for no apparent reason – none that I could fathom – except that he thoroughly enjoyed doing it. Our next-door-neighbour-but-one spent satisfying, oily weekends under his rust bucket of a car. And what did I do? I tinkered with people, trying to flush out a trait here, or slip in a quality there. My heroes were improbable men who acquiesced in this process – Mr Darcy, Mr Rochester.

Hah! Many a time I had wished that Michael were as pliable as Mr Darcy! But my husband seemed to be fond of his faults, clinging to them stubbornly.

The blonde's husband loomed on the screen now. A surprisingly nondescript rodent of a man – no chin, his mouse-brown hair slicked back from his forehead – he seemed to be called Mike.

'What would I change about her?' Mike mused. 'Not very much.'

'AAAHH,' sighed the audience.

'Oh, Netty!' exclaimed the compère. 'OH! HO! HO! NETTY! How does that make you FE-EL?'

'Pretty shitty,' Miriam volunteered.

'Miriam!' I said.

'We-ell.'

Anthea had a different problem, it seemed to me. Somewhere

along the line, her worship of her children had taken a different quirk to mine. Last year, the year before? I'd dropped in at her house one evening. Scott, her younger child, then aged seven, launched himself down the stairs towards me.

'GONNA play you the PIANO!' he announced to me, pushing through to the sitting room.

'Scott, no,' Anthea wheedled. 'Later. Ella wants to relax. We want to talk.'

Without warning, he launched himself onto the carpet, and lay face down, keening. 'Oh,' Anthea said. She glanced at me pleadingly. 'One doesn't know what to do, does one? All right. All right. But just a quick tune. Just the Bach. He's terribly keen. He's terribly musical.'

We sat through the Bach and two more of his own tuneless compositions before he was placated.

In my mind, I brought the piano lid down on his fingers.

Once he had left, I looked at Anthea, her tired face, the eyes rimmed in black and pearlised blue. She sighed. 'I'm scared of them not liking me,' she said rather plaintively.

'Oh,' I said. 'Well, you are divorced, it makes it hard.'

'No, it's nothing to do with that,' she replied. 'I was always like that, even when Sean was here. Maybe it's coming to motherhood late that does it; like you're old enough to know what you don't know, like the brash confidence has been bashed out of you.'

Miriam had flicked channels. 'Oh, cool,' she said, at an advertisement for the latest multimedia computer. 'In IT today, me and Kate . . .'

'Kate and I,' I said, but lightly. 'I don't know why we send you to that school.'

'Ah, but what else would we spend our money on?' Michael said from the corner. He always parroted this, and with infuriating good humour, whenever the photostatted letter arrived, informing us of another hike in the school fees. What else would we spend our money on? I could have given him a list of what else, if we had felt we had a choice.

But almost every parent in the street was in the same boat, some throwing more money about than others – up to three thousand pounds a term, some of them paid – and boasted about it, too. Jocasta rolled her eyes to the ceiling and drawled, 'Twenty seven k a year, for the three of them! Thank God for grandparents!'

It seemed to me that our neighbours were forever bragging of property values or clever deals, or how their offspring were 'gifted'. It never used to be like that, did it?

'And how is Miriam getting on?' Jocasta had said to me one evening, years ago, over the New World wine, the Italian food and the Marks and Spencer pudding. We were discussing secondary schools, both of us having reached that stage of child-rearing.

'Oh, Miriam's thick,' I said. 'Thank God. We can dump her in the state comp. with the high rise retards and an easy conscience. We're for the Caribbean this year. How about you?'

It was pleasant to make Jocasta blench.

Unfortunately, I was lying. Miriam wasn't 'gifted' like the rest of the street's children, but she wasn't stupid, either. She inhabited that middle ground in between, an averagely bright child with expectations of an interesting career, which her parents must help her attain. This was how she, too, came to attend the private secondary school with the fees that expanded covertly, like a forty-year-old woman's waistline.

Oh! it was small wonder that we worshipped our children, that we genuflected before their every flicker of usual intelligence. Small wonder that my conscious moments were occupied by Miriam. Small wonder that nightly I left Michael to die in the perpetual flames.

Chapter Two

One Friday in that balmy period when spring blurs its edges with summer, Michael returned at 8.00, which now qualified as early, and sat in his place in the kitchen shelling peas for me. Within a week of the redundancies at the lab, his job had invaded early mornings, evenings, weekends: it was that quick and deft.

I looked at him. He seemed to have turned mute. His eyes were puffy and his skin pale, greyish. He looked as if he'd forgotten to shave that morning. I'd always thought his face included just enough imperfection to save it from bland, knitting pattern handsomeness. His nose is not quite fine enough, his jaw not quite clean-cut enough, his expression not smiley enough; indeed, not smiley at all.

His hands stilled, one holding an empty pea pod, silvery on the inside, lurid green out. He was looking at it but he didn't see it. After a little while, he said, 'Do you ever wonder if it's worth it, El? We've turned out just like our parents and we promised ourselves it was going to be so different.'

He threw the pod on the pile and handed up the colander, favouring me with a belligerent look as if it were all my fault. I dedicated myself to washing the peas and pouring them into a dish ready for the microwave.

A pea lay on the table and after a while he flicked it with his forefinger and thumb towards the goal mouth of an empty carton of crackers. 'Yes! Banyer scores! Yea-hey!'

His fingers drummed a triumphant war dance on the pine. He caught my eye and smiled.

I said, 'Go and watch the football,' and got on with the dinner myself, stabbing the leg of lamb with a lethal paring knife and stuffing the incisions with garlic and rosemary. My industrious silence was punctuated by sporadic yells from Michael, muffled explosions in our sitting room; he would be in a better mood for it. I peeled potatoes, playing the game of my childhood, when, to make the task less boring, I had dreamed myself a gem dealer carving the facets of a pigeon-egg-sized diamond.

On Sunday evening, he said, 'I don't want to go in tomorrow.'

'Take a sicky.'

'Can't. Too much to do.'

'Don't grumble, then.'

He sat on the edge of the bed, peeled off a white sport sock and aimed it at the wicker chair opposite. 'There was a job in one of the scientific journals last week. Up in Norwich. A lot less salary, of course.'

I sat on the sock and gave him my attention. 'Norwich is a long way from Miriam's school,' I said somewhat archly.

'The point, El, is that if we're going to do it, we've got to do it now, before her GCSE courses kick in.'

'What do you mean? If we're going to do it? One minute you're contemplating a sicky, the next you're moving the family to the other end of the earth.'

'You'd like it up there.'

'I would not like it up there. I like cities. I like the grime and the noise and the stink of ambition. How do you know what Norwich is like?'

'I went there once, as a student.'

'Oh, two decades ago, eh? Norwich is a long way from my office, too,' I said.

'Don't you want to simplify? Don't you want to have more time, more quality of life, more . . . everything?'

'No,' I lied. 'I'm happy.'

He looked at me for what seemed a long time. I had said the last thing he had expected. He was trying to work me out. 'I don't believe you, sometimes,' he said, and he rolled into bed.

The next week he clocked up five sixteen-hour days: I suspected him of engineering them deliberately. All the same, I missed him; the rustles from his chair as he browsed the newspapers while I cooked. On the wall above his chair was the pinboard that featured a bright kaleidoscope of family photographs. I liked to watch him, sneakily, while he sat there, glancing up from time to time, from the news reports. And suddenly some Kodachrome image of our past lives would cease to be part of the unnoticeable background and his mouth would twist up at one corner.

There we were at our wedding, in the days when I fancied him something rotten, despite the Regency haircut, and me, looking quite pretty, if too safe, too open: that was the trouble with wide hazel eyes and a square jaw, you were never going to look sleepy-lidded or even gamine, which were the only two looks worth having, in my book.

There we were in the days when we had money to spend on ourselves: once more in Rio de Janeiro on holiday, on Ipanema shore, buying *maté* from the strolling merchants; and in the background, the beach footballers diving and dancing, like pagan gods in incongruous, fluorescent swimming briefs.

Here I was bulbous as a balloon and looking as if I might pop at any moment, pregnant with Miriam. And at the christening, looking thinner, looking as if I had suddenly got the answers to every question I had ever asked, looking, in fact, as I felt.

Thereafter, we rather faded from the parade, and the separate snapshots seemed to merge into a poster which advertised Miriam, her life and accomplishments. A plump preschooler in lurid frills for a ballet competition: in gingham check with her hair in bunches for her first day at school; in blue and white sheets, clutching a pink plastic doll, cast as Mary in the school nativity play.

There were fewer photographs as the years accelerated away, as she refused to pose, or cast us a look and uttered an exasperated exclamation. 'Oh, Dad, per-lease'. Sometimes these moments were captured – the second where she rolled her eyes to the heavens, or placed her fingers into a crucifix-shape and shouted, 'Back, back, you soul-stealing fiend'. For someone who acted so reluctant, she was surprisingly pleased with these images, examining them frequently, giggling to herself.

But now it seemed as if there was no continuation in the pictorial history, Michael was right about that. We were all so occupied, somehow, so that it seemed as if the rest of my life would be spent in the office or by the cooker, or dealing with some niggle of everyday existence, such as battling with Miriam about vegetarianism.

'How can I be sure you'll get nutritionally balanced meals?' I wailed. The mere notion of preparing a separate menu for her gave me the heebie-jeebies.

She saw through me in an instant. 'I'll cook for myself,' she said.

'No,' I said tersely, imagining what repercussions that would have on her homework.

The next evening, while I was reading she draped her arms around my neck.

'No,' I said again.

The arms withdrew; she was wearing that pouty, dead-eyed, injured look she acquired when I had wronged her. No one, I thought, is as good at self-righteous indignation as a teenager.

'Actually, mother,' she said in a high, prim tone, pronouncing every syllable. 'I was going to talk to you about a Saturday job.

'There was this woman, see, called Louise Carrington.' She rushed on, her face gradually relaxing into its normal, expressive countenance and her voice dropping to its normal pitch. 'She gave a talk at school. She runs this small, but really cool animal sanctuary, out in the suburbs. It's at the end of the tube line though, so I could get there and back really easily. And I'd really like to help out, Mum. You know how I really want to be a vet, so it would be good experience for me, wouldn't it?'

'Oh,' I said. A vet, I was thinking, I wonder how a Saturday job would interfere with homework? . . . A vet, well, that's a lucrative, secure career . . . It's very enterprising of her . . . I said no to the vegetarianism and I can't oppose her every wish. And perhaps it was the last notion that swayed me.

'OK,' I said, 'Subject to one of us going to have a look at this sanctuary.'

'Oh, brill, Mum!' She was delighted with me. She pounded off to telephone this Carrington woman, and I returned to the novel she had interrupted, which was by one of my favourite authors but was proving disappointing, an early work that failed to engage me. I gave up.

I hoped Michael would approve of my decision. I felt like a single parent, with no one to bounce these questions off. Then, I reminded myself how lucky we were to be a 'work-rich' family in a competitive global economy, and as I did so I could imagine smooth-skinned Asians, of great beauty and enterprise, in high rise apartments in one of the Pacific rim economies, Singapore perhaps, and I warned myself that the almond-eyed wives of my imagining were not so foolish as to grumble when their husbands worked late.

I fell for Michael the first time I saw him, in a university corridor, making a withering comment to someone who deserved it. It took assurance, I felt, to be rude discriminately. There were not many young men at university who had assurance, most of them were bashful, or adopted poses, or were pleasant lads and, therefore, boring.

I talked to him, all animation, my eyes glittering, at a party; monopolised him really, but I could tell he liked me. I could have devoured him that night, the line of his jaw, the slight prominence of his cheekbone, the way the muscles of his limbs were hard, where mine were soft.

Once we were a couple, accepted as such, we spent tracts of time in bed; we worked, we partied. We scarcely discussed what we wanted of life. The path which took us to number 39, Dryden's Avenue, was the result of deep programming by our parents. A childish fear that mine could read my mind had given way to a more frightening realisation: parents were so powerful that they could insert subliminal messages in your brain.

We left college and we talked about travelling, but somehow it seemed foolhardy to reject the not-to-be-sneezed-at position on offer to Michael. We might return to find he was yesterday's news, despite his 2:1. And if we were staying, we may as well buy a flat, before prices rose again, leaving us beached forever among the flotsam, among those who could not afford to own property. In this haphazard way, we had become who we were, members of the middle classes, as our forefathers were before us, and if we thought our outlook was younger, our dress trendier, our ideas more liberal, there was always Miriam to disavow us.

I remember, during one long vac, we drove to Wales in Michael's do-or-die VW Beetle to see friends of his, a former teacher and his wife, who had left the city, worked heroically in the third world and eventually retired sick, through some monstrous African amoeba lodged in their intestines, to a slate-roofed cottage on a damp and drizzly emerald hill. They owned fifteen acres of the lower slopes, which they had stocked with two yellow-eyed goats, chickens, some matted sheep. A vegetable patch which ran to half an acre or more was bursting at the seams in a vulgar profusion of holey cabbages and flowery herbs. Rows of onions sent up tall, tough stalks topped with spherical flower heads like wonderful satellite towers.

'Talk to me while I work,' Brenda, the wife, commanded me. She was banging elasticky bread dough onto a marble slab with her chapped, red fingers. Michael walked around the smallholding with Reg, his former biology teacher, the mentor who had infected him with the bug to study zoology. I could hear the rise and fall of their easy conversation outside.

'You're a city girl,' said Brenda, with a smile, as she tugged at a falling sleeve with her teeth.

'Oh, I don't know; at the moment, maybe.'

'Your age, I used to love the city,' Brenda said.

'Is it hell here in winter?'

'It's a bugger when the snow comes,' she said. 'An absolute bugger. We've seen half a dozen marriages wear away on this mountain. Utopia has its fair share of burst pipes, and ice on the inside of the windows, and the power going down for days on end. But it's not that that does it. It's the boredom. Round about the second winter, they get bored with each other. You need a bloody good education to do what I do, so you can gaze out of the window while you're washing up and think of Catullus and Lesbia or J Alfred Prufrock.'

Then Michael burst in at the plank door, saying, 'Brenda, what are you feeding us?' and I never got to ask her more.

We stayed in the tiny spare bedroom overnight and made love silently but with our eyes open. We were smiling as I wrapped my legs around his thrust and stab, and I can still recall the beauty of his young man's body.

When we drove away, Michael said to me, 'I really admire Reg. He hasn't done anything he didn't want to do. He's made a difference and now he's absolutely contented, in his corner of a Welsh paradise.'

I hedged my bets. 'A paradise in summer,' I said. 'Apparently it's a bugger when the snow comes.'

But he only stopped the car in a passing point, and gazed over his shoulder at the grey cottage on the green hill, his arm resting on the back of my seat, and I sensed that he was happy, truly, consciously happy, to be with me, in this place, at this time. It was, to him, the perfect spot, the perfect minute, the perfect girl in the front bucket seat of his car.

Miriam was doing her homework on the dining-room table. I perched myself on the chair in the corner, awaiting a lapse in her concentration.

Finally, she said, 'Mum, what to you think of these "e"s?'

I rose and examined the page she held up. She was always changing her handwriting, adding curls and flourishes, or just as suddenly, paring them away. It was as if she were trying on a new personality; does this one suit me? Do I stand out from the crowd? Or – horrors! – am I too different from my peers?

'Miriam, your dad has seen a good job on offer,' I said slowly.

25

'It wouldn't be so pressured for him – which is good – but it would mean us moving.'

'Come again?'

'Out of London.'

'You're kidding,' she said blankly. 'Where out of London?'

'Norwich.'

'Norwich!'

'Well, he's never really liked the city,' I said.

'He's never said anything to me.'

'Well, I suppose he's been too busy just getting on with it. I don't suppose he's thought about it for a long time.'

Miriam put her elbows on the table and pushed her fingers through her dark curls, averting her eyes, looking down at her rough book, at the doodles and the lines which read, again and again, 'This is my new handwriting. Does it suit me?' She poked at an ink blob with her pen nib, gradually gouging a raggedy hole in the page.

'This is unreal,' she finally mumbled. 'Bloody fantastic, isn't it? Parents act as if you're important, like you count, like your homework and your job counts, and then when it suits them . . .'

'Miriam, sweetheart . . .'

'Oh, not you, Mum. You see my point of view. But him!' She was working herself into a paddy. 'I hate him, sometimes. I really do. He's so selfish. Why does he think he comes first? It's not fair.'

Suddenly, she half rose and reached for me in a gawky-graceful gesture, wrapping my arms around her waist and burying her head into my neck. It had been several months since she had sought my embrace and I found myself inhaling her smell, trying to learn by heart her textures, the soft, springy hair, the fine bones under calf-soft skin. 'I like it here, Mum,' said her voice in my shoulder. 'I've got a life, here. I like my school, I like my friends, and I've just sorted out about Louise's.'

'I know,' I said, 'I thought as much. I felt I had to sound you out. Leave it to me. I'll sort it out.' I gave an extravagant sigh, kissed the top of her head and she drew away and poked me in the stomach.

'Mum?' she said, as she returned to her geography. 'It's just the overwork talking. Dad's circuits are blown. His system's overloaded. Take him away for a dirty weekend and he'll be fine again.'

'I don't think you can have a dirty weekend once you're married,' I said. Indeed, I was sure of it.

'You didn't say what you thought of my Greek "e"s,' she called through the door as I made my way to the kitchen.

'Oh. They look great,' I said. 'They really suit you.'

After his A levels, before university, Michael had gone overland to India in a minibus with a group of friends and acquaintances. His anecdotes had left certain pictures in my mind, of a perilous crossing through high passes on the fringes of Afghanistan, something to do with the likelihood of bandits robbing them, or worse. For some reason I particularly remembered what he had told me about Istanbul. On the outward journey, it had seemed to them to be the first truly alien city they had visited, but on the return leg they hailed it, hallooing, as the first outpost of civilisation.

Byzantium! For some reason I pictured them driving down a hill towards the city, and I could envisage its great blue-grey domes and minarets against a bluer sky; I sniffed its spice, heard its street cries, and I tried to convince myself this Asian air was homely. How rich and exciting life must have seemed to Michael, then.

As I considered this teenaged Michael, this boy-man who pre-dated my personal knowledge of him, as I remembered our pilgrimage to Wales, it became clear that his wish to change course had been a long time coming. But that was tough, frankly. He was committed. We were on our conveyer belt. Our daughter, her schooling and her fragile adolescent friendships, most of which would not last a year or two, demanded we remain where we were. Michael's dissatisfaction would dwindle into a mid-life crisis, to be managed and forgotten, a minor blip in the continuing middle-class passage from Silver Cross pram to stripped pine coffin. And yet it might have been different. It might have been a junction at which we

27

chose a different path, and who was to say it would not have proved happier?

The next Saturday, as we were gardening, he put down the shears with which he had been clipping some box hedges – my pride and my joy – and said, 'You love designing gardens, don't you?' Instantly I could read his thoughts, that he had hit upon my Norfolkian occupation, one that would keep me happy and silence my opposition.

'Go marry Vita Sackville-West. Stop trying to turn me into a rural wife,' I said and menaced him with a daisy router

This disarmed him, as I had intended. 'Oh, El.' He subsided onto the teak bench. He looked up at me, all grey eyes and a comic strip of personal memories. 'Doesn't it depress you? The thought that this might be it? You slog on for forty years and then you retire and then you die. This monstrous, monotonous comfort?'

'It beats monotonous poverty,' I said, thinking of my Pacific rim family. Couple, two children, gold-toothed mother-in-law, all sharing the same white-walled flat. They had an electric rice steamer, an American fridge and a wide-screened television . . .

He said, 'I know how ridiculous my restlessness is.'

'No, it's not. I understand it. I really do. But everyone goes through it. It's temporary. The grass may be greener in the verdant countryside but it's not, if you see what I mean. There's a life of drudgery out there in paradise.'

'Of course,' he said.

'And ambition? Promotion?'

'Ah, yes, promotion. As seems likely. I then get to oversee the department's down-sizing, phase two. Who shall I decide is expendable? Kay with her new flat? Or Bob, the empty nester? What a plum job! All that unpleasantness for an extra £2,500 a year. That's,' there was a brief pause, 'a hundred and twenty five pounds extra a month, after the government's had its slice.' He shot me a bitter look, as if I were to blame, and stonked off into the house.

I went back to the ground elder. I was seething. After a while, I calmed down and tried to think about what to do next, but the thoughts just milled around, colliding with each other in my head, and in the end the only conclusion I reached was that the trouble with getting older was that you were more aware of the underlying themes. You turn into one parent and marry the other, so the theory goes, and when you're twenty you think, Huh? Me? Never! But when you're forty, you begin to wonder, Well, is it me playing the victim that's leading to this? Am I becoming my mother? Or, Was I sub-consciously attracted to Michael because of his remote, untouched, broody quality that reminded me of Dad?

But where does that get you? Suspecting these things doesn't advance you any. Personally, I'd like to roast Sigmund Freud and his kind.

Within a week, Michael had made a good fist of persuading himself he was contented. No, this is not true. The fact is that for the next few days he wore a face like thunder. His conversation withered; he spoke in monosyllables or niggardly phrases, a grudging, judging presence. Stuff him, I thought. In my imagination I made a wax effigy and stuck pins in him.

'What's the matter?' I said, late one night, in an effort to clear the air.

'Nothing,' he said.

There are ways and ways of saying nothing. I knew what this nothing meant.

'For God's sake,' I snapped. 'Just grow up will you? You've been sulking for days.'

'Sulking? Who's sulking? I'm not sulking. I may be depressed. I can't just switch on "joy",' his fingers provided the quotation marks, 'at your command.'

'Oh, show me the subtle difference between sulking and depression, I would be fascinated to see.' I was quite pleased with this retort. 'This is a democracy, Michael. Two out of three members of this family are in agreement on this.'

He did not apologise (typical) but the next morning began making a heroic effort. I found him in the kitchen having made the coffee, helping Miriam with her biology prep, a picture of patience.

'Dad's really brill, sometimes,' Miriam said to me after he'd left.

There was a something in her tone that sounded a little smug, as if she suspected that, unlike her, I was incapable of fully appreciating his good points.

On Saturday morning, returning from Sainsbury's, I found them in the garden together; he reclining on the steamer chair with a beer in one hand, she perched on the edge, chatting to him animatedly. As I watched, she reached forward and patted him on the head, her smile fond.

I passed them on my way to the shed carrying an unwieldy stack of cardboard boxes. I said to myself, 'That's right. Bond away. Blame the messenger,' because it seemed to me that my intervention had been so selfless that it had allowed each of them to see me as the cause of their 'misunderstanding'. (I mentally provided the quotation marks.) I had rubbed out his blunders and been diminished in the process, like an eraser.

I slammed the kitchen door. From the corner of an eye, I caught them exchanging glances. They appeared directly to put away the groceries.

'Go and sit down, mother,' Miriam said, folding in an extravagant bow, wrist circling, finger pointing to indicate the back door and the lawn beyond.

That was it, I said to myself I was irritated at how little help I got around here. But that wasn't it: I just pretended.

When I had replaced Michael in the steamer and he had brought me a rather sickly elderflower cordial drink to which I had succumbed in the supermarket, when I had registered the sun dodging between high, friendly clouds, I was calmer. I asked them if they had any suggestions for a catchy title for a new rural magazine which a client of ours, a growing periodical publishers, was launching.

'Hamlet?' Michael suggested, and he and Miriam folded with laughter.

Later, she consulted him about her earth science homework. I heard them discussing the pros and cons of the Newbury Bypass. They both expressed a wish to become eco-warriors and I had an image of them, swinging through the treetops on liana-like ropes, their faces painted blue with woad.

I heard her say, 'Beats Norfolk, Dad. I'd be up for that one.'

He said, 'I don't think your mother would like to leave her home comforts, bean bag.'

There was a beat of my heart, it swelled, contracted and the blood was forced through narrow tubes; I could envisage this. I was almost, but not quite, conscious of the choices open to me. My first reaction was to explode with indignation at his portrayal of me as the family killjoy. Or I might reinstate myself in the family triangle.

'Too damn right,' I called through the French windows.

'You could visit, Mum,' Miriam called back. 'At weekends. You could bring us food parcels. Collect our dirty washing.'

I put my head around the billowing curtain, wagged my finger at her. 'Uh-huh.'

'Ooo 'eck,' she said.

All was good humour once more. We tidied away Michael's mid-life dream, Miriam's teenaged selfishness, my immature stabs of possessiveness, beneath family play. And I daresay they would have remained tidied away, had it not been for bad timing.

On Monday, shortly after I arrived in the office, there came a series of three phone calls, the first from my mother, in a tizz.

'I'm so upset, Eleanor,' she said. 'I'm allergic to fruit acids. New cream, cost a fortune, and my skin's come up in bumps. I'm all red, like a navvy. You really don't expect it, do you? You'd think they'd test these things out, wouldn't you? Have you tried them? Are you allergic? You just be careful. You may have inherited the allergy from me.

'And as if that wasn't enough, someone's stolen our fastigiate yew. Can you believe it.? Woke up Sunday morning, looked out of the window and thought, something's different. Then I realised. There was a big hole where it had been, pile of earth. I telephoned the police but they could scarcely stop sniggering. It may be small potatoes to them but there's no reason to act like that. Anyway, what do they do but sit on the bypass all day and try to catch poor motorists . . .' (My mother had been stopped and cautioned for speeding three months previously.) 'When are you coming down to see us? You never come. How's the family? Everyone all right . . . ?'

When my father came on the phone, I said, 'Must have been someone who gets up early. Have you got a horticultural milkman?'

'We don't have a milkman anymore,' he replied. 'We buy our milk from the supermarket. Virtually fat free.' His voice lingered in disgust at the words. 'May as well pour water on your cereal.'

At about 11.00, Anthea appeared in my doorway, emitting a comical aargh! of rage through bared teeth. I dropped my pencil on my pad. She prowled my linoleum floor, blonde hair bobbing down her back, each pale corkscrew indignant – a hairstyle too young for her face, her ex had once acidly described it, though previously he had crooned about pre-Raphaelite curls.

'I hate him,' she told me. 'You won't believe this,' she said, sounding like my mother. 'He called to say he wants to change this weekend's arrangements. It's been fixed for months. He insisted on it. He wanted to take the kids to see *his* mother for *her* birthday. Now, he wants to change the day to Sunday. I ask you! He's doing it to spite me, isn't he?'

I screwed my face into an expression of sympathy.

'He knew I was going out, didn't he? He deduced that I'd fix up to go out on Saturday evening . . .' She sat down on my visitors' chair and looked at me over the horn-rimmed glasses she wore for reading, which gave her tired, mutton-as-lamb face a scholarly air. 'Where did I go wrong?' she asked me plaintively. 'You're happily married. Tell me the secret.'

'Huh! Happily? I suppose so,' I snorted.

Anthea looked prim and rather shocked, and I suppose she had a point. It was a mystery to me why some couples stayed together and some didn't; look at my parents, look at her. Having observed both partnerships – one, I admit, much more closely and for much longer than the other – I could only conclude that there wasn't much difference between the two, if you were measuring for levels of contentment or rancour.

Why were Michael and I jogging on, and would we continue to? It didn't seem to me to be anything you could count on as firm and unequivocal. In fact, when you got right down to it, if you asked any woman if she was happily married, she might say 'No,' one week and 'Yes,' another, depending. Because there are some days when you begin to contemplae a life without him – the bachelor girl flat, the freedom from his dirty socks and underpants, his skid marks in the loo – and there are other days that bring back to you the reasons why you married him in the first place. Women, I think, should be more honest about these things. Scrunch the happy-ever-after. Marriage is one-day-at-a-time stuff, as perilous as an addict staying clean.

She went back to her room when my phone started ringing. It was Michael.

'Oh, hi,' I said, somewhat coldly. 'We've had some dramas here this morning.'

But he didn't ask the invited question. 'I just had my mother on the phone,' he said.

'My father's got liver cancer. He's got six months to live.'

There was a gap, the pause, the shock, the readjustment.

'Oh, shit. Oh, Michael. I'm sorry,' and I added, 'Are you sure?'

For days, I berated myself for the crassness of that question, but I know that Michael did not: I know he knew I just wanted to make it better.

It's funny how a day can change like that. How a day that had seemed so routine, indistinguishable from the others, like round beads on a thread, will take on a dreadful significance in a matter of seconds, in the saying of a few words. You know you will never forget that date, that the next time it comes around, the next time you flip the page of the kitchen calendar and see May 13, in bold, black letters, your heart will tighten. Unlucky May the thirteenth. That was the day Michael heard his father was dying.

Michael's parents were decent sort of people. Richard and Ann Banyer lived in a corner of Sussex which was, in many ways, similar to the area in which I had grown up, for it was an enclave of the English middle classes. Sussex, though, is slightly better mannered than Surrey, for the smart houses snuggle into woods, heaths and farms, so that the display of comfort is more discreet.

Richard and Ann owned a smallish Edwardian house, its lower half of red brick, its first floor white rendered with white painted barge boards. It lay along a narrow, pot-holed lane on the other side of which lay the village cricket pitch. So, a pleasant site, but hazardous in the cricket season. In the summer Richard hung nets from the gutters, pegging them on the front lawn, so that the house wore a veil like an Edwardian lady. Nevertheless, it was alarming to sit in their bay window and spot the smudge of red in the sky, speeding towards you. I always ducked. As missiles go, it was a homely one, round and shiny as an apple, but hard enough to break bones, blacken eyes; and that is how life goes, doesn't it? Someone lobs an unknown into your lap and you discover it is not as benign and ordinary as it appears.

For years, Richard worked at a firm in nearby Crawley where he drove everyday in his German saloon car. Ann did not work, not even when her children were half-grown. She occupied herself with do-gooding organisations and was a stalwart of Meals on Wheels and church flower arranging. She re-upholstered her ancient sofas and button-back balloon chairs. She tended pots and hanging baskets that sat on her porch and terrace, a tumble of colour. She grew a vine in her conservatory round the back. These were her pursuits.

There were four children, Michael was the youngest and the only boy. He believes these two facts are related.

'He'll be very spoilt,' a university friend warned me, as I told her of him in the squalid dorm kitchen.

'No,' his mother said, frying mince on her elderly gas cooker, a cooker with legs, during the first weekend I was invited to spend there. 'I don't think he's spoilt. I'd say he's used to being bossed by women.' I rather think she was fooling herself.

Ann might have been formidable; she was direct and somewhat patrician, and there lay in her manner the residue of something like disappointment. Richard had clearly been extremely good looking in his youth; still was. He had provided a comfortable lifestyle for them – two cars, two holidays, certainly – but it was grammar, not private school for the kids and Ann had no opportunities to wear her family emeralds. She took the necklace out of its fading red silk box and held it up to the light, great thick chunks of solidified ocean, deep and mysteriously green. I sank into the bedspread – William Morris's honeysuckle pattern – and watched her. She made me try on the square-cut ring.

'I might as well sell them,' she said sadly. 'We never go anywhere.'

'No, you mustn't,' I said, because it was what she wanted to hear. 'One of the girls may marry well.' And we both began to laugh.

Michael and his sisters were not close and I haven't tried to make amends. At that time, the two eldest, Phyllida and Jane, shared a flat in Guildford and the third, Daisy, was working on a kibbutz. Phyllida I found bossy but it was Jane of whom I was initially wary. She told bare-faced lies, without so much as a flush of conscience. In fact, I think she always believed what she said.

'Oh, I could have gone to university,' she told me the first time we met. 'But at my interview the tutor put his hand on my knee and I realised then how things would turn out.'

'Gosh,' I said.

But afterwards, Michael told me Jane had left school after her O levels and taken a secretarial course.

'But why did she tell me . . . ?'

He shrugged and grew tetchy, as much with me as with her. I didn't push the point.

Jane never lost this awesome mendacity, even when, like Phyllida, she married and became a respectable home counties matron, both of them settling for an approximation of their parents' lives. And I never lost my ability to believe her; whenever we met I would listen to her stories, rapt, with complete faith, brimming with righteous anger on her behalf, or with capering delight at some triumph. Michael disapproved faintly – I think he thought I was encouraging her deliberately

– which was why I learned to keep my distance from her. There was obviously a very thin line between my secret fantasies and her spoken fabrications.

But it was Daisy who emerged as the true black sheep, by settling in Frankfurt and becoming gay almost overnight. Not that this was ever openly stated. No one ever discussed her continuing spinsterhood, nor the female names who entered and exited her letters, forming a sequence that would have seemed wasteful and callous had they been platonic friends.

On that May 13, we picked Miriam up from school and drove straight down to Sussex, the pinhole in the exhaust emitting a low snarl of animalistic pain. Ignoring it, we sped along the motorway, under the silver-grey aeroplanes on their take-off trajectories, as they carried carefree families to gritty beaches and cool pools. Phyllida had told Michael, on the phone, that Ann would want her family there. We turned off through the villages and down through the woods. Flick, flick, flick went the late afternoon sun through the gaps in the trees, like one of those cartoon books, fooling your eyes, making you think it was a mild and kind summery day, a happy day.

The wheels made their nice, friendly, crunching-on-the-loose-chippings sound when Michael turned the Jeep into the lane. The cricket pitch rolled away to our left, a green triangle surrounded by twee houses. An elderly man, much older than Michael's father, was fussing over it with roller and hose. Last house along, red brick, white render, tulips in pots, just as always, except that Phyllida's van of a car, for carrying her three teenaged children and their friends, was parked on the drive. Michael eased the Jeep in beside it, carefully, for there was little space. Those two tank-like cars, the cars of busy adult children, parked there early on a weekday evening, were the only signs to the outside world, to the observant neighbour, that something was amiss in this neat house in this neat street.

We didn't bother knocking. They were in the drawing room. Ann was gazing through the French windows, partly enfolded in the sweep of one of her chintz curtains. There was an air of reverie about her, as if you had stumbled on her alone, daydreaming. Phyllida was perched on the pretty blue silk Victorian chair which stood at a right angle to the fireplace; her two boys and one girl, Lucy, were sprawled upon sofas and rugs. With their unruly hair and unlaced trainers, they seemed to be too big and clumsy for the room, as if they possessed too many sharp elbows and bumpy knees. Richard was in the high-backed wing chair, presenting us with a view of the back of his head, the pink, freckled scalp visible through the combed, silver strands. Then he became aware of us, as Phyllida's expression altered upon catching sight of us in the doorway, and the spaniel hauled itself to its feet, uttering a half-hearted yap.

Richard half rose from his chair.

'Why've you all come rushing down?' he said tetchily. 'I'm not going to kick the bucket tonight, you know.'

'Richard, please.' Ann came forward and kissed us each on the cheek. 'Would you like a cup of tea? Miriam, dear, you must be hungry. What about a sandwich? A slice of French bread pizza?'

'I'm fine, Grandma,' Miriam said, shooting her a look from under her long lashes. She was surprised, and relieved, at this show of normality.

'Well, I *don't* know why,' Richard mumbled. 'Lucky Jane's away or we'd be swamped.' And there was a long pause while he examined the backs of his hands.

Michael, too, looked abashed. He cleared his throat. 'Well, it's a bit early, but, erm, how about the pub, Dad?' he asked.

'Good idea.'

Phyllida's cheeks had turned pink. Michael and Richard left quickly, shouting their goodbyes from the front door. There was a noticeable diffusion of tension amongst those of us remaining. Ann went to make the tea; the children escaped to the garden from where their sporadic bursts of laughter could be heard.

'Giggs? Girly Giggsy?' I heard one of the boys shouting. 'He's absolute unadulterated, overrated crap!'

'Oooh-hoo! Who's jealous?' Miriam's voice replied. 'Who wishes Giggs played for Arsenal!'

'For heaven's sake,' Phyllida exclaimed. 'You'd think they could be more sensitive.'

She was going to remonstrate with them, but Ann, returning with a heavy tray, said, softly, firmly, 'Leave them alone, dear. They're only young,' so that Phyllida's cheeks bloomed red once more.

'I was only trying to help,' she sniffed. 'Trying to get things sorted.'

'What happened, Ann?' I said. 'How long has this been going on?'

She sat on the arm of the wing chair, balancing her cup and saucer, and sighed as she looked back into the past. 'I don't think we could have prevented it, if that's what you mean,' she said softly. And she told us about the early symptoms, her nagging of Richard to see the doctor, how he had ignored her for a while, until the discomfort had taken hold of him and propelled him to the surgery. She told us about tests and retests and the brusque professional manner that a doctor adopts when he has bad news to break. About the special room they take you to; the bad news room. Phyllida began to cry, noisily, her nose running, so I went to the downstairs loo to tear off a couple of strips of bog roll for her.

Miriam and Lucy were singing doggerel words to a monotonous tune and executing an elaborate coordinated dance on the lawn. I saw their slim arms raised and waving, like the corps de ballet in *Swan Lake*. They turned on the spot, took a step forward, a step back. A moth was fluttering by the lighted lamp on the pedestal table, hurling itself upon the translucent shade. The carriage clock chimed sweetly from the mantelshelf. It still surprised me to see my own face peering out from among the framed family snapshots that jostled for space beside it. I always felt like an impostor, someone Ann included for politeness' sake.

While I had tuned out, the conversation took a turn for the commonplace, for safer ground. Phyllida and Ann were chatting about the summer's vicarage fete, which Richard usually helped to organise, planning how to do it for him without his noticing. Their voices floated through the evening gloom like dust motes, circled the sagging sofas with their faded loose covers, landed on the good Wilton carpet, bought forty odd years ago and now about to outlast its purchaser. Life goes on, their voices seemed to say. I suddenly understood Ann's calm very well indeed.

Michael played the game because his father insisted. It was weird, he said to me later; all the pub regulars were greeting and ribbing Richard as if nothing had changed, because, of course, as far as they were concerned, nothing had. None of them knew. And Michael felt at a loss: was he supposed to pretend, too?

'It's not Sunday, is it?' the barmaid said, looking at her watch, because Richard materialised before her between 12.00 and 12.30 on a Sunday only, for two pre-lunch whisky and sodas. Regular as clockwork. That was that.

'Pushing the boat out, are we?' said Roger Falconer. He nudged Michael. 'Make sure he buys his round.'

Richard slapped his wallet on the bar and pointed to it, which sent Roger Falconer away tittering as if at a hilarious skit. While Richard was ordering a whisky and a beer, the vicar bobbed up at his shoulder.

'What brings you down here?' he asked Michael.

Cancer, Michael thought to himself. So bugger off so I can talk to my father, and Richard said quickly, 'Oh, this and that, this and that.'

'Cricket club banged any sixes your way?' the vicar asked.

'Sixes!' Richard snickered. 'They're getting worse. Watched them from a deck chair on Sunday. Went to make a cup of tea and when I came back the entire middle order had got themselves out.' He hunched his shoulders and gave his uncertain grin. 'It's early in the season, so I suppose they've got time to work on it.'

'We must hope and pray,' the vicar said, placing his fingertips together, and he made off in the direction of Roger Falconer. People, I had noticed, never lingered over chitchat with Richard, he was so bad at it, so tongue-tied.

Michael took a deep breath. 'Dad, why have you refused chemotherapy?'

'Hah. Your mother told you, too, did she? Well,' he sighed, 'It would only give me a year or so, don't you see, and it wouldn't be pleasant. Seems a bit pointless, sort of thing. Don't go on about it, will you? Phyllida's been kicking up a fuss.' He examined his whisky, swilling it around the tumbler, as fiery as medicine; and usually it made him feel better. He sighed and looked Michael in the eye.

'You know what I regret?' he said. 'My one regret. I know this'll sound daft. I'm sorry I never did the one thing that really fired my imagination. I wanted to go up the Amazon in a small craft. Up the Amazon. Across land. Down the Orinoco. That would have been something. That would have been quite something, don't you think?'

'Oh, El,' Michael said to me afterwards, at home, late at night, recounting this scene which I rewound and played again and again in my mind, adding the nuances of expression and gesture, looking for ways to help him. 'I couldn't believe it when he said that. I think my jaw actually hit my chest.'

'But darling,' I said, pulling my T-shirt over my head, holding it to my bare chest as if it were disrespectful to discuss Richard when deshabillé. 'You know full well, you understand that people have . . . impractical ambitions . . .'

'It's not that,' he said fiercely. 'It's not that. It's that I didn't know. I didn't know what my father's dearest wish was. He never told me. When I come to think about it, that conversation in the pub is the longest confidence we've exchanged for . . . well, for donkey's years, truth be told.'

He shook his head. 'He never told me,' he echoed.

And you never asked, said the voice in my head, but I knew better than to say so aloud.

He came across and kissed my forehead.

'Thank you for coming,' he said.

During the next day, an anger rose in me. A rage at doctors in quietly furnished rooms who pretend they hold the answers and then let you down. A rage at brave faces and words left unsaid. A rage that a man who had just heard his father is dying must repay the brief time he had snatched to come to terms with the news by working a sixteen-hour day on the morrow. Even a rage at how it is now normal for men and women in their plump middle years to lose their jobs and, with them, the routines with which they frame their lives.

Before he left home, at 6.00 that morning, I had asked Michael for Barbara's number. We had exchanged holiday postcards and Christmas cards for nine years, hellos in passing if she happened to answer Michael's extension, and I owed her that telephone call.

'I'm thinking of suing them. I'm going to see a solicitor; got an appointment the day after tomorrow,' she told me. My heart sank: my husband's interests, my interests therefore, were still bound to this company. She had received a pay-off. It was all legitimate, even if she found it hard to accept. Just as suddenly, I lost patience with her. I wished I hadn't called. But at the same time I was ashamed of myself. It was so craven of me, to think like a company wife.

There was bad news on the television that night. Children's faces in photographs; dead children, murdered children. I think there were many women that evening who heard the long, slow cry of the eternal mother, grieving; many people who raised their eyes from their family dilemmas and wondered about the sort of country we lived in. I went outside, into the dusk, and dead-headed the roses with sharp secateurs, cutting out the brown, rotten wood and sickening, spindly stems, a task I had hoped would prove cathartic.

Mostly, though, I was trying to come to terms with the idea of people ceasing. Of people going out, like snuffed candles. Of empty chairs and empty sides of beds. Of the smooth mound of the adjacent pillow. Of the tricks that the mind plays, when you look for someone in their old familiar place before the beat of remembrance. And I felt a new fury that it had been organised like this, because it seemed inhumane and wrong and evil. The old clichés.

Michael arrived home after 9.00, shattered. Miriam came down, kissed him, and returned to her long, lonely vigil over her homework in her bedroom. I had kept some supper warm, shepherd's pie, comfort food, and he wolfed it down. I was so pleased to have him there, in his rightful place.

'Mikey, I've had second thoughts about Norwich,' I said.

He stopped, fork poised midway, a neat square of mashed potatoes balanced upon the curve of the tines. 'You don't have to do that,' he said, very gently. I could see how highly he thought of me at that moment. 'We're fine.'

'Yes.' I sat down opposite him. 'I know. But I think you're right. I would like there to be time. I don't want to feel so indebted to your job that it's worth these hours you're working. I'd like to see you. I like you. I think you're the nicest man I've ever met. Well, most of the time, I do. And I always knew what you wanted. You didn't spring the Amazon on me.'

'Just Wells Next The Sea.' He said it lightly but there was a trace of bitterness in his voice, as if he was appalled that his hopes and his life had not soared higher than four walls and a field, but it seemed to me to be a good and laudable aim. He started to say something: 'My research, my job; I haven't done anything important . . .'

'Yes, you have.' I offered reassurance I hardly believed myself.

'What about Miriam?'

'She'll get over it. I was thinking, yesterday: she's fourteen, almost fifteen, she knows the words and the dance steps to the latest rap record, she asks for Calvin Klein underwear for her birthday or Doc Martens or Poison. But she doesn't know what to say to her father or her grandfather in a crisis.'

'Aw, she's a good kid . . .'

'Of course! She's not unusual in any of this, but that's not the point. I would like her to be unusual.' I had hit my stride now. I got up and went to the window, which overlooked the street with its ribbon of houses. I began to load the dishwasher, stacking each plate with great care, putting everything in its alloted place, taking some pleasure in imposing order. 'The one thing I promised myself when I had her was that I'd give her some sense of infinity. Of infinite possibilities. That the world held so much more than acquisition and attainment. I seem to have forgotten about that in the last four or five years.

I rediscovered ambition. I got that promotion. Well, stuff it. I want a different pace of life. You were right. I want a life.'

'We'll look into it,' he said, and at that point, just as suddenly as the familiar squeeze of affection had emerged, the familiar irritation bubbled up. I wanted to hit him, because he was acting as if downshifting were my idea, not his at all. He was adopting a wise, prudent stance, as if he had to rein in my foolhardy impulses.

And that is how it probably appeared to Miriam when he told her later that week. We had gone to the local Cantonese for dim sum, and while I was delving into a bamboo steamer, Michael suddenly declared, 'Miriam, your mum and I have been talking and we're thinking again about Norwich. We're going to suss it out a bit more. Nothing's definite, but we thought, well, let's not dismiss it out of hand.'

I was as astonished at this announcement as she was. She had paused, chopsticks halfway to her mouth, which had taken on that stubborn, sulky set. 'Have you applied for the job?' she asked.

'Today.' He glanced at me. This was news to me. Sometimes she was so much more perceptive than I was.

Magnanimously, I let it pass. 'I think we ought to go up one weekend and have a look around,' I said. 'What do you think?'

'A recce?' she said. 'Count me out.'

'I may not get the job, Miriam,' Michael said, and she rallied a little, but when he went to pay the bill, she shot me a look, just a quick, furtive glance because, as an only child, all her rebellions tended to be momentary.

'Oh, Miriam, please,' I said, 'Don't be self-centred.'

'Me? Me? What about you? You promised me. You always do that, you say one thing and do another. I thought you saw my point of view.'

Michael returned and she subsided into a pouting silence. She walked to the car, maintaining a distance as she strode ahead, staring at the pavement, her trainer laces trailing along behind her.

Chapter Three

When Miriam was young we employed a daily nanny, Debbie. She was with us for five years, and even after she left she made a point of sending Miriam a card on her birthday and at Christmas, with a fiver folded inside. Four years ago, the ritual ceased without warning. Miriam was not upset. The years had carried her far beyond her memories of Debbie's constant, good-natured jabbering, her tuneless warbling of pop songs. But I often wondered about Debbie's emotions. Had she suddenly realised that the child she remembered had been replaced by a lanky girl of uncertain moods? And recognising this, had she turned off her love – *click!* – in an instant?

I have keen memories of Debbie. I can recall her answers and her behaviour at our first interview, the way she took Miriam, who was then six months, onto her lap and began to chat to her – and how are you, little lady? – while clapping her hands together, so that Miriam smiled, one of her huge, slow, slightly cross-eyed grins. And I remember how I began to find fault with Debbie, over the years, though these grumbles were aired to Michael or to Anthea, rarely to Debbie herself.

But there is nothing of much substance beyond these sharply flavoured vignettes, for it is shocking how little I saw of her, how little, in the end, I knew her. She came and I left for work. I returned and she rushed off to the 'tween wars semi in Ilford

45

where she lived with her parents. The only time we shared the house was when I was ill, and must watch her do everything slightly differently from how I would do it myself – that time I was food poisoned; and the time I had 'flu.

That was back in 1986, when Miriam was four. I was off work for a week, feeling as boneless and pale as rolled pastry. I lay in bed sipping a mug of Ribena, which is all we had in the cupboards, and dazedly watching the cracks in the ceiling and the solitary cobweb that festooned one corner of the coving. Miriam was downstairs with Debbie. The radio buzzed un-heard, a garrulous companion. (Chatty, chatty, chat.) The sounds from downstairs were the ones that intruded, which suddenly loomed closer, then faded to nothing; Debbie singing, the rasping hum of the Hoover, the slap of a door closing, the rhythmic churning of the washing machine.

Time dragged its feet.

After a while, as the cracks grew infinitesimally bigger, the cobweb blew in the slipstream of an impossible draught, and the liquid crystal display on the clock radio blinked, winked and contorted from 12:05 to 13:22, I came to the conclusion that I must make the effort to get up. I should wash, brush my teeth. I would feel better. The washing machine had begun its frantic spin, forcing the clothes outwards on their wall of death, cuffs gripping metal drum.

I launched myself from under the duvet. The malicious February cold was far too canny for our central heating system; it slipped between the authentic Victorian cracks even though every door and window was stuck with strips of squashy plastic or tacked with funny fringes that reminded me of Hitler's moustache. In my drawer I found a thick cardigan. At the end of the bed I located my thick winter dressing gown, the one that Michael grumbled about, and in the absence of slippers, I pulled on a pair of his socks.

I was silent as I padded down the stairs – this was before we upped the mortgage for the first time, to convert the fourth bedroom to a bathroom. After I had brushed my teeth, washed my face and neck and wee-ed, I stood up, catching my reflec-tion in the mirror. I looked like shit. I felt like shit. Back to bed, back to the cracks and the cobweb; I would feel better.

Debbie was in the garden, wrapped in a Michelin man jacket, hanging clothes on the line. Where was Miriam? Dressed in a paintbox-coloured jumper and corduroy dungarees, she was standing in stockinged feet on the sofa in the bay window, overlooking the street, her hair a statically charged halo around her head. We could never do anything with those wiry curls.

'Hello, bean bag,' I said to her back.

She didn't answer. She was tracing patterns with her finger in the condensation clouding the panes. The reception rooms seemed chilly to me, so I lit one of the fires; turning the hissing tap, awaiting the quiet explosion and the flowering of flame around fake coals. We had knocked through the sitting and dining rooms, and restored the pair of fireplaces, one with its original tiles, both with stripped pine surrounds. Our house, at that stage, featured as much naked wood as a lumberjack's yard. Later, we painted over much of it, quickly, furtively, in embarrassment at our former taste.

Miriam cast me a look from over her plump pillar-box red shoulder, but returned, with wordless concentration, to her recreation. Feeling slightly giddy, I swayed over to her to examine her handiwork.

My middle-class heart did a little head over heels and sunk. Miriam was dyslexic. The symbols in the mist were letters, but distorted, back to front, gobbledygook.

Then she spoke. 'I'm writing back to front.' Of course she was. Perfectly formed letters, perfect sense, advanced for a four year old, even; back to front, mirror writing, designed to be seen from the street.

'How clever, darling,' I said. I worked it out. I AM MIRIAM.

Miriam smiled and waved. I followed her gaze. In the bay window directly opposite I made out the shape of another child, an impression of blonde ringlets above a fussy flounce of Liberty print.

'They've got good heating,' I said.

Debbie came in and, turning the fires off, packed me off to bed. It was odd how officious nannies became when they caught you deshabillé, as if your authority was good only for as long as you wore your grown-up suits and shoes with heels. Or maybe it was me feeling vulnerable.

'I'll take Miriam over this afternoon,' she said brightly, gazing at the vision in the window. 'It'll be nice for her to have a friend of her own age in the street.' Why did I infer a note of criticism?

So Debbie took Miriam over to meet Kim. Wrapped in the duvet, I watched from the window as the two figures appeared directly below, the one blonde with black roots – why didn't she do something about that? – the other miniature perfection. Hand in hand, they crossed the grey tarmac, negotiating the gaps between the parked car bumpers.

I noticed the micro-second's pause between Debbie's pulling on the heavy metal door knocker and the sound it made, like a battering ram on the panelled door of the house that mirrored ours; same bay window, same stucco detailing, same slate roof, same red and black tiles on the path. And down the street and round the bend, the string of houses continued, once built for artisans, now colonised by the stripped pine classes, each containing people like me – with hopes like mine, and similar fears.

Now, I could hear the melody created by Debbie's voice and the voice of the woman who lived opposite. The two of them went in. Miriam was making a new friend, without her mother beside her, although her mother was, for once, off work.

Debbie was a wonderful source of local gossip. In the evening, when I arrived home, she would pass on her knowledge. 'The man from number seventeen. No, red door, three houses up on the right – that's it – he's been done for fraud,' she'd say. Or, 'The woman with the blue Golf who's best friends with the fat one with the Daihatsu? Got her? Well, she's been having an affair with fat Daihatsu's husband.'

'Really?' I would say, astonished at the range of sin a street – according to Debbie's possibly unreliable accounts – can encompass. It was odd because I did not know these neighbours. Working all day kept me on the fringes of acquaintanceship, so that I could barely put a name to a face or a house number to a familiar figure, and yet I knew the rich details of their private lives.

Kim's mother was called Yvonne, and she had been abandoned by Kim's father, Jake, two months earlier, just after Christmas.

'He was a yuppie, very aggressive, done very well for himself. But she's a different kettle of fish, bit of a mouse,' Debbie said. 'You wouldn't like her.'

I recalled them vaguely from the 'garden party' Jocasta had held in the June, which had turned out to be a posh name for a barbecue in a back yard.

Everybody had talked about how much they were making and how their conservatory had added zillions to their property values, and Jake's voice had been the loudest. Michael and I were left beached on our old-fashioned upbringings. The one thing we never discussed – scarcely between ourselves – was the vulgar matter of money.

Yvonne was distinguishable only by the fact that she was perhaps more silent than we were. She sat to one side, fiddling with her daughter's ribbons, nodding at her extrovert husband's performance, like an individual claque.

Yes, I could place her. I hadn't liked her.

But it irritated me the way Debbie acted as if she knew me inside out. 'Why do you say that?' I snapped at her.

'Well,' said Debbie, 'She's just not your type. I don't mean to be funny but you are a bit snobby.'

Debbie had provoked me and the following week I engineered an excuse to work from home, saying I wanted to start writing a string of imminent press releases, spending a morning tapping away on the electric portable on the dining-room table, which was also, at that stage, stripped pine.

At 3.30, when I had exhausted my powers of professional fervour, I switched the typewriter off, excavated Miriam from beneath a pile of building bricks – wooden, not plastic – and trotted her across the road to the identical-different door. Yvonne looked startled to see me instead of Debbie.

'Coffee? 'S only instant.'

'So's ours.' I wandered into her sitting room, my nosiness antennae twitching, mainly because I hoped to glean some imaginative interior design ideas which would, of course, suit our house, too.

Yvonne must have seen my eyes sweep the room. ''Scuse the mess,' she said, whisking a magazine from the sofa. It was the cleanest, neatest room I had ever entered. The carpet pile showed the tracks of the Hoover.

Kim was sitting on the window seat like a china doll: her blue eyes, beneath the baroque curls, were almost as expressionless as a doll's and unnerved me.

'Hello, it's Kim, isn't it?' I said.

She gave me her baleful stare.

''lo, Miriam,' she said. She slipped off the cushions and silently led the way upstairs to her bedroom.

Yvonne reappeared with two china cups on a tray. The next hour was such heavy going that I suspended my resolution to establish warmer relations with the stranger neighbours there and then.

I saw her often, after that, standing in the bay window looking out, a beautiful child with a seemingly vacant life. I waved to her once as I left our house for the Saturday morning ritual of Sainsbury's. One of the neighbours passed by at that moment, the one who labelled her furniture, whose name had leaked from the sneaky holes opening in my brain.

Her eyes travelled past me to Kim in her vigil.

'Strange family. Your nanny's been taking Miriam over there a lot. Did you know?'

'Of course, I knew,' I said, bridling. 'Nice girl. Very quiet. Very well behaved,' I said in a pointed tone.

'Oh, do you think so?' she said, and continued on her way.

To my annoyance, her words remained with me, niggling. I had thought Kim acceptable, if a little odd. Miriam seemed to like her . . .

'What do *you* think of Yvonne?' I asked Debbie.

'Knew you wouldn't like her.'

She was putting on her coat at the time, glancing at her watch because she always maintained it was dangerous to use the tube after 8.00. 'Look, Eleanor,' she added, stuffing a couple of my glossy magazines into her macramé bag to read on the journey home, 'I'm not being funny but Miriam needs friends of her own age. Here in the street, not just at play school. If you're going to disapprove of all but the perfect child, she won't have any. That's all I'm saying . . .'

Kim did not go to nursery school, but, like Miriam, she was down for the local Catholic primary, which was the only half-decent state school in the area. I recognised the form on Yvonne's kitchen table, the black logo with its cross that looked curiously like an ankh. It was an advisory photostat; I had one the same at home. Confirmation of Place To Enter the Reception Class, it said. And then the details arranged neatly, in a list, so that my eyes flicked over it and read it unconsciously.

'Surname: Rogers. Given Name: Kim. Sex: Boy.

I was turning to Yvonne, who was ironing, my mouth open to say something like, 'Hey, they've made a mistake. You better do something about this,' when I realised belatedly that I shouldn't have read her letter and, in a rush, that there had been no error.

'Kim's a boy!'

'Yes,' said Yvonne. She teased the iron into an awkward corner of one of the many smocked, Liberty print dresses which she was always laundering. She looked up wearing a hard, defiant expression. It was as if, in an instant, she had grown a film over her eyes, so that I could not look through to her soul and see what she was really thinking. 'So he's got long hair,' she said and she shrugged.

I took a sip of coffee. I couldn't for the life of me think what to say.

'He looks gorgeous with long hair,' she continued. 'Those ringlets. He's going to have it cut off when he starts school. I'm not stupid. I don't want him teased, whatever Jake used to say. Anyway, it's only fashion. They used to wear long dresses in the olden days, boys did. They used to wear long dresses and have long hair. And he does look so cute with those ringlets . . .'

She went back to the ironing. I pretended the woven straw mat on the table was fascinating to me. 'What do you think of the school?' I said. 'I was quite impressed when I looked round.'

When I thought a decent interval had passed, I called Miriam from upstairs. Yvonne saw us out, though she and I avoided each other's eyes. We both knew that Miriam would not be playing with Kim any more.

'Can I go to Kim's?' she said the next day, which was a Sunday.

'Not today, darling.'

On the Monday, I warned Debbie.

'A boy! Who'd have guessed it?' she exclaimed too loudly, just as Miriam paddled in.

She looked at us. 'I did,' she said. 'I knew. I still like him.'

'How did you know?'

'He told me.'

'You should call the RSPC-thing,' Debbie said.

'What did Kim say?'

'He just told me. He doesn't mind. He doesn't want to have his hair cut off 'n' be a big boy 'n' sleep in his own bed.'

Debbie echoed the last three words, stirring dark mud from the bottom of her mind. She raised an eyebrow.

'Miriam comes in for a cuddle with us on Sundays,' I said firmly.

'And when I've had a bad dream,' she said.

'Some mothers. They defeat me,' Debbie said, as if as a breed we disappointed her, all falling short of professional standards; as if it had been me who had promoted the friendship, unbidden.

In the September, I saw him, wearing trousers with flies, his hair barbered into a brutal short back and sides, as he walked to school on the opposite side of the street to us. His neck looked pink and achingly vulnerable. Yvonne walked behind him, not holding his hand as she used to. Afterwards, she returned to the house that mirrored ours and closed the door. The following summer, they moved away. It was said she made a quarter of a million on the house sale.

Chapter Four

The nights grew lighter. When Michael dived into the house – always after nine, as a glance at the clock told me – there was still a corner of whiteness, over there, by the edge of the sky. Yet despite the long hours he was working, Michael now seemed remarkably happy, as if he was humming inside. He wore that tingle of last lap anticipation, oblivious of the shock waves reverberating through his family.

Was I happy for him? Was I resentful? Bit of both.

One Friday evening, Anthea dumped her son on me. She was going out and her nanny had the weekend off. She had been invited to a divorced people's dinner party, 'a sort of bourgeois blind date,' she said with a wild laugh. I had thanked my stars I was married when she told me this.

She pressed a sheet of paper into my hand, on which was scrawled, in her barbarian hand, the instructions for collecting her daughter, Samantha, who was at a classmate's birthday party.

'I'll pick them up at elevenish,' Anthea said. 'They can doze on the sofa.'

It was light enough, even at 8.00, for the boy, Scott, to amuse himself in the garden. I peered out from time to time, and saw him, stick-like arms poking out of the edge of his T-shirt, as he swarmed up the apple tree at the end of the garden. He straddled one of the lower branches, kicking his trainers back and forth, shrieking, 'Ba-boom-boom, Ba-boom-boom,' as if it were a battle-cry, or an identifying yell, like Tarzan's yodel.

Miriam peered over my shoulder. 'Is he deficient, or something?'

'He's eight,' I said, although inwardly agreeing with her. 'How are you, sweetheart?' I added, conspiratorially.

'Fine,' she said, contradicting herself by her glower.

At 10.00, I left Scott in the care of a disdainful Miriam who was crunching a sack of crisps while watching a faintly unsuitable video. I negotiated my way through the northern wastes of London, to a grimy church hall where, according to Anthea's note, I would find Samantha at a discotheque.

'It's the big thing, at their age,' Anthea had informed me. 'Aged eleven, they think a disco is the last word in cool. That and a sleepover.'

'I remember,' I said. 'But note: at fifteenish, they're too sophisticated. They've graduated to dinner parties.'

'Oh, God,' Anthea had groaned. 'It makes me feel so old. Aged fifteen, I'd have died to have gone to the local hop. I remember when my father took me to the sailing club dinner-dance. I was made up for a week.'

A large poster on the heavy oak door proclaimed, 'Let Jesus Into Your Life.' There was a lobby, swinging inner doors with glass panels. The hall was illuminated by a pulsing strobe; music throbbed. The girls were gathered at the opposite end of the hall, by a low stage, jiggling to the beat.

The lyrics ground out, low and deep, a male voice growling about 'doing it'.

'I hope they don't understand the words,' said a woman who banged in behind me. Side by side, we peered through the gloom at the slight figures, thin, breastless, their legs emerging, strong like trunks, from inch-long mini-skirts. They danced in a circle like a coven, their movements in unison. As we watched, they sank to their knees, wriggling their shoulders suggestively to the beat. The woman and I exchanged glances.

But there was one girl who hadn't got the timing right. It was Samantha; I recognised her, a pretty girl with her mother's fair, ringleted hair caught up in a ponytail. Her face was angled slightly towards the girl next to her, as she copied her companion's movements, but a fraction behind the beat, a gawkiness in every gesture. She was the only one in jeans, too.

The girl next to her straightened, said something, something disparaging, something excluding: I could tell, even at my distance, by the set of her head and the drooping of Samantha's.

'Last song,' shouted the disc jockey.

The shoal of precocious figures darted to one side and regrouped. Samantha looked up, saw me, and shrugging and grinning, clasping her elbows, clopped across the parquet towards me.

'Don't you want to stay?' I said, as if I hadn't noticed anything amiss.

'Nah. I don't like this song much.'

I put my arms around her skinny shoulders in the thin T-shirt as I steered her out into the evening, and I had to resist the urge to squeeze her tight.

Miriam had fallen in love, just this last Christmas. Well, I use the word love, but what I mean is that she had her first crush on a male she actually knew. A boy who for a fortnight seemed ravenously keen on her, too, who rang two or three times a day, to Michael's growing grouchiness. And finally, this boy arranged to see her at a friend's Christmas party. And then, when I had gone to collect her at that party, I had found her straining for self-control, her eyes flashing me wordless messages of misery as she located her coat amongst the mounds on the pegs. As she shrugged it on, the boy himself emerged from a side door, trailed by another girl, an older-looking, plumper girl, a blonde with a proper bust, who wore make-up.

'Forget him,' I told Miriam, in the small hours, when I had deduced by osmosis that she was awake and teary,

Her voice was quavery. 'I don't see how, when you have adored someone, you can stop adoring them just because they don't like you. It doesn't seem like a good enough reason.'

I fell silent. I quite saw what she meant.

She recovered within a couple of weeks, which was good – of course it was. But it was also such an irrevocable step in her growing up. She had learned a lesson in pragmatism. She was dressing herself in the armour that would protect her in adult life and that would hide forever the glorious shine of her younger self.

Anthea picked her children up at gone midnight when the rest of the street, including Michael and Miriam, was asleep in bed. I hoped the delay meant that she had been enjoying herself, but no.

'They took an hour between courses,' she whispered on my doorstep, 'and I was stuck between the two biggest bores of our time. It was horrendous. Never again.'

Samantha appeared, stretching drowsily in the hall behind me.

'I bet you had a better time than your old Mum,' Anthea said to her.

Samantha smiled wanly. 'Oh,' she said, 'it was cool.'

And Anthea looked so proud.

Michael had a look round the animal sanctuary one Saturday and I spoke to Louise Carrington on the phone. She sounded like one of those lonely, eccentric women who have given up on men and substituted packs of mewling cats.

'Well,' said a low, fake mid-Atlantic whisper, 'we started in 1988? With a couple of injured hedgehogs? But you know how it is: one thing seemed to lead to another.

'When people started bringing me animals I couldn't say no. It was fate. I'm very fatalistic, I believe in karma, don't you? So then, we started opening to the public and that brought its own trials. There was a God-awful battle for planning permission and if we'd have lost it, we'd have had to move, because no way was I going to give up my animals, no sirree. I kept saying to myself, if it's meant to be, it will be. But, oh lawd, the relief when we got it!

'Perhaps you should come over one evening. Do you like Indian food? I've got a wonderful aubergine recipe I want to try out.'

I had a picture of her in my mind now; someone gaunt and pale, a woman in her late fifties with the long fringed hair of a sixties' model, in jeans and cowboy boots. There was an odd, off-beat glamour about this image which for some reason raised in me a chafing dislike. I saw her sleeping in a four-poster bed underneath heavy tapestries, with twenty kittens curled in the nooks and crannies of her arms and legs. There was a fairy-tale quality to this image, too. It explained to me why Miriam seemed to be so enchanted by this woman, why she might find her refreshingly different. So I constructed this picture of Louise Carrington, and it seemed so real I never thought to ask Michael or Miriam what she was really like.

Miriam talked of her often. How Louise had praised her; how Louise had fed her an incomparably delicious, spicy lentil dish. (Louise, naturally, was a vegetarian.) Miriam now spent her weekends at the sanctuary and returned smelling of gamey animals, but with a glow about her, at least until she had been home for ten minutes and recollected her grudge against us. Louise lent her a book on Eastern philosophy, and Miriam began doing yoga in her room, first thing.

'May I have my allowance?' Miriam said one Friday. 'I need a new jacket.'

'Sure,' I said, 'But when are you going shopping? I might join you. Fancy a girls' day out?'

'Oh,' she said, and her face grew tight, discomforted. 'Oh, Mum, you see I arranged to go with Louise.'

A jolt passed through me. If she had said Kate or Twist or Becca, any one of her school friends, I'd have made a joky, long-suffering comment – 'Oh, I can quite see *their* appeal above *mine*; get along with you then,' – semaphoring to Miriam that I understood; she was growing up, she needed her tribe around her. But Louise?

But when I mentioned to Michael how crestfallen I was, he told me I was making too much of it, and I decided, on balance, that he was right.

I was due to fly to Ireland. We were handling the publicity campaign for the autobiography of a rock star and I had drawn the short straw. I drove out to Stansted, my foot on the pedal, smug as I passed the queues inching towards London on the other side of the central reservation. I always notice when I am travelling against the stream.

The morning was dull. A giant hand had spread a thick, grey eiderdown of cloud over the curve of the globe. I gazed through the airport plate glass at the variations of colourless shades – the sky, the tarmac, the planes – while trying to construct a campaign which would spark newspaper interest in a has-been. I didn't feel very inspired.

The truth was, I had drifted into my job, just as I had drifted inside so many of the other boundaries of my life. I had never asked what my history degree at a provincial university was equipping me for; it was part of the experience, like Michael's overland minibus to India. I was not cut out for teaching, which is why I had taken a post as a glorified secretary and worked my way upwards. Not that I disliked my job. There are popular misconceptions about public relations. The first rule, taught to me by an old hand very early in my career, is that you never lie. The second is that it helps if you like journalists, which I do. The best ones are always interested and therefore they are invariably interesting.

NML was Nicola's baby, its initials were hers – standing for Nicola Marianne Lyndhurst – with their neat reversal of the alphabetical order. It was largely her money which had funded it and it was made in her image, so that its accounts reflected her North London interests: books, a handful of big budget but, as she stressed, 'ethical' firms, and a couple of charities. Catherine and I had each pitched in £30,000 a few years ago in order to see the company through the darkest days of the recession. I did not have that sort of money to hand, you understand, but had had to top up the mortgage. This was a year or two after Michael and I had doubled it to pay for the attic conversion, the conservatory and a new damp course.

Which, when you came right down to it, was how Michael and I drifted through the weeks, the months, the years, unquestioningly servicing our six-figure debt. It was good that he had made me wonder why I had been content to plod on. I had never wanted to be a plodding sort of a person; nor to marry one.

Standing in the airport, I played out the scene in which I broke the news to Nicola that I was leaving for a rural future. As she sat at her desk, her face became immobile, as I had so often seen it when she wished to control her emotions, but her thoughts flickered in her eyes, the fast calculations visible. She decided to persuade me to stay. She offered me a whopping rise, a company car, a full partnership, my pick of the clients . . .

I returned from my fantasy, staring blindly at the runway. I had been tempted by her blandishments,

At Dublin, I found the car hire desk and went through the business of signing forms and proffering credit cards. The girl serving me was chatty and I told her this was my first visit to Ireland. She hoped I would like it. But when I drove out through the suburbs, into the countryside, expecting postcard cottages thatched with heather, and rich green fields dotted with cows, I thought the scenery as dull as the day. I sped past bungalows with aluminium frame windows, tacky modern houses, their square lawns edged with identical orangy-pink hybrid tea roses. Reproduction stone lions sat atop pink brick pilasters, trying in vain to add grandeur to the short, suburban drives they guarded. Outsize plastic butterflies basked above front doors. Here, without doubt, was a country with a rising standard of living.

The rock star had been christened Alan Watts but was universally known by his stage name. He lived in a large Georgian mansion outside a market town that also disappointed me by its shabbiness, though the countryside surrounding it was prettier and lush. I left the town behind, slid the car round a wide bend which skirted a copse, then the trees gave way, on my left, to a luxuriant verge, a low stone wall, and, beyond it, parkland. Eventually I came across a pair of princely wrought iron gates. I pressed the intercom several times, until a sudden electronic buzzing and humming forewarned me that the gates were swinging open.

The drive meandered, without much purpose, through fields choked with thistles, cow parsley and ragwort. Some of the trees, so judiciously placed as saplings by the landscape designer two centuries before, were now bleached skeletons. The house itself, when I crested the little hump-backed bridge and turned the final bend, was similarly neglected. The plaster was cracked, the paint peeling at the windows and at the great front door with the carved stone arch and cracked fanlight above. It was highly romantic, but it was also obvious to me that the hundred-and-fifty-thousand advance the book had commanded was not going to stretch far.

The rock star opened the door himself, which was startling. He was familiar and yet different. He was so much smaller and slighter than he had appeared in his artistic videos and publicity shots, a squat man in jeans and a sort of brocade jacket, his face sagging, his eyes bleary, his hair greasy. It was tied back in a ponytail. There was a white shower of dandruff on his maroon and gold shoulders. He was only six years older than me but he looked worn and lined, as if his skin were a garment that had been washed and wrung out too many times.

'Top of the morning to you,' he said, in mock Irish. He had a soft adenoidal drawl.

I'd had a dare with Michael who'd bet I'd be too chicken to call him by his stage name.

'Good morning, Virus,' I said, in an over-hearty way.

He led the way down a damp corridor, which skirted a central courtyard, to a large kitchen where his wife – Mrs Virus? – was supervising a pale toddler doing a jigsaw.

'Make some coffee,' Virus ordered. 'We'll be in the blue room.'

The kitchen was warmed by the Aga and I had to brace myself to leave it. Our footsteps echoed in the flagstoned corridor. I noticed more damp patches, two electric guitars propped next to an old pine armoire, a broad stone staircase scattered with toys, and, hanging above it, an enormous, alarming drawing of a nude man with a snake for a penis. The snake was curled within the crook of the knee, but its yellow eye was open. Long passages of Virus's autobiography were devoted to the tawdry proving of his potency.

He saw me looking. 'Me mate did that.'

'Oh,' I said.

Behind me, he turned the brass knob on a door that opened into a cavernous drawing room, furnished in the country house style. The fireplace was flanked by a pair of red velvet Knole sofas and a matching pair of mahogany side tables upon which dunes of books and records were capsizing. Thick wads of discoloured stuffing were emerging from holes in the upholstery. Above the fireplace hung a spotted looking-glass in a carved gilt frame.

Soft rain kissed the window panes. Beyond, through the thick, undulating Georgian glass, I made out a dappled grey Connemara pony in a field, its head down, its back to a blustery wind. There was an electric fire in the hearth but Virus did not turn it on even though the room was icy. I shivered, tucking my hands under my arms.

The coffee arrived while we were discussing the broad press campaign. Mrs Virus balanced the tray precariously on a pile of newspapers atop a stool, and went away directly. Her husband did not look up from his notebook. He was absorbed in a comprehensive list of the television programmes and the press which he insisted he would not do, either because of slighting reviews in the past or because of a newspaper's political bias.

'Look, Virus, if you want to sell your book you had better save your politics for the polling booth,' I warned him.

He capitulated instantly. 'Yeah, you're right. And I do want to sell my book. You read it?' he said. 'You like it?'

'Of course I've read it,' I said, and I managed some flattering words about its veracity and the vivid pictures it painted of life on the road.

He flashed a wide smile. 'Course I know it's not art,' he said. 'I need the dosh. Got this place to keep up.' He adopted a plummy accent. 'Staff are so expensive. And the west wing is crumbling. And,' he added, returning to his normal drawl, 'there's the alimony and the school fees. Fuckin' crippling me, they are.'

I gave a little surprised laugh. I hadn't pictured him being as wedded to the treadmill as we were.

We pitched in to the subject of his elder son, who was fifteen and attending an English boarding school which had recently been in the news because two pupils – one of whom was said to be a distant cousin of the Queen – had been expelled for dealing in Ecstasy.

'Do you talk to your son about the drugs you've taken?' I don't know what made me ask him that – perhaps the school hall lecture was loitering in my mind? – but after I'd blurted it out, I felt my ears go pink, and I busied myself pouring thick, bitter coffee from an old fashioned percolator into a chipped mug.

He wasn't in the least offended. 'Yeah, a bit,' he said. 'What can I say? It's a matter of public record. I was busted twice. Once 'ere – well, in England, I mean – once in Japan. The fuss they made. You'd think I was caught with a stash of bloody 'eroin.' He snorted. I knew that he had been caught with a gram or two of cocaine and a rather larger quantity of marijuana.

'Tommy said to me, "Dad, you took stuff and you're OK." And he's right. So I believe in honesty, total honesty. As you probably realise from reading my book, I grew up in the sort of working-class household where we never discussed a friggin' thing. Sat with our tea on trays in front of the telly. My dad forbade me playing with the group I formed after school. "Why?" I said. I did all my homework. I'd made it to the grammar, I was bright. I was on the O level courses, not CSEs. And he said, "'Cos I say so." Don't get me wrong, he wasn't a bad man, but that generation, that was the way they were.

'But how can I turn round to Tommy and say, "Don't do drugs . . . 'Cos I say so." He'd just laugh at me. No, it's a whole, brave, new world now, and for myself, I think it's a lot healthier.'

We had lunch at 3.30 in the afternoon in the kitchen. Mrs Virus, or Lucy Watts as she called herself, flitted between Aga and sink. She had been a professional girlfriend to a series of actors and rock stars, but not enough that you could call her a groupie. She had inspired several songs in her heyday, not all composed by her husband. I regarded her, curiously.

She spoke very little, was tall, thin and pale, the blue veins standing out against her white skin, her cropped white-blonde hair standing in little spikes around her head. There was something tacky about her, too; a suspicion that she had not washed her face or combed her hair. She wore a sad, wistful expression so that she seemed flimsy, ethereal, like a ghost that was haunting the house. But when she cut her finger while chopping tomatoes, she bled profusely enough, drips landing in the salad. She boiled the potatoes dry but served them anyway, with a brown, smoky crust.

'I hate 'tatoes,' the little girl, whose name was Patience, announced, standing on her chair next to me. She was a pretty, gamine child, with her pixie haircut a copy of Lucy's, but she also looked as sickly as Lucy, with blue shadows beneath her enormous blue eyes, a stream of slime flowing from one nostril.

'Well, don't eat them,' said Lucy. 'I love potatoes. And broccoli,' she said to me. 'Healthy, no calories, dream food.' She thrust forkfuls of vegetables into her mouth.

In the centre of the long, undyed, cheesecloth gown she wore, which reminded me of vampires, a large, dark, grease stain had appeared.

She took me on a tour of the mansion after lunch, wrapping herself in a padded jacket before she left the kitchen. It was a long, echoing procession through crumbling, faded neglect, except that in Patience's bedroom Lucy had painted a bright mural of jungle animals on the wall. And the master bedroom also provided a startling change of decor. The walls and ceiling were painted black. There was a camp, Elinor Glyn leopard-skin bedspread draped over black sheets. The mirror on the ceiling above spoke of mannered sex, an aging man's pursuit of a precarious erection. A bamboo birdcage threaded with innocent fairy lights hung from the ceiling rose and twinkled in the sloping mirror.

On the telephone Virus had warned me that the local inn

was a dive. 'You better stay the night with us,' he had said. So, that evening, Patience sat on my knee and played with my laptop computer while we finished talking about the publicity campaign. She had a hacking cough and in my opinion needed her bed.

Virus uncorked two bottles of wine. Finally, he pushed the plug of the bar fire into the socket and the two rods glowed through grey to orange. Patience launched herself from my lap and crouched in front of the fire, spitting at its curved metal back and giggling delightedly as the globules of saliva writhed in the heat and evaporated, leaving only a faint stain.

'Oy,' said Virus. 'Don't do that.'

'Why?'

'Because it isn't polite, that's why.'

'Why-y?'

The wine was fine and mellow, and I lay back in the Knole sofa, letting the imbibed warmth trickle through me like a balm. Virus had begun to tickle Patience; she lay on her back on the shabby rug, kicking her legs and gurgling. A soft clicking of needles, interspersed with pauses, arose from Lucy slumped in the other sofa, knitting. My eyelids turned to lead.

The chill of the corridor and my bedroom and the high-ceilinged bathroom next to it woke me briefly. The bathroom shelf was lined with those sample-sized bottles taken from hotel rooms, and the towel had a hotel monogram. I fiddled with a tiny packaged soap, dug in my own overnight bag for my toothbrush. From my window, the park rolled away in shades of grey under a darkening sky. I pulled the roller blind down with a rattle. The sheets were white linen and so cold they felt damp. I curled into a ball waiting for the warmth to build, and while I was waiting, I fell sweetly, deeply asleep.

The noise infiltrated my dream, and pulled me back to waking. I lay with my eyes closed, my mind swimming, gradually realising I was awake. I opened my eyes; the black was rich and almost solid.

The noise was love-making. The puff-grunt – uh-uh-uh-uh –

of a man, and the high breath-gasp – ahhh-ahhh-ahhh – of a woman.

Oh, no. I rolled over and slammed my head into the pillow.

The grunting grew urgent and louder, the gasping more agonised until it reached a shrill, sustained, half-strangled note. They had finished. But no. The grunting started again, and after a while the sibilant panting also.

I squinted towards my right, to my battered travelling clock on the bedside cabinet. The pale green luminous hands were caught somewhere between 2.00 and 3.00.

A rasping cough punctuated the animal sounds of sex. Patience. I could imagine her thin, bony shoulders wracked by the spasms. Then, her voice, plaintive and distressed. 'Mum? Mum?'

Uh-uh-uh.

It seemed they hadn't heard her, so buried were they in moments of obsession with flesh.

'MUM!'

The grunting stopped. There was a rustle and a whisper.

'Go to sleep,' ordered Lucy's voice, short of breath, drowsy.

Uh-uh-uh. They began again. There was a perfunctory urge in the sound of their sex which reminded me of dogs that you see copulating by roadsides. I sat up. Oh, what should I do? I sat up and scrabbled for my robe. Perhaps I might settle Patience, find her a drink to sip?

'MUM?' The grizzle was close at hand, on the landing outside my door. I paused. I thought that now Patience had got up, Lucy would recall herself, push her dog-husband off her belly and rush to comfort her daughter.

Aahh-aahh-aahh.

I stumbled from my bed, groping for the door handle. The light on the landing, though faint, made my eyes bleary.

The door opposite mine was open. It was the door to Lucy's bedroom. Patience must have opened it, for she was standing, looking frail and breakable in a white cotton nightdress, by the side of their bed. I could see too much through the door.

'Mum?' she said, and plucked at Lucy's arm.

Lucy's white arm and white leg lay wrapped around her

husband's sallow, hairy body, his buttocks pumping.

'Go back to bed,' Lucy said, glassy-eyed. She made a little shooing gesture with one hand.

'Patience!' I averted my eyes, examined the rug on the landing, pink and threadbare, while I called to her. It is rare that a stranger can divert and comfort a child who wants their mother, but almost immediately there was a flutter nearby and Patience stood before me. Her face was red, the cheeks shiny where the tears had not dried.

'I gotta cough,' was all that she said.

I softly closed the door to her parents' bedroom, led her back to the cheerful chaos of her own room, the soft toys spilling from shelves and abandoned on the floor, and brought her a drink of tapwater in the tooth mug from my bathroom. She had a slight temperature but it was nothing to worry about.

I opened a book which lay on the floor by her bed, which turned out to be *Peter Pan*, and began to read to her, and before Wendy had sewn on Peter's shadow, Lucy appeared, tying the belt of a white towelling robe.

'You shouldn't 'ave got up,' she said. 'She's always doing this. I put her down at night, and come two, three, she's up and awake again. Aren't you, you little blighter?'

I suddenly realised that the scene I had witnessed was a common one. I handed the book to Lucy and went back to bed. I tiptoed around my room, searching in my bag for socks for my feet which were cramping with cold, and for a book to read me back to sleep, wincing when a drawer in the heavy oak chest creaked. Heaven knows why I didn't want them to be aware of me. I knew I was being silly but I couldn't stop myself

In the morning, the rain had given way to hesitant sunshine. I slung my case over my shoulder and picked my way down the stairs and through the connecting corridors to the kitchen. The Watts family was already gathered there. I sipped a cup of coffee leaning against the wall by the high window. Patience, barefoot, was scooting over the tiles on her tricycle.

It seemed mealy-mouthed of me to keep noticing all the Watts' shortcomings as parents. What seemed to me to be shortcomings. Because maybe I was just being prim and Surrey-ish. You heard of people who thought it acceptable for their children to see them making love, that these children then regarded the act as something perfectly natural and did not invest it with the dark mystery of closed doors. But, somehow, well, it just seemed plain wrong to me. And how could you ignore your child's cries, even in the flush of sex; how was that for putting your husband before your child? That was a twist on Nicola's theories. What big ideas people like Alan and Lucy had had! How conscientiously they had pursued their inner selves. And all it had come to was a vague amorality.

But maybe Virus at heart felt as confused as I did. He showed me to the door and we both stood for a moment, blinking at the beauty of the new morning.

'My manor,' he said, and he swept his arm outwards to encompass the rolling acres.

The fields looked so beautiful glimpsed through the diamond net of the mist. The ghost of a rainbow arched over them, like a promise. Indeed, from where we stood, it looked as if the rainbow's end was to be found somewhere in the lower paddocks, beyond the river, though I had a feeling that the pot of gold had been dug up long since.

'I was going to change the world with my music,' Virus said, squinting against the reflected brilliance. 'Now I'm a member of the pop squirearchy. That's the real story of my life.' He had the same tone in his voice as Michael discussing Wells Next The Sea.

In the aeroplane cabin, strapped into a window seat as we droned above the earth, a great wave of tiredness washed over me. I closed my eyes. I longed for my bed, not just for a night, but for a day, a week. I wanted to lie on goose down and be stroked like a cat. I, too, was worn out by everydayness, and it did not feel like the normal lassitude which a holiday will fix. It felt rather as if my confidence were escaping, hissing through a pinprick, so that my face was collapsing inwards. I had no doubt that everyone could see what a ridiculous and undignified spectacle I was making, that they were watching to see when my feet would leave the ground and I would whizz off into the sky, leaving behind nothing but the high screech of a gaseous emission, foolish as a fart.

'Far to go?'

I jumped. It was the man next to me. Fortyish, hair on collar, white shirt, no tie, jeans, blazer. The sweet, sickly smell of alcohol burst from his mouth like vomit; I recoiled.

'I've got to get to Nottingham,' he said, without waiting for my answer.

A stewardess collecting the plastic glasses distracted him and I turned my back. The plane began its lilting dip towards the airport. I pressed my nose against the window, glad of the excuse. He leaned across, I felt his breath on my neck, smelt it.

'Beware,' he said in his chummy way. 'Men went to the moon and came back changed from gazing down upon the earth.'

'Is that so?' I hoped I sounded clipped.

At that moment, we pierced the dank monotony of the clouds, except for a few ragged tufts which the wings tore free, and which were finally blown back, like a flag from a car aerial. Below me lay the green fields and toy-town estates of Essex and all of a sudden I saw us very clearly, the limit of our lives. And what do our young want but less? They want compact starter homes with fully fitted kitchens and a hatchback sitting on the tarmac outside. They want an orgasm twice a week and they'll hunt foreign titillation on a satellite channel to achieve it. This is what it had all come down to.

People in strings of houses. People in strings of traffic. I sat back. The man next to me opened his mouth to say something, then closed it. Even he could see it wasn't the moment. There were tears standing in my eyes.

I had a couple of days off that week, to coincide with Miriam's half term. I was buried in trivia; I had to clear out cupboards, sew on buttons and name tapes, drop off dry-cleaning, telephone estate agents.

Miriam popped her head around my bedroom door. I was

on my knees by the closets, surrounded by black dustbin bags.

'I'm off to Louise's,' she announced, then performed a mock double take. 'Oh, wow! Eleanor Banyer gets to play house-wives.'

Indignation prickled my skin. 'I'd much rather not,' I said. 'Who do you think will do this if I don't? Your father? How do you think this home keeps running?'

'Don't be so dramatic, Mum. It was only a joke,' she said and withdrew. I heard her big bully boy soles assaulting the quaking stair treads.

'Be careful on the tube,' I yelled and the door slammed in reply.

I rested my head on a cool, slippery dustbin bag. I had planned to take her to Chawton, to Jane Austen's house, which she had wanted to visit. I had planned to take her shopping in the West End. I felt I was missing out, but Miriam did not. I tied up the dustbin bag, bumped it down the stairs. The closet was pristine. I should have felt a small glow.

Years before, when Miriam was four, I had had to go to the States for a week.

Debbie had brought her to the gate, that dear, small figure in blue corduroy trousers and an unravelling pink jumper, her hair in bunches.

'We'll be fine, won't we?' Debbie said, as I handed my cases to the taxi driver. And, 'Wave to Mummy.'

My last sight of Miriam, as the taxi pulled away, was of the sudden crumpling of her face, the way her mouth puckered, her eyes screwed up as the tears spilled down her cheeks. Debbie took Miriam into her arms, pulling encouraging faces at me over Miriam's shoulder. As for me, it felt as if a fist were squeezing my heart, there was all the pain of seeing her pain, and all the satisfaction of seeing how she loved me. Ten, eleven years ago, that was. It seemed a lifetime.

In the evening, Miriam arrived home in a flurry of high spirits, lugging a metal cage. Inside, was a small hedgehog. 'It needs a little more feeding up,' she said, as she set it on the kitchen table and fished in her denim pocket, extracting an eye dropper and a can of cat food. I put the cage on the floor. 'Then, we can release it in the garden.'

'The garden?'

'Good for slugs,' she said.

She ground the tin opener around the lid, took one of my best saucers from the cupboard and mashed a dollop of cat food together with a spoonful of water and a gritty substance she had brought home in a plastic pot in her other pocket.

'What's that?' I asked.

'Sluis.'

'Slewiss?'

'Dried beetles.'

She was using one of our everyday spoons.

'Where are you going to keep it in the meantime?'

'What? Here, of course,' she said.

'Not in my kitchen. Put it in the downstairs loo,' I said.

'Oh, mother,' she said. 'How about I put it in *my* bedroom.' But she clomped off to the loo, as bidden. 'There'll be some baby house martins, tomorrow,' she yelled, then, returning, her voice at normal pitch, 'Louise is amazing. What she doesn't know about raising wildlife . . . We had such a laugh today . . . I really like her, she's going to be my mentor, I can see.'

'What do you mean, baby house martins?' I felt a growing irritation. 'You'll be back at school next week. Or has the amazing, amusing Louise Carrington forgotten that fact?'

'They'll go back at the weekend,' Miriam retorted and she shot me a look. I went upstairs, drew a bath, measured three cap-fulls of foam bath into it, and then came down again and fixed myself a stiff gin and tonic with ice and slivers of lemon peel. It was only 6.00.

Fifteen minutes later, Miriam's face appeared around the door and, making a great play of waving away the steam, she plonked herself upon the closed loo seat. 'Are you in a better mood?'

'I'm always in a good mood.'

'Puh!'

But she wanted to talk, so of course I responded, made a daft face above the bubbles, raised eyebrows, rolling eyes.

'Do you know, sometimes I feel,' she paused, 'I feel as if I know the answers. There's a split second when I think I know all the secrets of the universe. And then, something happens, I blink, or somebody says something, or the sun comes out, and it all disappears. I can't remember what I knew. Do you get that?'

'I never feel I have any answers.'

'Do you believe in God?'

I was still struggling to extract my mind from a grumbling resentment focused mainly upon Louise Carrington, so it took me a moment to apply it to the weighty matters which had so suddenly claimed her. Did I believe in God?

'When I persuade myself I don't believe in Him, I feel sad about it.'

It was a fudging kind of an answer I thought, but she clasped her arms around her knees delightedly. 'Oh, so do I. Isn't that funny?' she said. 'That's what I like about you, Mum. You're always prepared to be honest with me.' There was something in her tone which suggested that she was comparing me with Michael, or even Louise, and that this time I was coming out on top. Finally, I felt that glow.

'You never think I'm silly,' she continued. 'You don't, do you?'

'Of course not.'

'I can talk to you about anything. Louise and me got started on this.'

Oh. – 'Louise and I.'

'I really like her. She said, "How do we know we're really here?" She's got a point. I mean, how do I know I'm not asleep and dreaming all this?'

'Because I'm going to pinch you if you carry on.'

I hate discussions like this. What is that question they put to school children? If a tree falls in a wood but no one is there to witness it, has it really fallen? Of course, it's fallen, I want to scream. It's common sense. Real is real and dreams are dreams; and I, for all my daydreaming, know the difference. But this speculation seemed typical of Louise, at least from what I knew of her, and I saw her again, in her jeans with her long, fine hair.

I bet she made love in front of her children.

'If I think a thought,' Miriam was continuing, 'do I think it involuntarily, or have I told my brain what to think? In which case, how do I know what I want to think before I've thought it?'

I smashed the side of my hand into the foam, karate-chopping the water, and a spray leapt into the air and darkened her white T-shirt. She blinked the foam away.

'Death!' she cried, wielding a cold sponge.

A few minutes later, we declared a truce. As I clambered out of the bath, she handed me the towel after first wiping it over her face and arms.

'I just had to do that,' she said, 'It was *so* satisfying.' This was one of her catchphrases, part of her construction of a droll personality that her peers admired.

'I love you, bean bag,' I said.

'You, too,' she said. She peered in the mirror at her damp hair. 'Blug.' Her eyes were on my reflection and I realised, all at once, that she was working up to something. She said, 'Mum, are we really going to move?'

I straightened, wrapped the towel more tightly around me. I could see her face in the mirror, and mine, similar but different, both perturbed. 'More likely than not.'

'How do you feel about it, really? What will you do?'

'Things I've always wanted to.'

'Like?'

'Like aerobics classes. Seriously? Like textile design.'

'Textile design?'

'Yes. I was good at art at school. That's where you get it from. So you see, you don't know everything there is to know about me.'

I had her attention now. There was so much I had to explain about India and Wales, about circling above Essex and wanting more for her than was on offer. I knew I had to help her construct a vision of what she would do in this altered future. I looked back at her as I opened the door. 'Come and talk to me while I change,' I said, and she looked happy. It was the right moment.

As we were crossing the landing, the front door slammed. Michael had, for once, come home early.

'Hi, there, you two,' he called. Footsteps up the stairs. He appeared, so glad to see us. He came to kiss me and pretended to tug Miriam's hair.

She smiled weakly, her eyes downcast.

'Hi, Dad,' she said and left, drooping. The moment had passed.

Michael collapsed on the unmade bed, tugged off a shoe.

'What's for supper?' he said. 'I'm famished.'

The estate agent was a tall young man with a shaving rash and a watch that beeped the hours to him. As he stepped into the hall, he looked past me, appraising the house already. His wrist chirped – 'Beep, beep' – so I knew he was prompt. He had said he would come at eleven.

'Name's Ray,' he said.

He didn't seem to speak in complete sentences. 'Good,' he said when he saw the conservatory tacked onto the kitchen, and 'Mmm,' when he examined the kitchen itself. He paused and sucked his teeth reflectively, frowning as he tried to figure out what was out of place, which was, in fact, the sound effect of chirping insects. I tried to steer him towards the bedrooms, explanation being beyond me.

The house martins, which had come and now gone, had had to be fed on live crickets. Miriam had brought home a plastic container, seemingly full of spiky, crawling lines, from which she extracted them singly, with tweezers, dunking them in water (she used one of our cereal bowls) and popping them into the gaping, tweeting mouths.

'This is gross,' I said.

'It's nature.'

But some of the crickets must have escaped for, though I never saw them, shortly afterwards, their merry singing began inside the kitchen. It was surprising how comforting, how inoffensive, this was.

'The Japanese keep crickets in cages as pets,' Miriam told me, and I could see why.

Before he went, Ray told me his guide price would be in the post within a day or two, but he could tell me – 'here and now,' he said, like a fanfare – that this was just the sort of property which was selling well. The market was picking up but only in certain sectors, he said. And one of those sectors was ours.

Curiously, I felt torn at this information; proud that our taste was somehow vindicated, but deflated, too. That was that. An obstacle had been removed on the flight into Norfork, the path to the unknown. To the inevitable rumpus with Miriam. And I loved this house, it had always been more to me than an investment. I loved the way the sun shone in the hall window on a slant, and was dissected by the bannisters into happy rectangles on the wall. I loved the fact that this was the only house Miriam knew.

Ray climbed back into his electric blue, curvy, city car, the very model I had craved for myself next time around, and accelerated away. His letter came two days later, a day after Michael heard the date of his interview. It said that, 'in the current market our house should be offered for sale at . . .' and there it was, the exciting figure of £285,000.

Michael exclaimed, 'Yes!' and waltzed me around the kitchen. 'We'll have almost two hundred thousand smackeroonees,' he exulted. 'We can buy somewhere outright. No more mortgage! No more overdraft! Oh, Lord, thank you! Thank you! I wish that all the world had problems such as ours!' And then his face darkened and he let go of me. 'Apart from Dad, of course,' he said. He went off to work, preoccupied, castigating himself for having forgotten, even for a moment, though it seemed to me to be an entirely natural thing to do.

Over the next few days, I rang around the estate agents in Norwich, saying we were interested in property between £150,000 and £200,000 situated in the surrounding villages. I spoke in the jazz of their jargon and they loved it.

I must admit that I adored opening the mail during these weeks. I am incurably nosy and other people's houses are a lure to me. Of course, the agents ignored my instructions: details of modern houses arrived, even though I had stated 'period'. They excused this by saying that they were 'character' houses. There was one memorable mock-Tudor monstrosity, so tall and thin it looked as if it had been condensed on to its narrow site. It was built of yellow bricks, white render and red tiles, Disney colours, with pretend black beams and leaded windows. Half the fun of house-hunting lay in seeing the exuberant tastelessness of other people.

'Look at this, Miriam. Isn't this hideous?'

She walked out of the kitchen.

Houses outside our budget came to tempt me at my breakfast table, houses at just £205,000 or £210,000, even, in one case, £265,000. But I rather enjoyed the games salesmen play. There were double-fronted flint cottages standing in unspoilt gardens, Georgian houses of soft, crumbling red bricks, Victorian houses under grey slates. My mind conjured up delightful attic bedrooms and sweet wood chuckling as it smouldered in wide grates.

There was one flint house that particularly appealed. On the back of its envelope, I doodled a design for a lino-print. My imaginary self held an exhibition, progressed to constructing great, colourful tapestries, was commissioned to make a hanging for an important medieval cathedral.

'This is a sumptuous work,' Sister Wendy said. We were standing in front of it, bright and heraldic against the ancient, dark stone, as the television cameras whirred. 'Sensual and erotic. You must be so proud . . .'

Michael caught me smiling to myself and offered me a penny for them, so that I flushed.

I bought a book on cottage gardens, whereas previously my shelves were filled with books about tiny, walled, town gardens, with chapters about creating outside rooms, the dramatic use of lighting, and the cunning tricks possible with *trompe l'oeuil* trelliage.

'What's trelliage?' I had asked the man from the garden centre.

'Expensive trellis,' he replied.

The flint house enjoyed 'approx. 0.75 of an acre', which excited me, though I had no real way of converting the decimal on the page into a plot in my mind. It sounded so large. You can plant trees in nought point seven five of an acre.

'We could have a wild patch,' I said to Miriam. 'For indigenous wildlife.'

'Oh, stop trying to jolly me, Mum,' she exclaimed. She left the room. She was forever leaving rooms as I entered them these days, and I trailed after her, trying to regain my magic power as the family conciliator but this time, apparently, doomed to fail.

> *Mary, Mary, quite contrary;*
> *How does your garden grow?*

Nursery rhymes and nonsense doggerel had followed me ever since Miriam's toddlerhood. Phrases had been left behind in my head, like an unmatched sock at the bottom of the drawer. That's what came of all those books telling me to chant Humpty Dumpty to her to benefit her vocabulary. Sometimes I thought I had a nonsense brain, forever erupting with limericks or caprices, so that I was never sure where it would lead me next.

The next day was balmy; Anthea and I decided to eat our expensive next-to-no-calorie sandwiches in the park, and Catherine announced that she would join us. Anthea and I, in particular, were feeling chummy. She liked the look of a man on the second floor and I said I would endeavour to sell Miriam's school raffle tickets to him and to ascertain if he was single. It was a teenage strategy that made us both giggle.

In the park, children were bicycling on the paths. People lay sprawled in the sun, tights and shoes discarded next to them. A moped hiccoughed along the street, the hum of the vast city overlaid by the immediate noises; it was all strangely soporific. Lulled by the sun and our chatter, I told Anthea and Catherine of our plans and swore them to secrecy. Catherine's mouth was full but she nodded.

After lunch I clopped down the linoleum-clad back stairs to the chrome and glass and the grey Venetian blinds of the studios below. I sold two tickets to the receptionist and three to the secretaries before I penetrated the inner office. The man in question was broad, hirsute, wearing a pink shirt. He had a fierce blue shadow of a beard. I told him my divorced friend fancied him, depending on whether he was single or not. Not. I think he thought I had invented Anthea as a cover.

Back in her office, I told Anthea what had happened. She let out what can only be described as a hen party shriek. 'You didn't! El! Oh my God! How will I face him again?'

Nicola stopped in the doorway, her face frigid; she didn't have to say a thing. She looked at me with what we called her death ray stare and then passed by. Anthea and I exchanged glancces. I knew instantly what had happened.

'You cow,' I said to Catherine. It was 6.15. I stood in her doorway with my coat on. She was still at her desk, and her phone was ringing.

She spread her hands wide. 'You never said not to say,' she protested. It was artificial, a ham actor's portrayal of innocence. I knew she'd heard my admonition, all right.

The decrepit lift took an age to crank from second to ground floors, packed as it was with high-spirited secretaries and their inconsequential, carefree chatter. I squeezed past them, walked out of the front door and then stopped in my tracks, feeling suddenly purposeless, as if I'd forgotten where I was going or how to negotiate the way. One of them cannoned into my back.

'Sor-ree,' she grumbled, tutting to herself

But all I did was stand there and sigh, my head thrown back, my eyes shut. What a fool I was! What a spectacle I made of myself! Nicola was not going to plead with me to stay. I was dispensable.

I opened my eyes; a brown speck hung in the evening sky, doubtless a starling, but it seemed to me to be my own deflating sheath as it shot off into the brown, soupy ether, and the city lights came out, one by one, to glimmer far below.

Chapter Five

I was fifteen when I began to rebel. It wasn't an obvious, noisy rebellion. It was done by subterfuge, so that I could even the score without my parents even knowing. It was, if the truth be told, a half-hearted, wimpish effort.

It began on the night of the school fireworks display. For days, the caretaker had been adding to the pile in the corner of the playing fields; old doors, paint flayed and blistering, discarded boxes, fallen branches that sprouted leprous growths. We watched the bonfire growing.

The sixth formers who were taking their Art A level had designed a guy and the fifth form needlework students, the duffers who couldn't manage an extra academic O level, sewed it. One afternoon, they bore him out to his pyre; a lumpy figure in a spivvy suit, who regarded us sadly from his chancy vantage point. His features were unmistakably those of President Nixon. They had sewed little blue knots over his chin like the President's perpetual nine o'clock shadow. Around his neck there was a placard which read, 'Revenge of the pinkoes.' The headmistress had them remove it. Miss Killen was a tiny woman who stood purposefully erect. We cracked jokes behind her back but we quaked if called to her study.

I had been eager to see the burning of Nixon's effigy but I arrived late, that Guy Fawkes night. All that was left was a mouldering pillow and two black brogues smeared with ashes. The bonfire licked languidly at the icy night with its long, red tongues. Its benevolent glow fell on the congregation gathered by its feet, mostly the younger girls, a handful of teachers and a few parents – the officious, chummy parents who sat on committees. A trio of fathers was in charge of letting off the fireworks; they lit them with long tapers and retired to a conspicuous distance, sidling back fearfully if they failed to ignite.

Marina was standing with her back to the fire, outside its circle of warmth, in the shadows of the belt of trees and scrub which lined the wire-mesh perimeter. She called me over, softly. I could just make out her face, a grin puckering the corners of her mouth. There was always a sly gleam in her eye as she explored the places forbidden to a teenage girl in stockbroker belt Surrey. In her hand, a butt glowed.

'Wanna drag?' she said.

I took the cylinder of paper between my thumb and fore-finger, gingerly, and my touch told me it was baggy, ill-rolled. I looked up into her witchy gaze, and she nodded.

'Go on,' she said, blurring the words, 'Ga-wn.'

A frisson of fear rushed from my stomach to my throat. I had never smoked a joint before.

I bent my head, puffed quickly at the acrid tube, and handed it back. My mouth seemed full of bonfire. My cheeks were bulging fit to burst. My lungs would explode.

I ack-acked into a cough and Marina tittered.

My eyes were watering so that as I leaned back, gulping iced air, the great silver stars smudged. I blinked, and they sharpened into focus, and there they were again, hanging in the black, whispering to me their chants of immortality. They always moved me. I was completely sober.

'Good stuff, eh?' said Marina, pretending to be an expert.

A figure loomed in the dark: large, female, authoritarian. Wordlessly, Marina and I wheeled to our right, away from the bonfire, strolled among the trees.

Marina was well-built, with heavy breasts and wide hips, the suggestion of a pot belly stretching her tight grey uniform skirt. Black mascara crusted her eyelashes and leached under her eyes. She had a mascara compact with which she busied herself in front of the lavatory mirrors, spitting into the black cake and twirling the brush, one, two, three, against her upper lashes. Make-up was forbidden in the school rules, but somehow the staff contrived not to notice Marina's.

I did not have to ask her where she had acquired the joint. She had long hung around with a group of young men – youths, my father would call them, with an inflection – in the pubs on Friday nights and in the coffee bar on Saturday mornings. She passed from one to the other, or perhaps it was they who passed through her hands. Her current boyfriend, Andy, who was in his mid twenties, was a labourer and, therefore, an alien being. Somehow Marina's stiff-collared father and Women's Institute mother did not forbid these relationships. Parents, staff, nobody made any attempt to curb Marina, although curiously, they reproved me for the slightest misdemeanour. When I told the careers advice mistress my ambition was to be a Russian spy, she sent me to Miss Killen for a dressing down.

'How do your parents get on with Andy?' I asked Marina as we strolled through the scrub.

'Get on?' she said. 'Oh, fine. They've come round to rather liking him. I've been studying more since I started going out with him. Thought it might pacify them. Now they're under the illusion that he's a good influence.'

We both snickered. Marina handed me the butt without my asking, and this time I took a deeper drag; a languid whirligig danced across the surface of my mind. I giggled again.

'You mongoloid, Ella, don't get silly.'

There was a soft explosion of pink and green stars flowering above us. I wondered for a moment if I was hallucinating. I handed the butt back to Marina, a scant inch left; she licked her fingers, tamped it, tossed it away with a flick of her wrist. It landed in the long jump pit.

'That'll give them something to think about,' she said. 'We better scarper. Miss Thorley's coming. If they find that roach tomorrow, she'll remember you lingering here.'

She would? But Marina had gone, had melted into the

undergrowth like she was a member of the Vietcong or something.

'Who's that? Oh, Eleanor,' said our form mistress, as she loomed out of the grainy night. She sounded disappointed. 'Help to tidy up, will you?'

I made as if to go towards the trestle tables where they'd been serving paper cups of thin tomato soup and those rubbery frankfurters which dripped hot water into soft rolls, but when Miss Thorley had passed safely on, I doubled back. I stood in the trees like an idiot, wondering whether to search for the joint in the pit. Fine if I found it, but what if I didn't? What if someone marked me on my hands and knees, sifting the sand? I wandered to the edge of the pit, as casually as could be, kicking at the soft ridges. And there it was, visible because it was still faintly aglow. Marina, perhaps on purpose, had not extinguished it properly.

I stooped, retrieved it, ran giggling to my hiding place. Pinching out the end, I put it in my pocket. I was invincible. The last of the fireworks, soft, fizzing imitations of the planets and suns and moons high above, bowled up into the sky. The sour smoke of the bonfire, the smoke of a thousand Surrey bonfires, crept across our patch of the earth, clinging to it sadly, a foggy shroud.

All at once, I felt young and vital and achingly sad.

I leaned my back against the bumpy bark of a tree, sharp on my sharp bones. It always caught me by surprise, the way the questions burned, the way the loneliness expanded. My mother said it was being a teenager that did it, but I didn't see why it should grab me like that. When I was young I used to get aches in my legs, growing pains she said; but it didn't seem fair that you should get corresponding pains in your soul. After all, my soul wasn't growing, was it?

I made my way through the trees, my feet crumbling the drifts of dry leaves, and left by the low, metal, back gate. It was only a short walk home, through the quiet avenues of substantial houses. From back gardens there came the occasional hiss of a rocket, or the excited cry of a young child. Buttery lights gleamed at windows, through which I glimpsed sitting-rooms like ours, similar beige, tweedy sofas and heavy curtains in safe, neutral colours. I felt so alone.

When I got home, everything was as usual; the television murmuring behind a closed oak door. The clock chimed a quarter hour. I dived into the downstairs loo to check my face in the mirror, sure that my activities must be written upon it, in red-veined eyes or drowsy pupils as round and black as two caves. Potholes, I thought and my reflection sniggered.

My mother said it was so easy to tell when a young girl lost her virginity; you could see it in her eyes. She said this in a warning tone, casting me a glance. What a mimsy specimen I was. I believed her; or else I did not put it past her to deduce these things mysteriously. And perhaps the sly artifice in Marina's sideways glance proved her point.

As a child, I had believed she knew my thoughts. Above my bed there hung a small disc enamelled with bucolic lambs gambolling across a field, a leftover from nursery days. At night, this became the secret gizmo of my controlling parents, the device by which they collected my brain waves, using electro-magnetic forces. In their newly-installed built-in bedroom furniture – white with gilt mouldings – there was hidden, I knew, the consoles and the television screen upon which they tuned into my dreams and my private thoughts. Although, naturally, I grew out of such fancies, an aura, an echo, remained, enough to fear that my mother would see that I had loitered in the woods with Marina, succumbing to temptation.

But now as I confronted my new self, the person who had smoked a joint, I looked just as I always did. I grinned and my reflection grinned cheesily back. There was nothing cunning about me. It was a relief – and a disappointment.

I called out, 'I'm back,' as I ran up to my room.

Text books lay open on my desk; I checked the essay in my exercise book, sardined the lot into my bag, closed the curtains. I checked on my face again in the dressing table mirror, I took the stub of the joint from my coat pocket and for some reason secreted it in a glass jar which was intended for cotton wool balls.

I had an inviolable bedtime routine. After my visit to the bathroom, the washing of my face in anti-bacterial cream, the hundred strokes of the hairbrush in front of my dressing table, I extracted my diary from the right-hand drawer of my bureau and turned to the day's page. I wrote, 'lst j'; then, after considerable wrestling, on a new paragraph, 'I have come to believe in the intrinsic nobility of man.'

'Something I am determined on,' my mother announced one day. I was strolling in the garden on a spring morning, eating toast and jam, and she came to join me, carrying her little trug and the trowel and fork set I had bought for her birthday.

She peered at me through narrowed eyes. 'I am determined,' she continued, 'that you will have good skin.'

I reached for my cheek and stroked it. It felt smooth, it felt fine.

'I noticed your friend, Jenny is it? Have you seen the acne on that girl? I'm going to teach you to cleanse, tone and moisturise, as the Europeans do.'

She didn't mean to make me anxious. She was trying to treat me – nicely is the word that springs to mind – as a fledgling woman, is more accurate. She began to buy me surprisingly adult gifts, which reflected her own attitudes towards femininity and which I have never fully escaped: make-up, cold creams and perfumes. When I was twelve she had bought me, and my best friend, a whole set of nail varnishes, from deep red to light pink, ten bottles in a see-through zipped bag. The best friend's mother, who was a Scottish Presbyterian, was aghast.

In my teens, she bought me a whole set of expensive eye shadows, layer upon layer of bright colours in a black plastic case with a silver motif. Appearances matter, she would say to me, and I believed her. It took me years to see the more important truth: that people took you – more or less – on your own valuation. My lack of confidence was as garish as my lipstick; no wonder I had never acquired the popularity that came so easily to some. No wonder I never achieved as much as my talents had promised.

How we prinked and preened – I and all my friends – before we ventured out! Heather used to cut little strips of false lashes to glue to her upper lid, then she dipped a fine sable brush in black liner and painted lines on her bottom lid, fanning them outwards like a doll's. If her hand wobbled, she turned crabby – a sharp hiss of breath, a pout in Cinnamon Kiss – then she blotted out her mistake and started again. There was a possibility – never yet realised, but awful in prospect – that one day she would simply run out of time and have to appear half-painted at the disco or the party in some friend's sitting-room (the parents having conspicuously taken themselves upstairs after we arrived).

We used to get ready at my house, the ritual becoming a part of the social event. I would paste white gloop on my cheeks and lie back, two plump tea bags on my eyes. I felt the tea bags grow warm, the skin on my cheeks and chin tightening as the clay dried white. Two rivulets of tea trickled down each of my cheek bones, eroding the powdery chalk, staining my yellow bedspread. Fifteen minutes of immobility it took; for a crack in the face pack mysteriously negated all benefits.

The routine was always the same, I believe, but the episode I remember was when Heather provided me with final proof that she had left me far behind. Ah, Heather! We had been to primary school together, Heather and I, but even I could see the gulf that was opening between us. Heather with her lips pursed together and her blank, blue eyes, so full of herself, so precocious, so alien. Heather whom I admired because she so admired herself.

'Time's up,' she called to me.

I removed my tea bags and rose carefully. In the mirror my reflection was startling. I looked like an Elizabethan, my stern complexion lead-powdered, my lips alarmingly red and moist in comparison. In the bathroom, it always took me ages to wash my skin clear; the powdery clay clogging in the fine hairs at my temples and above my ears.

Back in my bedroom, Heather had plugged her curling tongs into the socket by my bed and crouched beside it, gnomic.

'I'm going out with Dieter,' she informed me. Dieter was

her elder brother's foreign exchange student; he was staying for a fortnight from Cologne. She had fancied him from the start.

I paused in the business of rubbing cream blusher above my cheekbones. 'Gosh,' I said. Then, 'What does your brother think of that?' I vaguely imagined Jonathan's peevishness at being unable to practise his German.

'Don't be a moron! Why should he care?' There was a swishing sigh from the tongs as Heather pressed the steam button. 'The three of us met some friends, went up to a concert at the Rainbow, went on to a party in Reading. It was really something else,' she said. There was a silence while she tugged at the curler where it had caught in her hair. One side of her blonde head was ringleted; the other smooth and flat. 'Dieter and I went up to the bedroom and petted,' she said.

It was lucky she had waited to tell me this until after I had removed my mud pack. Surely otherwise the cracks would now be splitting my face, great chunks crumbling in astonishment onto the carpet. I stared at her reflected face, the careful way she arranged her expression, her set shoulders. I could see it was a dare, like that time she bet me I wouldn't free-wheel my bike down the hill outside our primary school. To this day, there was a sort of hole in my knee where I had hit the tree at the bottom. But I had never regretted that dizzying, sickening ride, even though I'd known my brakes weren't working. You didn't refuse one of Heather's dares.

She was studying me, too, in the mirror and she caught the avidity in my expression. 'You're not to tell anyone,' she ordered, fiercely. 'Not anyone. Got it?'

'Of – of course,' I said, fervently.

Pacified, she brushed out another strand of hair and clamped the tongs around the end, drawing them downwards, winding them round and round.

'Was it heavy petting?' I said. I had no idea where the demarcation lines between 'ordinary' petting and 'heavy' petting lay, but girls like Heather, girls like Marina, they knew; they had travelled right to the brink and made the decision whether to cross over, or remain.

'No,' she said, shocked. 'I haven't known him long. Light petting. I let him take my bra off.' Another part of my face seemed to flake in stupefaction.

'What did he do?'

'What do you think he did? He touched them, of course. Took them in his hands.'

'What? He sort of weighed them?'

'Oh, you're such a moron sometimes!' Heather slammed the tongs onto my bed and I watched in agony, lest they brand my pyjama case, which was in the shape of a black poodle, and which lay in its customary place with its chin on the side of my pillow. And indeed, when I said, 'Sorry. Only joking,' in a small voice, and she picked up the tongs once more, there was a faint smell of singed nylon. Heather examined Talbot. A strip of fur, like a lash on his back, had withered and turned a light golden brown.

'I'll report you to the RSPPC,' I said. 'Royal Society for the Protection of Pyjama Cases.'

Her eye caught mine and we both began to giggle. We were friends again. You never knew with Heather. There had been, for example, that business when she had passed comment on my legs.

'You should wear trousers, you know,' she had said, 'Your legs are such thin, weedy stalks.'

I glanced down at them and silently agreed.

'Oh, well,' I sighed, 'at least it's better than being fat.'

She didn't talk to me for a fortnight after that. I had to ask Pam Bates what I'd done wrong and Pam had to collar Heather in the cloakrooms, and then she relayed the message. I had called Heather fat.

No, I hadn't, I said in my mind.

'I'm sorry,' I had told Pam wearily, who had told Heather, 'I didn't mean it.'

At the discotheque that night it was the usual story. Although objective analysis suggested to me that I was at least as pretty as Heather, although the mirror as I searched it, questioning it, seemed to say, you look OK, I still ended up sitting out a number of dances, and otherwise was asked only by the grammar school dorks. Not for the first time I wondered how I might acquire my friends' knowingness without, well, having to know. As for Heather, I hold a few images of her from that night in my memory. I see her snogging with Dieter, who turned up later, the pair oblivious on the edge of the dance floor. I see us walking through the dark streets afterwards, me trying to keep up with her scornful eighteen-year-old brother, as I was always struggling to keep up at that time. Heather and Dieter, however, lagged behind. Once, I heard her carefree laugh, and looking back, I saw him piggy-backing her, as one might a child. It was a gesture at once innocent and affectionate, and yet also describing sweaty sexual exertion, as she clamped her legs around his back. And I also hold the mind image, implanted while talking in my bedroom and just as powerful, of him holding her breasts in his hands, balancing them in his palms, a quizzical look on his face, as if he were deciding which one was riper.

'What did it feel like?' I had asked her.

She had wriggled her lips and thought. 'Well,' she said, after a while, 'all I can say is, he certainly seemed to enjoy it.'

I was flattered that Heather chose me to accompany her to the family planning clinic; I remember that clearly, too. I followed the great events of the year – miners' strikes, the massacre at the Munich Olympics, the break-in at Watergate – in a desultory manner, for I retained some sort of political curiosity as a kind of defining edge to my persona. I argued with my father. I bought a paperback by Che Guevara and learned how to make Molotov cocktails. For some time I viewed each of my mother's empty milk bottles as a potential weapon in urban guerilla warfare. Even today I could give you the instructions to make a petrol bomb although other lessons carefully taught to me (trigonometry, the life cycle of the liver fluke) have vanished into the spongy matter of my brain. But 1972 remains for me the year of Heather's sexual awakening, the year in which, one by one, we turned sixteen, and sent each other cards scrawled with feeble jokes about the age of consent, flaunting our fake adulthood.

'I've decided,' Heather said to me one day that March, when we were supposed to be revising. Her hair was bright against the faded spines of fusty books on the shelves of the school library. 'I've decided I'm going all the way.' She tipped her chin up, pouting, as she made this statement, appearing defiant and mysteriously female. 'I'm in love with him.'

Dieter was returning for the Easter holidays and had written urging her to go on the pill. 'Take the pill' was the phrase he used. I heard his voice, low and mesmeric: Take ze pill, Heather. Take ze pill.

And Heather was in love. I had never been in love; not unless you counted Che, who was even more than usually unobtainable, being dead.

'You will come with me, won't you?' said Heather in the library, and for a moment something sad and frightened peeked out from behind her rapturous, hormonal stare.

We met on the station, platform four, having decided it was too risky to visit the local FPA where we might bump into a school mate, a friend's mother or worse, a teacher. I had not imagined married women attending clinics. Surely they could go to their own GPs without embarrassment? But Marina said she had once had to hide behind an FPA door for thirteen minutes in order to avoid Mrs Briggs, the biology mistress.

'Mrs Briggs on the pill?' I had said. 'But she's got wrinkles.' And we had all snickered.

'You're late,' Heather said when I clattered down the covered stairway onto the platform. She was standing next to the railway buffet.

'No, I'm not.' I checked the big clock. I wasn't.

'Well . . . at least you're here now.'

She was wearing a checked smock dress which hung from her pouter pigeon bosom, a tip-tilted cloche hat, and red leather clogs on her feet. This was the fashion of the moment and it rather suited her. She carried two magazines, *Honey* and *Petticoat*, but, when the train arrived and we settled down on a flocked seat that smelled of warm dust, we merely flicked the pages. The train rattled its way laboriously to the next town on the track. I turned my attention to a splodge of nail varnish

that I had dabbed around a small hole in the knee of my tights.
I picked at it with my nail. You were supposed to use colourless varnish, so the mend would be invisible (this was the
theory), but only peach had been to hand. It looked highly
conspicuous.

There was no one else in our carriage. 'Do you know where
the clinic is?' I whispered to Heather.

'Of course I do. I've looked it up. I've got an appointment,'
she whispered back.

We fell silent. Eventually, she nudged me; the train was
changing tracks, its wheels screeching in protest; we had
arrived.

It was a drab day, the sky as grimy as the pavements under-
foot. To our discomfort, a group of boys, fifth formers from
the local secondary modern, hailed us.

Heather knew them vaguely from a dance she had been
allowed to attend at the Hacienda ballroom.

'Hey, lucky Heather! And one of her grammar school friends!
Whaddya doing?'

They approached of course. The grammar school girls had a
reputation; supposedly we felt the deprivation of belonging to
a single sex school; supposedly we were slavering for males.

'You gotta hole in your tights,' one of them drawled, flicking
his eyes up and down me. He was already growing stringy
muscles at his wrists and in his neck, though his cheeks were
downy and innocent.

'I know,' I said, chilly as could be.

'Where else you gotta hole?' he retorted, and they erupted
in chortling derision.

Heather and I marched side by side, eyes front, faces like
pokers. That was what you did. The boys swaggered and
heckled. The girls kept on walking. It was such a predictable
pantomime, and yet experience did not make us less appre-
hensive, or less humiliated.

We knew they would fall in around us. I glanced at my
watch, which had a face as big as an egg cup, in the current
fashion. We had quarter of an hour before the appointment. If
we were lucky, they would lose interest. Otherwise, what

would Heather do? Would we pitch up at the FPA with a raggle-taggle mob of jeering youths behind us? I felt my ears burn red.

One of the boys, walking backwards in front us, bumped into a middle-aged woman coming out of a shop doorway. She was jamming her purse into her laden wicker shopping basket which was why she, too, had not been looking where she was going. Seeing us, she hammered it down even more firmly, and pursed her lips and shot Heather and me a look of disapproval, as if it were our fault that we had attracted the attentions of this raucous lot.

'Excuse me,' she said, in that old-maidish way.

I pleaded with her with my eyes. Please see that I am not usually the sort of girl who hangs around with boys who bump into old ladies, or make vulgar comments. Nor are many of my friends on the pill, yet. In primary school, Heather hadn't been like this; she was like the rest of us, she collected gonks and trolls, and wished she were Marion Coakes, the show-jumper. If not Stroller, the pony. But of course the woman didn't decipher any of my message. She hurried off, shoulders hunched.

Shortly afterwards, the boys got bored and peeled away. One of them ran towards the benches that faced the river, climbed on the low grey wall and beat upon his chest with his fists.

'Yo-yo-yo-yo-ow!' he called and pretended to teeter on his tiptoes, windmilling his arms.

Then all the others took off after him, in a wheeling flock. They screamed and called like gulls. And then they rebunched – some sitting, some standing with one foot on the seats. They made a great play of shaking cigarettes from packets and lighting them.

We turned the corner. Neither of us referred to them or their coarse comments. Beyond a sigh and a click of the tongue, you never did. You just pretended you were immune. And we were already at the entrance to the clinic, which was sited next to a newsagent's in a terraced house, a perfectly ordinary house, except that in the bay window, where you expected to see net curtains, or perhaps a Coronation cup on a white doily in the dead centre of the sill, there was instead a flotilla of VD posters stuck to the inside of the glass. Worried About Gonorrhoea? one proclaimed.

Gosh, no. I hoped I never would be.

My impression of the waiting room is tinged by the anxiety that gripped my shoulders and propelled me through the maroon front door after Heather, and up the narrow, gloomy stairs. It was a light, cold room, painted aquamarine. The pale vinyl chairs were arranged in a row with their backs to the door, which was unsettling. Also, they made rude noises if you shifted your weight quickly. In front of them, on a low Formica table – white, sprigged with black leaves – lay untidy rows of magazines and pamphlets.

The receptionist, a slight, tired woman with watery eyes, sat to one side at an ordered desk. Behind her were two cubicles, also made of Formica, with curtains on rails for a modicum of privacy. One was occupied and I began to fret that we would hear what was going on inside but after a while, apart from one metallic clink, which made me jump, the worst that emerged was an inaudible murmur.

So. Not so bad. I relaxed a little.

I turned to the notice board on my right, which was bristling with more information about sexually transmitted diseases, abortions and help for drug addicts. I was both thrilled and terrified. This was the nearest I had ever come to low living.

Heather was given a card to fill in before being called to the empty cubicle. I grinned encouragingly at her. She regarded me soberly, widening her eyes a fraction. Swish! She disappeared.

Alone, I sat in an agony of eager dread.

A motherly-looking doctor emerged from the one booth, cracked a joke to the receptionist, winked at me – I grinned again and shrugged – and disappeared behind the other curtain with Heather's card and a stethoscope. A motorbike roared down the street outside. The telephone rang. The unknown patient emerged. She was thirtyish and looked well groomed; incongruous, somehow, in these surroundings.

The woman looked at me for a beat longer than politeness allowed. I found myself slouching. I made as if to examine the tips of my fingers, slightly puckered with the unseasonal cold. I was running her face against a checklist in my mind. I didn't think that I knew her, even by sight.

'Thanks,' she called and clicked off down the linoleum stairway.

I didn't know her. I blew out a breath.

Heather's consultation went on and on. I picked up a pamphlet from the table. *The Right Contraceptive For You*, it said. Inside there were drawings of curly coils and descriptions of caps which were boggling beyond belief.

Finally, Heather came out. I snapped to attention the moment the curtain rings jangled. She was smiling. She handed me her squashy hat and various bits of paper and returned to the desk to arrange a second appointment for a month's time. The receptionist was emitting perceptible waves of nonjudgemental friendliness as she leafed through her big black diary, offering a selection of dates and times. At last Heather flung her coat over her arm and turned to go.

'Take the pamphlet,' the receptionist said to me, and I started. I was holding it still.

'Oh, thanks.' I stuffed it into my deep patch pocket. I felt I would cause grave disappointment if I told her I had no need of it.

We tramped down the stairs, Heather's clogs echoing brazenly on the thin wood. In the station waiting room she extracted the foil packets from her bag and we both gazed solemnly at the pills in their plastic bubbles. Heather was a grown-up.

I did not see Heather once over that Easter break so I was unable to tell her that my mother, finding the pamphlet where it lay forgotten in my coat, had jumped to the worst conclusions. I was in my room, reading *The Lord Of The Rings*. My door burst open. She flung the pamphlet towards me and it fluttered to the carpet, lying limp and pitiful on the blue velvet pile. My heart lurched.

'What are you doing? What do you think you are doing?' she screamed.

I managed a 'but', before she lurched towards me and slapped me across my cheek, hard.

There was a moment of absolute silence and stillness. My cheek burned. My eyes filled with tears.

'It wasn't me, it was Heather,' I said and I put my hand to my face, but I think I was really trying to disguise my disgrace.

She drew back. She knew I was telling the truth. But all she said was, 'You bloody little fool! Clinics? I'll give you clinics! I don't want you mixing with that little tart ever again. Do you hear me? Not ever again! Half the golf club goes to that FPA!'

I waited on my bed with Talbot, as striped as I was, on my lap. I waited for my father to come home. I knew that then I would be straining to distinguish the words and phrases in the music of their conversation, straining to hear what they thought of me. I hoped he might prove kinder. He was kinder to me than to her. And while I waited, I resolved that I would never behave like that towards my daughter, if ever I should have one; and I decided this resentfully even though I could see it was fear and relief that had jerked her hand upwards, as automatically as a puppet's.

So that is one reason why I did not see Heather again until term started, and she, preoccupied with Dieter, did not call me either. But on the first day of the summer term, she sat next to me at lunch. We didn't talk much as we picked through brown stew and scoops of mashed potatoes, the lumps visible on the surface like islands on a globe, but when those nearby had scraped their plates into the metal swill bin, we sat on.

In the course my life I would discover that there are two places which smell of boiled cabbage even if no one appears to be boiling it; apartment block stairwells in St Petersburg and all school halls. I will never smell this smell without thinking of Heather and her tales of lost virginity. The two seem to go together, the one a background to the other.

'I did it with Dieter,' she said. She was looking at her lap, drawing patterns on the serge of her skirt with her fingernail. A first former sped past, panting. Running inside the building was forbidden by the school rules but neither of us reprimanded her.

I adopted a confidential kind of an expression. 'What was it like?' I asked, agog.

'It takes a bit of getting used to,' she replied. 'All he said was, "Use your muscles." Well, actually,' she stole a quick glance at me, 'What he said was "Use your muskles." '

Use your muskles!

I gaped at her.

'Which muskles?'

Her shoulders began to shake. She buried her head in her hands. She let out a snort. For a minute or two, I sat, stupidly, unsure as to whether she was laughing or crying, and when she surfaced, she seemed to have been doing both because she was dabbing at her eyes with her forefingers, while her teeth were bared in a skeletal grin.

'Anyway,' she said, when she had recovered, 'he's gone back to Cologne and good riddance to him. He was really quite immature.' She bent her head closer. 'The thing I really hated was the way he kept his eyes open when he kissed me. He looked so sloppy and twittish.' She pulled a gormless, moon-struck face, boggling her eyes and sticking out her tongue. 'Barry – do you know Barry? He's a friend of my brother's. He kisses me with his eyes closed. He's just gorgeous . . . No, I know I can do better than Dieter,' she said.

It was May and Heather was in love again.

In the sixth form, Heather and I were no longer friendly and I suppose the only surprising thing was that we hadn't fallen out sooner. Heather palled up with Isabel, a galumphing, ugly girl with a shaggy mane of wiry, mouse-brown hair who was every bit as inexperienced as I was, but considerably better at hiding it.

I remember Heather saying to me, 'You realise I'm going to sit next to Isabel next term?'

I blushed at the cruelty of her defection and said, 'Of course,' because, of course, I had seen it coming.

Marina's pot belly bulged and strained at her tight, grey skirt.

'Are you all right?' I asked her, and she said, 'Fine,' as her eyes slipped past mine to examine the wall.

There had been a case like this before, a girl whose stomach was a scandal. As it grew, her back hollowed and her gait changed, so that she teetered along, chest first, as if charging towards her moment of truth. How much longer before the staff twigged? we said, one to another.

One day, I was walking along the corridor. It was a lesson period, for it was very quiet and empty, but for some reason I was not in the class. My feet tapped a dancing rhythm on the polished tiles. Every now and then, I stroked a few sweeping paces on my new leather soles. In this way, I glided past the heavy glass doors of the main entrance on my right, and the bronze sculpture of three bright, purposeful girls, arms entwined; I passed the wooden door to the gymnasium on my left, approaching Miss Killen's study.

And there she was, the girl with the swollen belly, standing outside it, waiting to be called in. Her face was taut, white. I have never seen anyone so frightened, or so vulnerable.

'Oh, please,' she said, when she saw me, 'Would you take a message . . .'

But I skated past her on the tiles, my pace quickening, pretending not to hear, as if her condition were catching.

For that is what women – mothers and teachers – fear, isn't it? That is why they warn you off girls like Heather. Or, if they spot them, girls like Marina. But Marina did not keep an appointment outside Miss Killen's study and then vanish from the school once and for all. Marina merely disappeared in a discreet fashion for a few days, and reappeared, looking happy, and we neither of us alluded to her absence. To this day I do not know for certain whether I was right in my conclusions, for she left after A levels and the last I heard of her, she had married a civil servant and moved to Potters Bar.

At that period, I wrote in my diary: 'The most promiscuous girls are the most romantic.' I must have thought this profound. Jessica was my best friend by then. Sensible, arty, quirky Jessica, she used to come round on Saturday evenings and we would talk till late, about literature, art and the problems of the world. About the convoluted love lives of our con-temporaries. Once, we worked out that we constituted two of the only six remaining virgins in the sixth form, and as the other four were dumpy, frumpy, born again Christians, who witnessed for the Lord in the school corridors, this was a truly remarkable feat. But we were both determined that there should be some link between love and making love, and we were so sure that we would recognise true passion where our peers had failed.

I showed Jessica the entry in my diary and she said, 'God, El. You're such a cynic.'

I glowed with pride.

Shortly afterwards, I went up to university and I lost my virginity to one of the tutors, a married man with a shock of greying curls and a sardonic take on the origins of feminist thinking. We smoked a large joint in the back of his family estate and I tumbled over, onto my back. All that holding out, all those conversations with Jessica, all that hoping for something real and right. But it wasn't such a big deal. It didn't bother me half as much as other things that happened to me in childhood.

I had two unsatisfactory love affairs after that, the latter with a married man whose idea of a gift was a twist of paper which looked innocent as a sweet but which contained cocaine. I very quickly realised that cocaine was dangerous to me; it would be my drug of choice. The iced paralysis and the bitter aftertaste at the back of the mouth, these I loathed; but the feeling of unassailability, of control and power . . .

Years later, I would see Anthea sniffing cocaine at a party, and be shocked. It was a recreational boost, like a drink, to her, just a London party accessory. But to me there could be no reason for the degradation of rolled bank notes and sniffing long and loud unless it was a deeper one. That was why it had frightened me so. In my five-year diary, which I had brought to university with me, I wrote for the same date on the next year: 'If my life has not changed for the better by now, commit suicide.' I was so fragile and I craved the illusion of strength. I was miserable.

But in a year's time I had forgotten that entry. I had forgotten the diary. I had met Michael and I was happy. His love now gave me the illusion of armour; the loneliness shrank or was disguised.

The rest you know. I became a respectable cog in the machinery of the community; I became a mother, that is to say, a woman with secrets. My life turned predictable, with all the satisfactions and frustrations that that implies.

Chapter Six

A sawing moan drenched the air: a violin played tentatively.

I lingered at the foot of the stairs. The same phrase was repeated, more smoothly and surely this time, then gave way to a plucking pizzicato. The melody was familiar, a piece Miriam had been set by her violin teacher months ago, but had barely practised since. Oh, but I had been tippytoeing towards this resumption for so many weeks, anxious not to nag but eager, too, to encourage her. I had tried all methods, playing the CDs which included particularly poignant violin phrases; proffering the temptation of seats to a concert, straightforward reminders of how long she had not practised. At last. One of the approaches, perhaps all of them, perhaps simple maternal patience, had worked.

The bow resumed its lilt. I mounted the stairs, feeling suddenly restored, pausing in her doorway to watch her.

She was poised in front of her music stand by her bedroom window overlooking the garden. She had not changed out of her navy-and-grey uniform; the V-necked jumper, the checked shirt, the navy skirt hitched to six inches above her knee. Her elbows protruded from their worn, transparent sleeves, the loopy stitches gaping, the bone sharp. I could never see Miriam in her school uniform without being achingly aware of the contradictions inherent in her age; she was tall and slender, sappy somehow, beautiful as a streamlined colt, and she was also gawky and angular, straining at the confines of childhood.

Her face was a quiet study of concentration as she gazed at the music, her arms cutting angles in the air. Then her eyes flickered as she became aware of me, the music faltered and went out.

'That was lovely,' I said, my Pavlovian reaction.

'Thanks, Mum. I thought I'd try it again. I was rather inspired by something Louise said.'

I don't think my face fell, though my spirits did. 'Oh,' I said. 'Do you know Messiaen?'

'Not intimately,' I said, somewhat coldly.

'There's this brilliant piece she played me. Can we get the same CD?'

'Oh, sure,' I said and drooped down the stairs. It was ridiculous to mind as much as I found myself minding.

Having opened the French windows, I slumped into my favourite armchair and gazed at the high summer abandon of my patch of a garden, drunken lilies and capering roses. Summer sounds competed with the renewed lament of the violin; a blackbird, a faraway dog, the further away rush and hum of the city.

The thought slipped through my mind, unchecked. How much easier it would be if Louise Carrington were a bad influence on Miriam. It would be easy to talk to Michael, to have him do something, risking his popularity with Miriam, rather than mine. It would justify my antagonism towards the woman, too, and how satisfying that would be. But no, Louise Carrington had Miriam practising the violin again, seemingly with a subtle, tactful word.

I would meet Louise Carrington at last tomorrow, when we dropped Miriam off. She was working there all day as usual, then staying the evening as Michael and I were finally going to Norwich.

'Won't you come?' I had asked Miriam.

She shook her head.

'I don't want you staying on your own,' I added, more sharply.

'Then I'll stay with someone.' The words were elongated for emphasis – 'Then I'll . . . stay . . . with . . . some-one,' – for the easier understanding of a simpleton.

'I could ask Kate's mum.'

'I'll ask,' she said. But in the evening she told me she had arranged to stay with Louise.

'Oh,' I said.

'Is there a problem?' The question was put belligerently.

'Well, not really, it's just that I don't know her.'

'You don't know Kate's mum, not really.'

'Well, I've been inside her house.'

'Huh. Only into the kitchen for a coffee. For all you know, Kate's father could be a child molester.'

'Oh, please! Kate's far too well adjusted.' She had hit on a raw spot; I had often wondered over the years how you could tell whether the smily, exterior faces of the school friends' parents hid deeper secrets. As far as I could see, you sniffed your way by instinct, like a canny animal.

Miriam was continuing with her grumble. 'You can come into Louise's kitchen for a coffee if you want. It probably has the same units.'

Mothers with teenagers are adept at picking their fights, and I knew that this wasn't mine. But I had noticed that it was with increasing frequency that I backed down.

Oh, well. Tomorrow. A part of me shied away from an encounter with the woman who seemed to be my rival. Did she guess how I regarded her? If we did not get on, as it seemed certain we would not, would Miriam frown, appraising me in that unnervingly objective way?

At about 8.00, Miriam clattered about the kitchen, fixing herself a Pot Noodle and yoghurt supper. I snoozed for a while, unwittingly.

When Michael came home at 9.30, I was still slumped in a corner of the navy armchair, stroking the nap of a ruby velvet cushion.

'I've had a very bad day,' I said in a tragic tone.

He bent and kissed the top of my head, went to make us supper, a chicken stir-fry, a familiar dish because his repertory was limited to five or six recipes. He brought the plates in on trays.

'Is it OK?' he asked me as I forked in my first mouthful.

'Delicious,' I said.

This was part of our unvarying repertoire, too; he could never take a turn cooking without hinting for my approval, like Miriam really, or as if I were a claque of one. A commentary accompanied all Michael's domestic efforts; 'I've put a load of laundry in for you,' he might inform me. 'Thanks, darling!' I would declare. How it had begun to niggle at me over the years! The way he said, 'For you,' as if none of that laundry was his. I reversed the parts once. 'I've done the dusting for you,' I told him. And he looked at me as if I was mad.

Oh, I was certainly in a fractious mood tonight. It did not bode well for tomorrow.

Curiously, I awoke and knew instantly that I felt better. I lay stretching in the rumpled sheets, orientating myself with the morning, the susurrus of a nearby shower; the downstairs jangle of a radio tuned to Virgin. The sun glanced in at my window and melted my heart with its eternal cheeriness. Well, I had burned my bridges at work so there was no point fretting any more. I sat up and beamed at the Eleanor in the closet mirror. She looked just as gangling and easily discernible as ever.

First, we took the detour to drop Miriam and her lumpen nylon bag at Louise Carrington's. She insisted we go in to see some of the animals she was tending, and, although Michael was reluctant, eager to be on our way – 'before the traffic built up,' he said, as if the whole of London would be streaming north to Norwich today – I backed Miriam.

'Oh, come on, "Dad", it won't take long,' I said, as if butter wouldn't melt in my mouth.

We ducked under a low willow tree, following a beaten earth path. There was a rank odour in the air, that smelled to me like dog fox and the marking of territory, though there were no caged foxes visible. Miriam led us to a small shed where a tawny owl made odd clicking noises at us, a sign, so she said, of warning; and then to two kestrels, which sat, regal and uninterested, at the back of their enclosure, regarding us with hooded, yellow eyes.

Miriam stopped by a wire mesh cage, inside which, sitting on a branch, was a small monkey with a tuft of hair like a toupee above sad, intelligent, human eyes. 'This is Tony. He's been maltreated,' Miriam said, 'He hates men. In fact, I'm the only person he's really bonded with.'

On the other side of the wire, the monkey began to pull faces, grinning like a corpse, and manipulating his eyebrows, up and down, up and down, very fast. Miriam stretched up towards him on his perch, her fingers entwined in the wire of the cage, and began mimicking his movements.

'What does it mean?' I asked her.

'It's a sign of submission,' she replied.

'How useful,' I said. 'If only humans would defer so readily.' She ignored me and it dawned on me that she thought I was having a dig at her. I was not yet an expert at filtering *everything* I said for offence to a teenager's sensibilities.

As we walked away, the monkey began to bang on the side of the wire and to twitter shrilly. We stopped and cast him a backwards glance. It was so sad to see an animal in such hysteria. He was running back and forth along his branch, straining to see Miriam. I recognised one of the reasons why she so liked it here: what a validation of yourself to be needed so fiercely!

I had almost given her up, when Louise Carrington intercepted us as we made our way back to the car.

'Michael!' called a voice. 'And it's Eleanor, isn't it?'

She was nothing like the Louise of my imaginings. She was almost matronly: shorter, stouter, with a heavy bosom. A little list scrolled through my mind: she's greyer, fatter, dumpier, older than me – for there were rings around her neck and, just as with trees, you can gauge a woman's age by their number. So I won. But it was galling how little satisfaction that brought me.

Her hair, a faded shade of blonde, darker near the scalp, was shoulder-length, cut in layers which she had blow-dried away from her face. Her eyes were her best feature, grey-blue, round, slightly bulbous. She wore lots of pink, jammy lipstick on a small, dolly mouth. She was wearing a scrunchy, blue cotton Indian skirt. A white T-shirt, tucked in at the waist band, meant that you could not avoid seeing that her bosom was supported by a small shelf of padding. Tied to one side of her neck was a long tangerine chiffon scarf, which she fiddled with as she spoke, running her thumbnail along the fine seam. When she remembered herself she would pat it down as if alarmed at her own nervous habit.

'I'm so happy to see you both,' she said in that mid-Atlantic whisper. 'I've been just busting to tell you what a joy Mirry has been. I don't know how I ever managed without her! You must be so proud of her. Oh, lord,' she said, 'I'm prattling. You're off to Norfolk, I hear; for good, I gather. I shall be so distraught when Mirry goes. I only ever managed sons and they're not a bit interested in the sanctuary. They have such ambitions, far beyond my feeble attempts to change the world.' She gestured to the cages and green lawns behind her. 'Ah, well, *che sera*. I do hope you'll let her come see us in the school holidays. Or maybe, Miriam, you can open our Norfolk branch,' she added.

She walked back with us towards the entrance. 'What sort of a house are you looking for? I'll come and check the feng shui on any house you want to buy, if you like. I studied under a Chinese friend, did Miriam tell you? After he taught me, I realised that my bedroom was just as wrong as can be! It was draining me. I had to have it completely redesigned to make the most of the forces and enhance my energy, you know. You may scoff,' she shook her head at us, but we both were keeping admirably straight faces, 'you may scoff but it really did work. I suffered from seasonal affected disorder until then. It was so bad, some winters I could scarcely put a toe out of bed, but the winter afterwards? I was so much better, it was like a miracle. So now when anyone questions ancient belief systems, well, I just have no patience with them. It worked for me, I say.'

Michael's mouth had tautened, his eyes half-closed; she was just the kind of woman who got on his nerves. But I was beginning to see what Miriam might like about her: the lazy, hypnotic cadence of her speech, the unswerving enthusiasm.

Back at the car Michael asked Miriam, a comment filtered through his lips, 'Is she always like that?'

Miriam gave a slightly embarrassed grin. 'Well, she wouldn't have done all this without the energy and the belief,' she said. But her expression said: I know what you mean, Dad.

I was glad I hadn't been the one to say something.

Although she ducked my kiss, as she habitually did, Miriam seemed cheerful enough as she said goodbye to us on the pavement. I felt a squeeze of gratitude and pride. I watched her dwindling figure as the car pulled away; brown curly head, cropped white T-shirt, blue jeans. As ever I was suppressing the great tide of love which rose in me whenever I noted anew how she was growing, her lankiness, the illusion of adulthood belied by her frantically waving hand, her eyes following me, checking that I was still watching her until finally the car swung round the corner and we were out of sight.

We headed out on the trunk road north in a cool morning that promised to split apart into a fine, ripe day. The city stopped abruptly where the motorway began. It bisected acres of green corn waving fringed kernels gracefully, like a hula hula dancer's hands. The wheels grumbled about the ridged concrete surface as Michael steered us past chunks of exploded tyre, past an articulated lorry which thrashed the hatchback in front of us in a tidal wave of displaced air.

'You see why I insisted on the Jeep,' Michael said, as the hatchback careered into the inside lane.

'You insisted on the Jeep because you're a city type posing as a country bumpkin,' I told him, and he grinned his lop-sided attractive grin.

I turned the radio on, tipped the seat back and half-dozed. Michael began telling me more about his job interview, which had taken place earlier in the week, and which seemed to have gone well, and I nodded and smiled at the right moments.

'Difficult question . . .' his voice said. 'Knew they were impressed . . .'

And I went, 'Uh huh. Really? Oh, good.'

Being interested, truly interested, seemed like too much hard work. I let my mind drift and Louise Carrington popped up in front of me, her slightly pursed lips, the tilt of her head, the soft, continuous, yankee doodle lullaby of her conversation. She reminded me faintly of my mother. She had my mother's artificiality, her mannered air, all of it desperately trying to disguise the great black vacuum underneath, the lack of a strong, structured frame of confidence. We had something in common, then. And yet neither my mother nor Louise were stupid women, when I came to think about it. The poses each of us adopt to face the world! The roles we construct! When you are young you are completely taken in; it is only when you are older that you spot the slight shake to a voice, the complete absence of serenity.

Once, my mother opened a window onto her inner self for me to glimpse through, not that she had intended to. It was in the middle of a rather trivial, rancorous discussion. I was trying to persuade her that she need not mind the signs of aging so much, need not take them so to heart, need not invest so much of herself and her will in combating them.

'Oh, Ella,' she said, using my old childhood pet-name. 'You don't understand. You don't understand how ... diminishing it is. There's a defining moment, when you realise it's all up for you.' I was about to interrupt with a jolly, pooh-poohing remark but she waved it away. She gave me a sad, blank stare. 'It's so humiliating,' she whispered. 'It's when you find your first grey pubic hair.' She inserted a pause between each of the words, so that they emerged with a certain weight, 'first ... grey ... pubic ... hair,' and her eyes turned shiny. 'It's then you see yourself turning into a scrawny old bird, all sort of *plucked* and *withered*. Oh, I know you think it's hilarious, or just plain pathetic.' And she placed both her forefingers against her lower lids in an attempt to staunch the tears without disturbing her mascara.

I couldn't think how I'd replied to her. It would have been nice to believe that I had shown her how I suddenly understood, how close I felt to her at that moment. But I probably just said something joky, offered some insipid attempt at reassurance.

An hour or so later, as we reached East Anglia proper, the corn gave way in places to homely cabbages and little copses in a whole palate of greens. The white flowers of bindweed, like a parading band of gleaming trumpets, oom-pah-pahed across the grass verges. Only the poppies seemed discordant, blood-red spattered at the edge of fields. I saw everything in terms of colour and texture, like a painting or a tapestry.

The East Anglian skies, of course, claimed me, a wash of poster-paint blue, a child's idea of how blue skies should be. The high clouds were bruised purple at their edges where they had bumped against each other. Two sleek, knife-shaped fighter planes slit through them, silently.

Michael said, 'Lakenheath, I think, unless they've closed it,' and I deduced this was an airbase and his local knowledge was pretty dated. He had spent a few weekends here at a friend's parents some months before we met, and I inferred from his reticence that this friend was probably a girl.

'It's not as flat as they say,' he added.

'I don't mind flat. This is pretty.'

'There's a saying here, it comes back to me; any fool can find beauty in a hill.'

I gazed upwards again, at the great arch of the sky, and I had the sudden vision that we were caught beneath a tinted glass dome, specimens observed by someone larger on the other side.

'Then I'm not any fool,' I said.

Norwich announced itself with the usual debris of city out-skirts; pylons, roadside diners decked in lurid logos, rounda-bouts daubed with bedding plants, a cacophony of colours. We stopped at a traffic light; from the car next to us came a low, heavy *stonk*, *stonk*, *stonk*, so that our car seemed to vibrate to the beat of its music. The driver inside, a young man with slicked up hair, like a porcupine's, was nodding his head, even his shoulders, rhythmically, and drumming a pulse on the steering wheel with his forefingers. When the light changed he accelerated away in a flash, and disappeared left at the next junction without signalling. It crossed my mind that Michael had once driven like that, and the transformation to sedate speed limits and reliable signalling had arrived so gradually that I hadn't noticed it until now.

A black-and-white sign at the side of the road declared, with all the self-importance of a civic dignitary: 'Norwich: A Fine City.'

'There, you see, it's not just me who thinks so,' Michael said dryly, slipping the car from fourth to third.

I pressed the button and the window purred open. 'I think I can sniff the sea,' I said.

This was not as fanciful as it sounds because elegant, white gulls wheeled above the streets as we penetrated the city centre, following the signs to a high-rise car park. Michael edged the Jeep into a narrow space, the fine bones of his hands standing out as he whirled the wheel. He killed the engine.

I watched him as he stepped down from the driver's side, placing a map and his keys on the roof of the car while he stretched, shrugged on his jacket and took off his sunglasses. In that moment, I saw him afresh, as if removing his glasses had removed a darkened lens from my sight. His familiarity fell away, and I was aware, all at once, of how he looked. His face wore a slight frown, his chin was clamped, tense, his eyes aware, heedful. Most people are unobservant and seem so, but there was often this sense of coiled energy about Michael; it was one of the qualities about him that was still intriguing to me.

I was very aware, at that moment, of his separateness from me, that however long and well I had known him, he was distanced from me by his otherness. It was also a moment of vigorous physicality. I was drinking in his solidity, his face and body. I slipped my hand into his as we walked, where it felt small and fragile as a bird. This was something I had not done for a long time, and it reminded me of when we were young, before we had Miriam.

I liked the look of Norwich. It was not so much its obvious

charm, though I smiled at the remaining medieval streets, their buildings propping each other up companionably, each painted a fruit gum colour. It was rather that it seemed to be inhabited by singular people. A woman in a man's suit, sporting a short back and sides, smoking a cheroot, strode past me purposefully. When we stopped at a shabby café for baked potatoes, an old man with a bleached blond crew cut, which made him look like David Hockney's father, or how I imagined Hockney's father to be, sat at the next table. The waitress who served us wore black eyeliner and green nail polish and looked as if she had sprung from the dark imagination of Roald Dahl, though her voice and manner were suprisingly fey. This impression of non-conformity struck me favourably, probably because I had feared that the provinces would be nervous of it.

After lunch, we found the streets where the estate agents had gathered, and wandered along them. We did not plan to view any houses until Michael had definitely been offered a job, but it was fun to see what was on offer. We exclaimed once more over the difference in prices, sharing the excitement between us, feeling as though we had stepped into another world, where we were rich, where we cut substantial figures.

Sucking an ice cream cone, I trailed Michael through the market, a warren of tented stalls, like the grand bazaar in Istanbul, but selling ordinary, English items: kettle leads, flowered Crimplene dresses, rawhide bones for dogs, prickly net curtains. Eventually, leaving the market behind, crossing a busy street, we made our way through an ornamented gate to the beautifully mannered cathedral close, all clipped grass and courteous, upright, red-brick houses. The cathedral lay on our left. We wandered towards it, stepping firstly, by accident, into the cloisters, where we surprised a wrinkled flock of picnicking nuns. Two of them were bickering.

'But where's the Magdalen?' one wailed. 'We haven't seen the Magdalen!' – and she stepped backwards onto Michael's foot.

A little ripple of dismay spread through the group, quite

111

disproportionate to the accident. Indeed, the old nun was so frail, with her bird bones and stooped back, that she must have hurt Michael very little, if at all. I believe it was his maleness that disconcerted them. They were acutely conscious of it, much as I had been a little earlier. And Michael was so calm and gentle, courtly, even, in his manner to the little nun as he waved away her apologies, that she grew flustered and girlish. He took her elbow gently and steered her up a short flight of smooth steps to the right, where some of her companions had been beckoning to her.

I followed him through the doorway – he cast a boyish, apologetic glance back at me – and I found myself in the cathedral, by one of the transepts. There was that immediate awe which comes from the smell of ancient stone and the sound of hushed voices lapping faintly at high walls. To my left I saw Michael shepherding the nuns to a counter where guides and postcards were on sale. He almost bowed, a little nod of the head, with a half-smile, as he left them. As he returned to my side, they stared after him, waving.

It sounds silly but I felt proud when he put his hand in the small of my back, and we walked away, towards the nave, our faces upturned to the glory of a stained-glass window. I felt myself caught between sexual pride and spiritual longing. Somewhere, a rich, contralto voice was singing foreign words. We were silent. Sitting near the nave, I gave myself up to the peace of old stone.

The builders awed me; not the architects, not the founder whose bones lay under polished black marble near the high altar, but the little people, the masons who had hacked out this vault, who had balanced stone on stone. I was suddenly aware of their vision and that through it they had transformed their everydayness, and I felt impoverished in comparison. I slipped my arm through Michael's and leant my head on his shoulder; I felt the muscle on the bone and the warmth of him, and I was aware, too, of how little we were in the vastness.

' "All shall be well, and all shall be well, and all manner of things shall be well." ' Michael said it softly, like a chant, or like something hauled back from the brink of memory.

'What's that?'

'Julian of Norwich,' he said. 'Medieval mystic. It was her great affirmation. A declaration of faith after suffering, you might call it.'

He smiled, stooped, kissed my forehead. I don't think I have ever loved him better.

Leaning on Michael's shoulder, I said a prayer for Richard. Oh, I knew it was silly to pray for a cure, or perhaps you would say, I lacked the necessary faith. But I told the ribbed vault high above me, 'Give him some peace,' and 'Don't let it be painful,' without so much as a please or thank you.

We were due in Sussex the next day, as Michael and his sisters wanted to check that their parents were coping. Telephone stories had reached us of nurses visiting to monitor pain relief, and we were perturbed. We hadn't expected such a fast deterioration.

Michael and I had booked ourselves into a Suffolk hotel for the night; we had planned a detour through some of the villages which looked so enchanting in the estate agents' brochures. On Sunday morning, we intended to cut across country, picking up an Essex trunk road and from there, the curve of the London ring road.

When Michael turned through the hotel gates, we found ourselves passing along a smooth gravel drive under an avenue of beech trees as tall, grey and lofty as the ribbed cathedral roof. After a little while we emerged, startled by the low sun, between yews clipped into the shape of heraldic devices.

The hotel was a fine old building, rendered and pargeted, under uneven tiles eiderdowned with moss. Its idiosyncracies had been exaggerated for the tourist market, with hanging tapestries of long-limbed white dogs and longer necked, whey-faced damsels. Our room, which overlooked a sweep of perfect lawn and a deep lake, sported fake crewelwork curtains and a four-poster bed. But I rather like overblown hotel decor; the more arch luxury they wish to pile upon me the better.

'My day is complete,' I crowed, enfolding myself in a thick, white, towelling robe after my shower.

Swaddled and damp, I perched by my pillow on the four poster and called Miriam on the bedside phone. As I waited for someone to answer, I doodled smiling flowers and a happy, buzzing bee on the scrap of paper on which I had written Louise Carrington's number. Miriam answered, which I had not expected. Somehow, this suggested that she was already completely at home.

'Good day?' I asked Miriam brightly.

But she was being laconic. 'Yeah. Fine. We're going to draw up some plans for a new fox enclosure afterwards.'

'After what?'

A sigh, as if I was being unreasonable and prying. 'After dinner.'

She didn't ask the questions courtesy demanded and temporarily I was at a loss. Should I play along, as apparently she did not want to talk about Norwich? Or might I seem secretive? She had recently been complaining that I 'hid things' from her.

I drew a breath. 'Norwich was beautiful,' I said. 'It's not nearly as provincial as I'd thought.'

'Oh, mother, please. Of course it's provincial. It's in a bloody province.'

'Don't swear, Miriam.'

There was a titter, conveying that she thought this a bit rich coming from me.

'Anyway, Mum, I've got to go. Louise's son is back with the curry.' In the background I heard the sound of doors, voices, palaver, the clatter of cutlery and plates. 'Have a really filthy weekend, Mum,' Miriam called.

'Take care, bean bag,' I said, but my words were met by a click and a hum as she put the phone down. It pierced me, that sound, and for a few seconds I sat disconsolate before shaking the feeling off. I knew I was being silly.

Instead, I went down to join Michael for dinner. He had changed into his dark suit and gone for a stroll around the lake. He met me in the dining room which overlooked the grounds. The table was dressed in a thick, white linen cloth and eighteen-inch square linen napkins folded into bishops' mitres. In my plain silk dress, I rather felt as if I let it down. The waiters sirred and modomed us, parading by regularly to ask if we were enjoying our meal. We were by a bay window overlooking the lake, and Michael ordered champagne which was very cold and went straight to my head.

In the lift coming up, I leaned forward, nuzzled his neck and slipped my hand inside his jacket to undo all the buttons on his soft white shirt, from the stiff collar to the one below his belt where the skin, stretched over tight muscle, was warm and smooth, and a golden beige against the white of the cotton. As I did so, he exhaled, with a smile, put his arm around me, and I felt his mouth pressed hard against my temple.

Well, I said to myself, when I awoke.

Well-ell.

Michael was pretending to be asleep but his lips were turned up at the corners. I stroked the mound of his chest down towards his stomach, kissed his forehead, slipped from the bed.

In the shower, I washed away the sticky sap of the night before, humming to myself under the hot, thrumming water. Since Michael's hours had elongated, our sex life had shrivelled to nothing. That week, in the newspapers, there had been much noise about Britons working the longest hours in Europe; I wondered what effect that had on the nation's libido,

So, I thought, snickering to myself, downshifting might have unlooked for advantages.

We reached the house first, just before midday, but Jane and Phyllida, who had driven down together, without their husbands or children, arrived soon after us. I heard the dog barking, Phyllida hello-ing, then the clink as she bumped into a milk bottle on her way past the back step to the garden, where Michael and his parents were strolling, admiring Ann's garden, which had abandoned itself to its high summer revelry. A deep red climbing rose ramped its way through an apple tree and the perfume of regal lilies was a tide so strong it rippled through the French windows which stood slightly ajar.

The three of them had left me in the sitting room, because I wanted to try Louise Carrington's number again. There was a thump against the magnolia door, and Jane's bottom nudged into view. She was manoeuvring a large cardboard box. I put the receiver down. It had been over six months since we had last met, on Boxing Day, here, in this very house.

'Lovey!' she exclaimed when she saw me. She always acted as if I were her best friend. 'How are you?' The last two words were drawled, conveying that it was simply ages and it wasn't her doing.

I got up and kissed her. 'How are *you?*'

She passed her fingers through her frizzy brown fringe and collapsed on the edge of the sofa. She was slimmer than Phyllida; her skin was very white, translucent, the network of blue veins clearly visible underneath. Like Michael, she had inherited Richard's grey eyes and extravagantly long, dark lashes. They gave her face a pleasant, open look, so that people always responded to her. You would never suspect this face of dissembling.

Jane wrinkled her pale, freckled nose at me, hoisting her box onto Ann's treasured Pembroke table, prizing open a flap with a fingernail painted with clear polish. I peered inside. A rainbow army of knitted pixies nestled within, each with a malevolent grin, likely to give a nasty fright to any child who received one.

'My offering for the vicarage fete,' she said. 'What do you think? Cute or what?'

'Gosh, yes, very cute . . .'

'My neighbour, Mrs May, gave me the pattern. Dear old thing, she knits her way through piles of toys and matinee jackets for all our village fetes.' Jane lived with her husband, who was something in corporate insurance, and her weedy beanpole of a teenage son, in a Surrey village not far from my family home. She was always pretending she knew the same people as my parents.

'How's Dad?' she hissed. 'Not good about this morphine lark, is it? Phyl is livid. She thinks we should all join together and make him have the chemo. But I keep thinking, why's he going to listen to us, when he won't listen to Mum?'

I shook my head. As far as I knew Ann had accepted Richard's decision, had made no prolonged attempt to dissuade him from it.

'My friend, Bob,' Jane said, 'was cured at Lourdes, you know. He was complaining of fatigue and stomach pain. Doctors opened him up, took one look, sewed him up again. Beattie, his wife, carted him off to Lourdes and next check-up they couldn't find a bad cell in him.

'Nobody would believe it, of course. Doctors are so arrogant. Remember the time I had that lump in my breast?'

I nodded. I did have a vague recollection.

' "Could it be cancerous?" I asked. My life was falling apart! "Of course it could be, but we can't tell until the biopsy." That's what he said to me, can you believe it? A woman in that position? I sued them, you know. Sued them for mental distress.'

That was the obviously mendacious section of the anecdote. I think she just got carried away, hit a point of inspiration. She started with a real, true happening and then swooped off, on higher flights of emotion to the flash point where imagination met fact.

'I hope you succeeded,' I said. 'Shook them to their boots, at least.' I was getting carried away, too; I always wanted Jane's stories to be true, there was often a magnificent flavour to them, as she battled her way through smug bureaucrats or the even smugger, unchangeable facts of physical science. Inoperable cancer? That was no problem to Jane's fancies.

She smiled at me. She liked me, with my ability to listen, agog and credulous. She scratched at her head, then, quite unconsciously, examined her fingernails for traces of scurf, and just as suddenly came back to reality. 'I can't believe this is happening to us. It just doesn't seem real. It always happens to other people, doesn't it? You never think it will happen to you.'

'Don't you?' I was astonished. 'I do. I always think it will happen to me. Every time Miriam has a headache, I wonder if she's caught meningitis. I'm forever going, "If it's still this bad tomorrow, I'll take you to the doctor." It's a kind of talisman.'

'Oh, children,' said Jane. 'That's different. We all do it for children.'

Phyllida had put on weight. Her two round bosoms hung heavily in her white polo shirt, her rounded belly swelled underneath the gathers of her droopy, print skirt. She bustled in from the garden, intent on forcing a family conference. She directed a speaking glance at Jane, so that Jane sprang into action, and I knew she had been pre-programmed in the car.

'Sit down, you lot!' Phyllida declared. 'Jane'll make us coffee.'

'I'll help you,' I volunteered, rising from my chair.

'No-no, you'll stay where you are,' Phyllida said quickly.

She turned to her father, who was lowering himself carefully, as if it might hurt, into his favourite wing chair.

I examined him covertly. I expect we were all doing that. But Richard looked much as he had always looked – thinner, of course, his arms and legs suddenly etiolated, the weak, spindly limbs of an old man, and there was a deep line between his eyebrows, an invalid's querulous frown, the mark of some-one who is losing patience with a failing body – but apart from that there was very little change. It was his gingerly movements that gave him away. I saw him measuring each day's deteriora-tion, the perambulation which ended a street, a corner, a tree, sooner than it had the day before, the turn for home creeping nearer and nearer to the front door. I imagined his slow, shambling plod to retrieve the mail after hearing the squeak of the letter box. I imagined the horror of finding that even to sit in his favourite chair had become tiring. I suddenly understood that death may have to be faced in such small, daily erosions. My heart gave a little lurch of pity.

But the sight of her father seemed to move Phyllida not to sympathy but to exasperation, as if it were his fault, as if they must do something to alter this decline towards the skeletal, as if the magic chemo would put flesh on his bones. She leaned on the back of the sofa where Ann and Michael were sitting and looked Richard in the eye.

'You know why we're here, so there's no escaping it,' she said in an accusatory tone.

Michael sighed, placing the tips of two fingers on his own forehead, running them up and down the bridge of his nose. Phyllida was his least favourite of the three sisters. Mine, too.

There was a V-shaped frown appearing between her eyebrows, and her little mouth, surrounded by pudgy flesh, was set in a small, neat clamp. She stroked the back of the sofa, outwards, twice, preparing herself, and then launched into her speech,

'Look, Dad, you've got to have the chemo. We're not taking no for an answer, are we? You can't just give up.'

'I'm not giving up,' he said, very firmly, emphasising the last two words. 'Treatment will give me a year and at what price?'

'You don't know they've got it right,' Jane, who had returned from the kitchen, blurted out. 'They make the wrong diagnoses, miracles happen all the time. There was this friend . . .'

Michael rose suddenly from his place and turned to her, his face stormy. He seemed to be on the verge of saying something, but instead, after a moment's pause, in which he simply scowled at her, he stalked to the garden windows, let out a breath and remained there, a brooding, menacing presence. Indeed, despite his restraining his comments, the whole interruption was so alarming that there was a ruffling and a silence which followed it. The sound of the kettle bubbling furiously allowed Jane the excuse of loping back to the kitchen.

Eventually, Phyllida picked up her thread. 'There're new advances all the time,' she said, but sullenly rather than with smooth persuasion. She was such a prickly person. 'I mean, you could just rethink it, couldn't you? If that's not too much to ask, from your own children. One of us,' she glanced at Michael, 'could go with you to the oncologist, talk it through, ask all the questions.'

Neither Richard nor Ann made a reply. Ann was fiddling with the link chain of her watch strap. Perhaps this calm gesture annoyed Phyllida because she turned on her mother. 'How can you allow this?' she exclaimed. 'Your husband's dying, don't you care?'

Much to my surprise, and Michael's, too, I suspect, for he turned suddenly and tensed, neither Richard nor Ann bridled.

119

Richard just said softly, 'Phylly, Phylly. You can't cure every-thing with a brisk kiss and an Elastoplast. Do you remember? You playing at nursing the dog? Tying its legs in splints so it goose-stepped round the garden. My little Miss Bossy Boots, always trying to mend something . . .'

And Phyllida, instead of pressing her point, said, 'Oh, Daddy,' and blundered round the sofa, across the rug, as her face crumpled. She looked so clumsy, so inept, so stripped of every adult dignity at that moment. Then she knelt by his chair and buried her face in his lap, and the sound of her sobbing was terrible.

Michael glanced at them, then stepped out of the French windows into the garden. Ann reached for the lace-edged handkerchief tucked into the cuff of her cardigan. And me? I think I looked at the rug for a while, before making my way to the kitchen to help Jane with the coffee.

In the event, we cooked the Sunday lunch, all four of us women, while Michael and his father talked in the sitting room. Phyllida fixed gin and tonics so strong they blew the sorrow from our brains in a bout of inane elation. Jane, who was stuffing the chicken, one of those super large birds which look faintly obscene, took it by the wings and made it high step into the roasting tin. ' "If my friends could see me now," ' she warbled, and we all cracked up, the dog capering at our feet, yapping and wagging its tail at our ebullience.

The mood settled into a semblance of ordinary cordiality through lunch. We discussed the two sets of neighbours who were arguing whether a boundary fence should be moved by one and half inches, somehow diversified onto noise pollution, and from there to the state of the British economy – on which Phyllida had many robust and slurred opinions, none of which seemed to be very well informed – and whether we thought the feel-good factor was truly back.

Smears of gravy were congealing on the surfaces of the plates. Jane lit a cigarette and exhaled noisily. Then Ann made some comment, quite innocuous, about the garden, her eye caught by a clash of colours outside.

'I think,' she said, 'I should move that day lily. It's so strident, so municipal park. I'll transplant it come this autumn.'

There was a sudden clatter as Richard hurled his knife and fork onto his plate. We all jumped. He was struggling to rise from his chair and it toppled backwards. He wavered rather precariously, so that Michael rose to support him.

'That's just it,' Richard stormed, and his face was red.

I saw Ann's face, her eyes round and startled, her napkin half way to her mouth. 'You just want me to die quickly so you can get on with your bloody gardening,' he raged.

'Daddy!' Jane was aghast. 'Oh, Daddy, you know that's not true!'

'Oh, do I? Oh, do I indeed?' Richard bellowed.

'It's all right, Jane,' Ann said.

Phyllida blushed; plainly she suspected she had planted this seed of doubt earlier. Richard laboured through the open door to the sitting room, Michael at his elbow. His eyes flashed a speaking glance at me before he adopted the unreadable expression he liked to hide behind. We heard the murmur of their voices and, after a while, the click of the front door as they went off towards the cricket pitch. I knew that Michael had engineered it. The team was playing at home this week and he had guessed the match might distract Richard.

Ann was resting her elbow on the table, her chin and mouth cupped behind her hand.

'I'm sorry, Mummy,' Phyllida said. 'I'm sorry.'

'He didn't mean it, Mummy,' Jane added.

Ann nodded and got up herself, scraping plates, carrying them to the kitchen. I followed her.

'It's the morphine talking,' I said.

'I know,' she said quietly. She was standing by the sink, wiping the stainless steel drainer down. 'I know, Eleanor. It's just that he's never actually shouted at me before. Not in the whole of our marriage. And now, in the last few months we have together . . .'

Her voice tailed off. The dish rag in her hands was dripping into the stale, grey water in the sink, *plop, plop, plop*; a sad sound, like tears.

* * *

By the time we left them that evening, it was dusk. I allowed myself to be hypnotised by the rhythm of the headlamps of approaching cars. I gazed at the yellow lights flickering above the motorway and the neon strips outside fast food shops, where vehicles clustered and litter lay strewn. We hardly talked on the return journey. All the affection and intimacy of the weekend had fizzled out. I suppose we were both groping towards a way of making the day's silly, ugly scene acceptable: we would qualify it with exterior knowledge about the effects of pain relief, the stress of terminal illness. But I knew, in my heart, what I had seen. Richard was striking out at the person closest to him.

I had always sensed his inarticulate resentment in the face of her condescension. There had been intermittent scenes over the years when she had put him down in public, once, when he had offered his opinion about something – something trivial and soon forgotten. But Ann's reply was never forgotten. 'How would *you* know?' she had drawled. And he had flushed and I had felt a flood of pity for him, this reticent man. It was true; he had never shouted, he had always swallowed the comments down.

Ann had always assumed that *he* was the lucky one in their partnership, fortunate to have found her, and for the most part, Richard agreed with her. But it was at moments such as these that I saw the flicker in his eye, his teeth grinding. I suppose that these were the moments when they wondered why they had married, and if they should continue together, until a change in the mood, a distraction, restored them to good humour. In death as in life: a marriage holds its shape to the end.

Once, when we reached the outskirts of south London, when we were stuck at the traffic lights by the big supermarket in Purley – this route was so familiar – I ventured a question. 'How do you feel about your father refusing any treatment, Michael?' It seemed odd to me that I had never asked this before.

There was a long silence, and I wondered if he had heard

me. Finally he said, 'Oh, mixed feelings. A part of me feels that it's his choice and should be respected.' There was another pause. 'And a part of me wonders if I have really grasped what's happening. My father is dying, I say to myself. But as long as he is still there, at home, in his place, well, death seems disputable, somehow. I can't believe in it.'

'I understand.' I did, completely, though I had not faced the death of anyone close to me and did not want to. My parents, with all their sharp corners and their acidic irritations, were vital to me. Their death would be the final act of growing up and I had always preferred my daydreams.

After that, we didn't talk. We were past talking. I was spent by all the seesawing emotions. Michael looked dishevelled, bristly, dog-tired. It was a relief when we reached the home stretch, the streets belonging to our patch of London, the landmarks that dictated a turn right or left, the tube station with its threatening, empty stairs leading down, the shops we used, now shuttered and silent.

I picked my handbag up as Michael finally swung the Jeep into our street, edging carefully between the double rows of parked cars. We were both hoping for a space outside our house – our parking space as we thought of it, our bit of the kerb – and thank goodness, it was empty.

I turned and looked at the house as he reversed in, one arm slung over the back of my seat. All the lights were on. Would Miriam never learn to switch off a light?

I inserted my key in the lock; the door stuck on the pile of post which lay, uncollected, on the mat, and I had to push to get it open, concertina-ing the corner of a large brown envelope as I did so.

Miriam came bounding down the stairs at the sound of our arrival.

I was bending to pick up the mail. 'Can't you do anything around here?' I said to her. 'Are you incapable?' and her face fell into the lines of resentment.

Michael was silent, absorbed by a thick, cream-coloured envelope which he had plucked from my hand as he entered. In the left-hand corner was a red and black logo which I recognised. I laid the rest of the mail on the side table, unread, and followed him through to the kitchen, where he sliced the letter open with a knife. He read silently. I watched his face but it was, once more, his stern mask.

Then he looked up. 'I've got the job,' he said.

It was odd, that moment. I felt pleased and deflated, both, but I said, 'Oh, Mikey, that's fantastic,' and went to embrace him. I could smell the faint spice of his new lemony aftershave, and that reminded me of our interlocking limbs on Saturday night.

'Well done, Dad,' Miriam's voice said, from the doorway, and I extricated myself. She was leaning on the jamb, her eyes with the faint shadows beneath them, the same colour as the edges of East Anglian clouds.

'Oh, darling,' I said.

And then she sprang upright, with a toss of her head, and said, 'Don't worry, Mum. It's cool.' I breathed again, turned to the sink. 'I've got everything sorted,' she added.

I was reaching for the kettle and I remember stopping, one arm half-extended, like the movement which goes with the rhyme that children chant, ' "*I'm a little teapot, short and stout . . .*" '

'Sorted?' I repeated and I put my arm down. 'What do you mean?'

'I've got the perfect solution. I've talked to Louise about it. She says I can stay with her.'

Here's my handle, here's my spout . . .

'She says she already feels that I'm a bit like the daughter she always wanted. So it makes sense if I go and live with her,' Miriam said.

And in my head the lines were completed . . .

Tip me up and pour me out.

Chapter Seven

The next morning, I had to stop at the supermarket to buy the evening meal. I grabbed a basket and strode in, fuelled by righteous indignation. The shop floor was almost empty, except for a stooped, grey-haired couple, the woman in pink, fluffy, zippered slippers, as if she was so senile she had forgotten to change into shoes. Or maybe she had bunions? They shuffled behind one of those special shallow carts. I dodged past them, throwing a net bag of peaches into my basket so violently I must have bruised the fruit. On the next aisle I encountered another harassed woman cramming in her shopping on her way to work, another woman who seemed tense, coiled as a spring.

By the first chill cabinet I came to a halt. Hummus and pitta bread was one of Miriam's favourite afterschool snacks. Normally I piled the cartons into my basket as a matter of course, but that morning I hesitated. It didn't seem to me that she deserved a treat. Seemed to me that she was spoiled. I took a step, then turned back, my hand already reaching for the carton. Why should I be forced into acting mean, leaving Louise Carrington the generous, munificent role?

I was early for the office, but Anthea was there already. I overheard her as I passed her half-open door. 'Oh, Robert,' she was saying – Robert was the junior – 'I'd better warn you.

Eleanor had a real go at Catherine on Friday night. There's going to be a sticky atmosphere around here, today. I'm just glad I can keep out of it, and I suggest you do, too.'

So much for friendship. So much for loyalty. It was typical of Anthea to be so superficial. This was the woman who proudly told me how her daughter put a glass in the freezer at 5.30 exactly, to be chilled and ready for her evening gin and tonic; a woman who ordered her cleaning lady to wash out the plastic cutlery tray in the kitchen drawer weekly. Now that I thought about it, she had this habit of clearing her throat and pursing her lips at the same time – 'ahem, ahem,' she went – which was unbearably affected. And the way she always jangled her pearls with her right hand!

She drove me batty. I banged my door loudly, to give her a start. I sensed rather than heard a rustle, a muffled whisper; I knew she was peering out of her office, aghast, and I smiled, inwardly.

On the bowing metal shelves in the dustiest corner of my untidy office, I found the reference book I wanted. At my desk, I ran my finger down the 'family' organisations until I found one which seemed to fit the bill. A lady with an upward lilt to her voice answered on the third ring: 'Advice centre.'

'Oh,' I said, 'I wonder if you can help me?' I sounded tremulous. I was scared of what she might tell me.

'Oh, teenagers,' she drawled, when she heard my babbled explanation. 'I have two at home. Many's the time I've thought of leaving them,' she snorted. 'Just up and leave them to it. Huh! Just how would they cope then? I bet Mum wouldn't seem like such a bad old stick then.'

She surprised me. I have never imagined leaving home. Oh, I've often thought of walking out on Michael, gloried in the vision of him gaping at the empty wardrobe, the shelf where the suitcases were kept. But the illusion always disperses when Miriam walks into the room. The prospect of *her* taking it in, stooping to gaze at the shelves, bare but for sorry balls of dust; well, it's too much for me, even in my secret thoughts.

The woman was telling me that Michael and I were

responsible for Miriam until she was eighteen – 'it goes without saying.' Of course, she added, Miriam might go to court for an order allowing her to live with Louise, 'but she would be highly unlikely to succeed'.

This image unsettled me. It was the sudden notion of it being possible at all, with the pictures it conjured of wily and in-formed children fighting their cases through the courts, of there being aid and advice available to them. And it tore my heart, too. I could imagine it so clearly: Miriam standing in front of a judge, saying in her husky voice that she did not want to live with me anymore.

'How highly unlikely?' I asked.

'Oh, very. I mean, scarcely credible. Even if it came to such a pass, in this country we have not yet reached the stage where children may divorce their parents.'

Afterwards, I telephoned Michael on his mobile. He was on a train to a conference in Liverpool, and would be away overnight. I told him what I had learned, but he merely hur-rumphed with irritation. His grunt had a lopped, secretive quality, because he thought it rude to talk loudly on the phone in public places. In any case, as far as he was concerned there was nothing that could not be solved by his looming im-periously on Louise Carrington's doorstep and dragging his daughter home. He was certain that she would submit to this sudden – and novel – regulation. Whereas I was not. How much easier it had been when parents could bark, 'Go to your room,' and 'I'll give you Louise Carrington,' and other meaning-less expressions which we, as sentient, enlightened adults, had consigned to the ark.

There had been a scene last night, while he tried to calm me. Why couldn't he realise that I didn't need calming? I needed him to be as outraged as I was.

'It will sort itself out,' he said, whereas I knew it wouldn't.

'You're not surprised, are you?'

'Oh, Eleanor,' he said. 'You make it sound so . . .'

'You don't care, do you? As long as you get to Norwich. No matter that it disrupts the family for good and all.'

'Look, it's about time she did as she was told. I told her

when she first. . .' He wasn't going to continue.

'First what?'

'First discussed this with me.'

'When?'

'What do you mean, when?'

'When, Michael. It's very simple. When did she talk to you about this?'

'I didn't keep a record, surprisingly enough . . . One morning we were talking, chatting . . .'

'Why didn't you tell me?'

'Do I have to keep you informed of every detail of my life?' He was growing irritated, now.

I ploughed on. 'You didn't think to tell me.'

'Eleanor, it wasn't worth telling. It didn't seem to matter that much.'

I sat on the edge of the bed with my head in my hands and he manoeuvred around me, not knowing how I might react, not, after all these years, having a clue of what was important to me and what was not. And all of a sudden I seemed to have lost that wifely attribute of being able to forgive him his daily inadequacies. The river of heaving red anger that I had directed at Louise Carrington was now deflected towards Michael. In my mind's eye, it engulfed him and his head went under, gasping.

There we are, Miriam; he's dead now. We don't have to move to Norfolk, any more.

Today, the day after I had killed him, he had retreated behind his gruff crust, as if he knew what I had done.

Replacing the receiver, I wandered into Anthea's room, needing to talk, needing to *spill*. She jiggled her pearls nervously when she saw me.

'You're not having a very good time of it, are you?' she mewed at the end of my account. 'Talk about never rains.' But the curious thing was that even as she emitted understanding noises, I could see her inner self triumphing. Her two would never act in such a fashion. Somehow I was not as good a mother as I had assumed. In short, I was not as good a mother as she was. We were in a competitive race to the end.

'Oh, stop it, Anthea,' I said crossly, addressing her true self. 'I can see what you're thinking, and I wouldn't be so smug, if I were you.'

She flushed and sat back. I could see her wondering if I had extrasensory perception or something. Have you ever noticed how some people are so easy to read? Their thoughts just flick up there in their eyes, clear as day, while others – Michael, for example – are stony and distant,

I rested my head in my hands. My eyes had that weak, watery feeling that comes from too little sleep. Not only that, but I felt sticky and dirty already. I had swopped to a new deodorant which did not appear to live up to its advertising, and my armpits prickled with damp sweat. It was one of those baking hot summer days when the heat bounds from wall to pavement, when it collects under the thin, tiled roofs of old buildings, like our offices, and swarms in the rooms below.

There was a fan on Anthea's desk, swivelling towards her, towards me, towards her again. It ruffled her curls slightly, then alternately blew her garlic-scented breath to my nostrils.

Until recently, I had been as complacent a mother as Anthea. I thought I had it covered. I worried about car crashes and anorexia; every modern danger. There was an element of superstition involved in this, as if by naming each evil, I could ward it off, so that I could rest easy that mine was the sensible child refusing the tab of E, or the bottle of alco-pop, the girl who wasn't fumbling with some boy's underclothes at the back of the public loos. And now, the one misery I had never suspected had crept up on me. I had assumed a little foresight would protect my child, and thereby my heart. Amazing how naïve mothers are! But I suppose, if we were not, we would never embark on such a great and hopeless endeavour as attempting to raise the perfect human being. Which is, after all, what we are about.

'It's like you can't win,' I said to Anthea's moon face in the intermittent wind. 'It's like when I was a kid and I couldn't work out why my brother always won at noughts and crosses. Got mad because he chuckled when I marked my innocent little cross in the middle square. How did he know I was going to get beaten when I didn't? I couldn't work it out and yet I knew, whatever I did from then on, I was going to lose.

'I don't suppose you remember, but you once said to me that you were scared of your two not liking you. And I despised you for that. I wasn't going to mind if Miriam, in a fit of pique, or awash with hormones, decided she didn't like me. And I didn't. Until she began to like another woman better.'

Anthea looked at me, chastened. 'Oh, El,' she said, 'I'm sorry. You're right.'

I returned to my office, retrieved my bag from its drawer, walked straight past Nicola, though she clearly wanted a word with me, and caught the tube to the end of the line; I went to confront Louise Carrington.

A small shed stood on the right of the entrance to the wild life sanctuary; two posters, depicting battery hens and a horse with its ribs protruding through its dull, muddied coat, were taped in its sliding glass windows. Somebody had written in blue biro, in fat, cushiony capital letters shaded roughly, the word: 'We offer a home to the abused.'

A white postcard stated that visitors were welcome during daylight hours and requested a contribution. Beneath this, a bit of change had been thrown onto a square of kitchen towel folded inside a clean ice cream tub. I had the feeling that these coins were Louise's, like those you see in saucers on the counters of hat check girls, placed there deliberately to encourage a donation. For the sake of the hens and the horse with the sticky-out bones, I threw a pound through the half-open window and it clunked, a hollow, dead sound.

There was no sign of Louise Carrington. I followed the path looking for her. In the field on my right there was a mixed flock of sheep, some of them with long matted dreadlocks that looked as if they had been dusted with soot. For the first time in years, I wished I had a sketchbook with me, so that I might draw them, the texture of their wool, the curve of their horns, their light, cloven feet. Two delightful small goats were play-fighting in a corner of the field, rearing and butting, wagging their tails happily like dogs. I watched them for a few seconds before following the path through the shadow shed by a thicket of trees and scrub. It was even hotter now and the cool shade was welcoming. Shiny, iridescent flies buzzed above a discarded apple core.

There were a number of enclosures in the wood, each like chicken coops, with a shed for sleeping and a wire-mesh cage for the day. I was searching for the capuchin monkey, I think; this other creature that so yearned for the presence of my daughter. But I must have taken a wrong turning. I passed a pine marten which gazed at me, curious and unafraid, its translucent bat-like ears cupped, alert, as I clicked my tongue and sucked high-pitched kissing noises through my teeth. Further on, there were two squirrels, small, shy red squirrels, and I wished, with a pang, that Miriam were with me, so I could tell her about how England used to be, when I was young, and the word 'squirrel' still meant these creatures, not the bigger, bullying greys. It was astonishing, really, how quickly the landscape had changed, for in my childhood I had walked to school through corn fields which in summer blazed with red poppies, blue cornflowers and white daisies. I had picked great bunches of those glorious flowers, taken them home, sheaves of countryside in the crook of my arm, to my mother. I willed her to place them in the drawing-room but no, to her they were kitchen flowers and on the kitchen windowsill, in jam jars, they remained; and too quickly they drooped, shed petals and faded.

I picked my way along the track. There had been a brutal thunderstorm overnight and the damp seeped through my city shoes. The leaves smelled sharp, like a new beginning. At the edge of a small pond, a rat whisked from the cover of brambles, intent on a fat moorhen. There was a moment of stupefied shock before the moorhen gathered up its skirts and legged it, in a clucking flurry, for the safety of the water. I must have squealed, inadvertently, for the rat spun round and for a second looked at me, its sharp, yellow eyes on mine, before disappearing in a rustle of thick leaves. I wondered what the neighbours made of Louise Carrington's sanctuary crammed into her acre and half of garden on the edge of the green belt;

and even as I did so I knew that this was the sort of speculation which would have incensed Miriam had I voiced it. It was so middle-class, so selfish; it expressed such a petty concern with suitable sanitation and property values.

Once I had been an individual who would have lauded a venture like this; now I was the sort of woman who would sign a petition to the planning department, grumbling about noise and nuisance. I could see my reflection in the pond: a woman with a short haircut because short was easier, a woman in a trouser suit because she was too old for brief hemlines; a woman with a slightly thickening waist whose chin should not be examined in profile. I was simply seeing myself as I truly was; for the me of my imagination was normally twenty years younger. I had avoided mirrors for some time, the tale they told of the passing of years was not one I wanted to witness, and I had long given up that teenaged habit of looking into my reflected eyes in search of answers. I knew myself, didn't I? I did not need that game. I had changed but not changed. I looked older but I had grown no wiser; indeed, I remained quite as maladroit as ever.

The wood had petered out, the last tree stubbing its toes against a large enclosure that blocked my path. On a rope swing, rocking back and forth, hung a monkey, but not the mistreated capuchin. A plate, screwed to the door, read, 'Crab-eating Macaques', and, now that I examined it, the cage housed not one but four downy, humanoid figures.

By the cage there was an uneven tree stump which had soaked up the rain water like a sponge; despite this, I perched upon it for a while, shifting my weight from one seat bone to the other, and I watched the little group.

A nursing mother, hunched over a tiny infant, had her back to me. Crouched at her side was another young monkey, an inquisitive, interfering sort, which poked and twitched at the baby in her arms. Whenever she moved, this monkey swung after her, as close as the ripple of a cloak. It grew rough, yanking at the infant's arm, which was red, hairless and wrinkled, and reminded me of the arms of premature babies, lying inert in incubators, in hospital documentaries. Once, the boisterous youngster tried to insert itself into the cradle of the mother's arms, as if he could replace the infant, assuming its place and its shape. Once, it cartwheeled over the baby, slyly biting its foot as it did so. The mother cuffed him but then turned away, looking tired, as if she had simply run out of energy. She bunched over the baby once more and her face was a picture of sadness.

'Poor Christina,' said a squeaky, breathless voice behind me. 'She only gave birth yesterday. She's fucked, poor thing.'

I turned round. An enormous youth stood behind me, more than six foot tall and with a girth seemingly wider than his arm span, so that he reminded me of one of those grinning dolls that bounces back whenever you smash it down. He was wearing jeans, dirty trainers, a capacious white T-shirt whose lager brand logo rested, aptly, on the globe of his beer belly. He was all curves, long, curly hair, rather unkempt, rounded cheeks, round wire-framed glasses. He seemed entirely benign. Beside him, I felt petite and fragile. With a huff and a puff, he squatted beside me. We watched the monkeys companionably for a while.

'Who's the rowdy monkey?' I asked him, as he seemed to know the family details.

'That one? That's Bill. Christina had him last summer.'

'Ah,' I said, 'So he's jealous. Poor Christina, indeed.' The female macaque ignored us with a sort of heroic concentration, as zoo animals do.

'It's partly that,' the roly-poly teenager said, sucking his teeth. 'Actually, it's quite dangerous for Bill at the moment; Tina might turn on him. She could bite him, do some real damage.'

'She doesn't look as if she has the heart.'

He pushed his lips out and nodded, conceding the point. 'Or Bill might hurt the new baby,' he said. 'He could pull that baby about a bit. He's curious, you see, doesn't really know what it is. In the wild, they'd be in a community of . . . ooh, say, thirty females to one alpha male . . . lots of company, lots of other youngsters, they learn how to play. Here, it's like a dysfunctional family. There's the alpha male, his dad, there's

Tina, and there's another male . . . him . . . George,' he pointed to the monkey who sat on a branch at the far corner of the cage. 'That would never happen in the wild.'

'What? You mean Bill would grow up with a mother, a father, lots of aunts and sisters and surrogate mothers, masses of siblings? And that's normal, is it?'

'You've got it.'

I began to giggle. 'I can just imagine what it would be like, living in an extended famly with Phyllida and Jane. They're my in-laws, I should say.'

'Oh, shit,' he said, 'so can I. With mine, I mean. I mean, it's like when they all come for Christmas and Mum gets in a flap and buys out the whole of fuckin' Tesco's, packets of just-in-case food falling out of every cupboard when you open the door, and then what? They all turn up and Grandma sits in the corner whingeing about how cold our house is, and the uncles eat until they feel sick and then, when it's washing up time, they sink into an armchair with the newspapers, or fall asleep in front of the telly, and by the time they've all gone home, Mum says, "Thank God, that's over. Never again." And we go, like, yeah, yeah. Like, we believe you. And then she starts taking it out on me. Nag, nag, nag. Fuckin' hell! What a nightmare!

'You know what? I reckon you should be able to get rid of your parents, when you reach a certain age. Eighteen, say, or sixteen. It's a chemical thing. Nature arranges it so that you begin to dislike each other. So you should be able to admit it. Say *arrivederci* to the relations. Nice knowing you and all that, but I'm off into the big, wide world, now, and it's best we don't meet again.'

'Or fifteen, why not?' I suggested bitterly. 'If you want to take that view. Of course, the younger ones would need some adult to take care of them, but hell, let's all swop children like suburban middle managers are supposed to swop wives. Isn't it monkeys that act as surrogate mothers to each other's off-spring? I wonder how Christina would feel about sharing her baby with another female?'

He shot me a sharp, interested glance. 'I'm Adrian Carrington,' he said, in that odd, high rasp.

'Miriam's mother,' I said.

'Oh, shit,' he said, with a slow grin. 'Awesome.'

I couldn't help smiling. Clearly, he guessed why I was here, but all at once I didn't feel in a hurry to see Louise. I turned back to the cage. 'Why do you have these monkeys here?' I asked. 'I thought you were dealing with native wild life?'

'We do, we were. Most of the non-native animals would have been put down if we hadn't taken them. They come from labs, other zoos closing down, that sort of thing. My mum can tell you more,' he added deliberately.

I rose from the stump and found my backside was soaked. Grimacing, I pinched the fabric away from my skin. 'I thought . . . at least your mother implied you weren't interested in the sanctuary?'

He got up to lead the way. 'Not when measured by her standards,' he said, and he raised his eyebrows in a way that reminded me of the capuchin, although this was not, in Adrian, a gesture of submission.

There was a fledgling in an incubator on the dresser, a pile of newspapers on the floor by the back door, a smell of rubbish ripening in the black sack, loosely tied, next to it. I would have liked to have dismissed Louise as a sloven, but in my new frame of mind it seemed possible that it was I who was infected by a suburban devotion to clinical hygiene.

Louise was talking on the telephone in another room; I saw Adrian stand in the door, semaphoring to her, saw him mouth the words 'Miriam's mother', and jerk his thumb towards me. Then he gave me a thumbs up sign and disappeared upstairs.

'Well, darling,' Louise's voice said, 'it's a nightmare for you . . . Mmm . . . Mmm . . . Well, you could try it? It's got to be worth that.' And a thought knifed me: that this was Miriam on the telephone, that she had called and Louise Carrington was counselling her while I sat, unawares, oafishly, in her kitchen. 'I do think it's unreasonable, I admit it,' she said; then, 'I must go, hon. I have a visitor. Mmm. I'll took forward to it. Bye. Lots of love . . .'

She came into the room, pulling her hands through her hair, adjusting a trailing scarf.

'I'm so sorry, I've called at a bad time,' I said, fishing for information.

'No, no, not at all,' she said warmly. 'I was just going to make some herb tea.' She said it in the American way – 'erb. 'You'll have a cup with me?' And I realised that I would never discover whether it was my daughter or not on the telephone, and I told myself that of course it wasn't Miriam, she was at school, although in fact, as I knew perfectly well, there was a pay phone in the entrance hall, by the staff room.

Louise made tea in much the same way that she spoke or dressed: with flowery movements of her hand as she warmed the pot, spooned in quantities of perfumed leaf tea, poured each cupful through the strainer, pursing her lips. It was good tea, served in giant, colourful cups. I had reached the stage – this is shameful – where I wished to discover her wanting in every detail including the most trivial of domestic arrangements.

I made myself say, 'This is lovely. Thank you.'

'I used to only drink iced tea in summer, but when I came here I got converted.'

'So you're American?' I said. It seemed I didn't even have the satisfaction of her accent being fake.

'No, no, I'm English but my parents lived there when I was young. We came back, when I was eighteen or thereabouts.'

She looked at me and clearly came to a decision, suddenly laying a little, freckled hand on mine, so that I flinched. 'You're angry with me,' she said. She squeezed my knuckles and I shifted under this physical contact, from Louise of all people. It was a dilemma to work out how to withdraw my hand casually, so as not to let her know how much she had discomposed me, in case this had been her intention. In the end, hers fluttered upwards of its own accord. Swiftly, I removed my hand to my lap, below the table top.

'You're a fiery sort of a person, I can tell,' she said. 'Oh, I don't mean any harm, so don't be offended. It's just I can see straight through people. A gift, my Chinese teacher called it. A curse, I said, in this day and age, to see to the heart of people, see the black and awful centres of them when the outsides are so clean and powdered. Oh, Lord! I don't mean you.'

'Mrs Carring . . .'

'Louise! Please!'

'Louise, I'm here to talk about Miriam.' I was trying to be very controlled and I took a hot gulp of tea which scalded my mouth and made my eyes water. The warm damp seeped from the seat of my trousers and I shifted in my chair. There was a faint pinging, a sensation of release, as the flap on my white body burst.

'I know, I know,' she said. 'Oh, I know. But it's like . . . you know how it is when everything seems to be going wrong? It's that time for me, with knobs on. The drive shaft's gone on the car, the zoo inspectorate are demanding we build a new fox enclosure, I can't pay the feed bill. The post brings disaster every day! And now this . . .'

She stirred her tea purposefully, so that it spiralled outwards and lapped the rim, cascading on to the floral oil cloth covering the kitchen table. She pulled a crumpled, grey tissue from her sleeve to sop up the spill. I wondered how she had edged things around so that I was feeling sorry for her.

'What happened was this,' she said. 'When Miriam came off the phone on Saturday, she said you'd liked Norwich. She'd been hoping you wouldn't, was rather banking on it.'

I propped my chin in one hand, covering my face up to the nose.

'As I keep reminding myself about my boys – it's just their age. You must *not* take this personally. You know how it is with teenagers; it's like a law of nature that she will feel there are things she can tell me that she can't tell you . . .' A spasm of emotion passed through me. 'I'm sure Adrian tells his girl-friend's mother things he'd never dream of telling me. Oh, that poor woman's weighted down with his dark secrets, that's for sure . . . Oh, well.' She sat back, pleating her scarf reflectively.

I considered this for a second. I didn't know how it was with teenagers. No one else's child had felt the need to confide in me, and had they, I would have been uneasy. 'Well, no,' I told her. 'And if I was ever in that situation, I like to think I'd say, talk to your mother. In fact,' – I thought about it – 'I'm sure I would.'

Louise looked at me, faded, baby blue eyes over the top of the cup. 'Oh, sure,' she said. 'But I did. At once? But then, Miriam, she . . . well, I guess we better not go into that.'

What had Miriam said? That she couldn't talk to me? That I didn't listen to her? That I never had time for her?

What was it Jane had said? You never think it will happen to you, and she was right, because no matter how many dreadful possibilities you ran through internally, trying to deflect them, there was always the one that slipped your mind. And now, here it was, looming in your life. All of a sudden, you remembered how, at the same age, you sat in some friend's bedroom slagging off your respective parents, deriding their middle-class ways. You never thought how disloyal you were being. 'You never think,' my mother used to shriek, and she was right, too.

A large ginger cat had appeared, leaping blithely onto the table where it lapped at the spilled tea. 'So,' Louise Carrington was saying, 'it all just poured out, and while I felt sorry for her – it's certainly amazing, isn't it, how teenagers take things so seriously – I can promise you I never would have offered to have her, but that she asked.'

She asked?

'Well, I said, straight out, didn't I, Roger? – he is my witness and he is a very truthful cat, in general – I said, "Won't your parents mind?" And she said, "Mind? Why should they mind?" And then she said that she was sure you wouldn't object to paying me for her board and lodging, if that was what I was worried about . . .'

We would pay her?

'And I said, "Oh, Miriam, of course it's not. There's no need to talk about things like that for now." I mean, a little contribution towards her food, perhaps . . .'

It was time to interrupt her. 'I'm sorry, Mrs Carrington, she is coming to Norfolk and that's final.' I sounded like my mother.

'Oh. But she doesn't want to.'

'It's none of your business.'

'But Eleanor, it is my business. Now, it is. Because Mirry made it my business. We are genuinely fond of her, and, heaven knows why, she is of us, too. There was all that trouble with her school friends which Adrian sorted out, you recall . . . ?'

But I didn't remember. I had no idea what she was talking about. Miriam had informed the Carringtons of some major calamity in her life which she hadn't spoken of to me. I was a stranger to my daughter's interior landscape, and Louise Carrington, of all people, was her chosen confidante. Not self-appointed. Chosen. And all these shifts had happened in a matter of weeks. I digested these facts as I sat at Louise's kitchen table.

'The thing is,' Louise continued, 'we have a lot in common, you and I, if you come right down to it. We both want what's best for her . . .'

'You don't see it, do you?' I suddenly exploded. 'You really don't see it! Are you always this thick-skinned or do you put it on when it suits you?'

Louise Carrington put down her cup and her eyes widened. 'Eleanor! There's no need for that sort of talk. Oh,' she sighed, 'Eleanor, Eleanor, please don't take me all wrong, but are you sure you're acting in Miriam's best interests? In your heart of hearts, can you swear that this is not mere possessiveness? Because I understand! Truly, I do. We all want our children to form mature, confident relationships with other adults, and then, when it happens, it comes as an awful shock.'

I rose, fumbled for my bag.

'No, no, don't go. Eleanor? The problem's not going to go away with you.'

I began to pace, approaching the Aga aimlessly. It was switched off for the summer and the cold which emanated from it was almost solid, like the cold that comes from a tomb. Or that is how I imagined it. I turned and my heels squeaked. The other limit on my pacing was the rubbish bag with its lush, fetid smell. Quite unconsciously I picked it up and placed it on the brick terrace by the back door, next to a broken flower pot and a pile of garden sweepings.

'Eleanor, let's not argue,' Louise said, trailing me to the door and – I almost cannoned into her – back into the kitchen. 'My father always used to say, "Let's not argue, let's compromise." He was a wise old bird, I miss him still.' She looked off into the middle distance with a smile on her lips, pleating her scarf dreamily. 'I remember once, when I wanted a dog, and my mother went mad. "A dog?" she said. "Over my dead body!" She said, "Who's going to clean up the hairs? Who's going to take it for walks?" And I was going, "I will, I *will*, you never trust me." And dear old Pops, he shushed us both down, he said, "Let me suggest a compromise . . ." And you know what happened? We got a poodle. They don't shed hairs, you see. And I did walk it.'

I looked at her and I think my expression must have conveyed that I thought she was raving, because she stopped herself with a cough.

'Anyway, what I mean to say is, none of us have any idea if her staying here would work out. It's no use me kind of assuming that once she gets here she'll want to stay. With teenagers, who can be sure of anything? So, how's this for a Popsish compromise? Why doesn't she come to us for a fortnight, say, this summer, before you move? Why don't we just see how it goes? She may hate it, you may not mind it as much as you think. After all, children go away to boarding school all the time. I mean, the crunch question for you, Eleanor, is if Miriam wanted to go to boarding school, would you mind as much? Without the personal element. Without feeling we were in competition. Yes, well, anyway . . . shall we just give it a trial run?'

She had taken my breath away. I stared at her.

'You see, when Miriam is sixteen she can pretty much live where she likes, anyway. It sounds outrageous, but when a sixteen year old runs away from home, the police, the courts, they do precious little to recover him. With two teenaged sons, I know about this, believe me. So she's almost fifteen now, you drag her screaming and kicking to Norfolk, in a year's time she turns up here anyway, only now you and she are not friends, only now her schooling is disrupted, only now there are major repercussions. I promise you, it's true, check it out.'

Adrian pounded, clattering, into the kitchen, his largeness obscuring light and air, as if a black hole corkscrewed in the corner of the room.

'Have you two finished?' he said, chummy as family, and the thought struck me that he would constitute an unlooked-for, honorary member of the family soon, if all went as Miriam and Louise wished. I would have to get to know him. I would have to be nice to Louise. 'Phew-ph! I could hear you two going hammer and tongs from two floors up,' he continued. 'Mothers! Who'd have 'em? No wonder Miriam and I both want to leave home!'

'Oh, you!' huffed Louise, prodding him in the centre of his paunch and adding tartly, 'Are you planning to go with Eleanor to Norfolk? I have to warn you, I think she's had enough of our family. Who can blame her? Lord, who'd be a mother if you knew in advance?'

And that was the most peculiar moment because, just for a beat, I found myself identifying with her.

I went home. The green light on the answerphone was flashing. I pressed the button and the tape whirred. The first message was from Nicola.

'OK, Eleanor, we have to talk. I'm out all afternoon so I'll see you tomorrow.'

The second message was from Phyllida. 'Mikey? It's Phil here. Did you see that report in the *Mail*? There's a new wonder drug in America . . . or Russia . . . urm, anyway, I knew there would be new developments. There aren't any side effects. Michael, you've got to speak to Mum or Dad. They'll listen to you. It's no use you sitting on the fence. I tried you at work but . . .'

'*Beep*,' said the answer machine and Phyllida vanished. I tried Michael's mobile but it was switched off. Reluctantly, I telephoned Ann. Although he never normally did, on this occasion Richard picked up the phone.

'Eleanor!' he said, in a tone that suggested hearing my voice was a great treat. 'I was on the verge of ringing you.' I was flabbergasted. An ungracious silence greeted his announcement. Richard never rang me, only Ann rang, on occasion, and even then I had the impression she would rather talk to Michael or Miriam.

'I've been wondering whether you would help me out of a fix,' his voice continued. 'I hope this doesn't sound like an, urm, imposition. Ann's wrenched her shoulder rather badly and I have to see a specialist in London tomorrow. I wondered if you would possibly come with me, Michael being away? And then afterwards,' he said hurriedly, 'we could go for some lunch. What do you say? Can you get the time off?'

Richard came to London on the train the next day, and I jumped in a taxi to join him at the hospital. Firstly, though, I endured my interview with Nicola in which she asked, coolly and civilly, for me to make my mind up about my future within a month. Even in the middle of my agitation, I could see that this was fair.

'I assume Catherine is eager to buy me out,' I said.

'I assume so, too,' said Nicola. 'But that doesn't mean that I agree with her.'

She wasn't such a bad old stick.

'You'll cope,' she said briskly, rising from her seat.

Richard was sitting on a bench in the waiting room, beneath a sentimental print, a blond child feeding blond ducks in front of a blond thatched cottage. He, in contrast, was grey: grey suit, grey hair, and grey smudged his eyes. I hated to consider how much the journey from Crawley had taxed him.

I was still somewhat uncertain about his requesting my help like this; it seemed so intimate somehow. I wondered if there was a hidden motive. I dreaded being asked to make a vow: he might make me promise to carry out some unpleasant duty for him after death, something that he would not ask his children to do. During the taxi ride from Islington, my fancy had conjured up a long-term mistress who must be comforted, and perhaps presented with an adequate cheque – although Richard being unfaithful was a farcical notion. He was precisely the sort of man who you could safely say had never looked at another woman, a man in the underwear and shirts which his wife bought for him at Marks and Sparks. He was an Englishman to his Y-fronts; in drip-dry poly-cotton, with easy-care emotions. But I do not say this derisively. I felt, indeed, a surge of affection for his reliability and essential decency.

When he saw me, Richard rose, with an effort, and kissed me on one cheek. I examined him covertly, his features, which traced Michael's, were stronger now he was a little gaunt, so that with dreadful irony he looked more courtly, handsomer, as the soft pads of flesh dropped away from his bones. His linear nose, fine mouth, the line that ran from the inside corner of his cheekbones to his jaw – he looked to me like a marble figure on a tomb, and the pertinence of this image made me shiver.

'I asked you, really, to put Ann's mind at rest,' he said, as if he had read my thoughts. 'Not meaning to be rude, sort of thing, but I am perfectly capable of seeing this through on my own. But she said she'd worry. She always comes with me, you see. Well, I certainly wasn't going to put you to the trouble of meeting my train, but I told Ann you were acting as my escort and that did the trick. Pretend when you see her, will you? Probably this is going to be a great waste of your time, as far as I can see, and mine, too, but at least we can have a decent lunch afterwards.'

And he was right. I sat on the bench while he was called off by sturdy-legged nurses clutching clipboards; then he returned for an interval before being summoned again. I flicked through magazines from the low tables in the centre of the room. A woman sauntered by; she was wearing a beautiful cobalt blue sari, embroidered in gold, and the chiffon flowed behind her. More and more people arrived and sat there, patiently, fanning themselves with the edges of magazines and books. The line of heads, I noted, was mostly grey.

Richard stood before me.

'All finished?' I said.

'Mmm hmm. Tests done. Everything as expected.' He took

143

my elbow to help me to my feet, such an old-fashioned gesture, so typical of him.

We made our way down the corridor; he was leaning on my arm. 'Do you remember when my mother died?' he asked me.

'Yes, yes I do. It was about . . .' I thought back. Miriam had just started school; events were often dated according to Miriam's life. 'It was ten years ago.'

'That's right. You do remember. Well, that was the last time I was in a hospital, sitting by her bed, waiting.'

I had dropped in on that vigil, from time to time, and found Richard, sometimes joined by Ann or one of the sisters, in the chairs arranged about the bed. Michael and I took a few of the evening shifts. At the beginning, when she had first been admitted with pneumonia, Flora would chatter to us, all of the talk mundane, nothing consequential touched upon. She was worried about her grass, a tiny handkerchief of lawn at the back of her terraced 'tween-wars house at the fringe of the city. 'It's going to have grown so long when I get out of here, I'll never be able to mow it, I don't have the strength.'

'Don't worry,' we said. 'We'll see to it.' We didn't, of course, we just told her we had. For when she was admitted, they had discovered the great growth on her leg that she had been ignoring through fear. Week after week went by, and at first she looked much the same, bird-bright eyes, her girlish, yellowing smile beneath the patchy grey tufts, but then, towards the end, she turned sallow, the colour of Dijon mustard, and her face sunk back to the skull, the eyes in their sockets fluttering open only briefly.

'You won't forget to do my lawn,' she said, the last time we visited.

'I'll never forget that,' Richard was saying. 'The waiting for week after week, until you were almost wishing that she would hurry up and die and let you get on with things. They were giving her drugs for the pneumonia. "Why are you doing that?" I said to them. And they said, "Oh, we didn't know what the family wanted." I lost my temper then. Told them to stop. She died a day later. I've always felt guilty about that. I felt like I hurried her death so I wouldn't have to wait around any more, so I could go back to the office, get on with life.'

I held the swing door open for him and he patted my arm before relinquishing it.

At the hospital entrance, we hailed another taxi, which ticked its way irritably through the obstructed traffic. The restaurant Richard had booked was wildly unfashionable, one which for decades had served roasted meats to men in tribal ties seated on velvet banquettes and uncomfortable chairs. Richard used to come here on his occasional business forays to the city before he retired.

When we were seated, he said, 'I must admit I had an ulterior motive for this lunch.'

I stared at him. 'Well, it was a lovely surprise,' I ventured.

'Surprise? . . . Hmmm. Well, that's just it, as it were.'

I looked at him blankly. I had no idea what he was getting at.

He was staring at me, the corners of his mouth turned up in what was more of a grimace than a smile, and he was nodding slightly, as if willing me to comprehend and spare him the business of explaining, of searching for words, of describing emotions. I frowned, shook my head, nothing came to mind. But at least it didn't appear that he was going to spring a mistress on me.

'I feel as if I've never had the chance to get to know you properly, Eleanor,' he eventually said, hesitantly, picking over the words. 'All these years and when have we talked? If you put it all together it would add up to a few hours' conversation at the outside. Not a very good record, I feel.'

I wanted to blurt out, 'Richard, you never really *talk* to anyone,' but what I actually said was, 'Oh, but you've always been so kind to me . . . so gentle and considerate.'

He interlinked his fingers and cracked his knuckles loudly. 'No, Eleanor, you mustn't try to be nice about it. It's rather getting on my goat, you know, the way everyone keeps pussy footing around me. "Richard," they say, "you must come to dinner." B,b,b,but,' he stuttered, 'they never ask. Too embarrassed. Wouldn't know what to talk about. Well, I thought to myself, it's no use getting mad, you can do something about this. So now I say, "I'd love to! When? Let's fix a date now, I may not be around much longer." That throws them, I can tell you.'

'I can imagine. I mean, they wouldn't expect you to . . .' My voice trailed away.

'Yes. I understand,' he said, amiably. 'But I'm growing grumpy and assertive, at least in patches. Ann blames the morphine. Anyway, Eleanor, I am very aware that I haven't paid you very much attention, especially when you think that I know my two sons-in-law so much better than I know you. You see, I sort of took pains to acquaint myself with them when they were courting my daughters, assuring myself their intentions were honourable, that sort of thing. That they might support my daughters in the style to which they were accustomed.' He paused. 'But you, well, although it is a little late in the day, shall we say, I wanted an opportunity to . . .' He paused, again, 'To say this to you, even though I know it's a bit late in the day, sort of thing,' he repeated.

'I feel as if you've made a declaration,' I teased him.

'You're a good girl,' he said. 'And as you probably realise, Miriam is my favourite grandchild,' he added.

Out of the blue, I found myself gasping for breath, my shoulders heaving, my pulse racing, the room spinning like a whirligig.

'Are you ready to . . . ?' The voice petered out. 'Is Madam all right?' the waiter asked Richard.

'Oh, dear,' Richard's voice replied.

Richard's handkerchief appeared within my sphere of vision, which was confined to my place mat and the king's pattern flatware. I heard him order two gin and tonics and, shortly afterwards, mine appeared, inserted onto the place mat between my navy elbows by Richard's hand in its neat white cuff with the simply dreadful watch of which he was so proud, a bulky object which told the time in the centre of the earth and if stamped on by a herd of elephants. I coughed up a few gasps of fond laughter.

'I didn't mean to upset you, my dear,' he said, all concern.

'I'm sorry, Richard,' I said. 'This is ridiculous. We have what you might call a domestic crisis.'

'Oh I see,' he said, sitting back. I had to fill him in but all the same, I kept my account brief, it was so obviously insignificant when compared with his cancer.

'For what it's worth, I think you're a wonderful mother,' he said warmly. 'Wonderful.'

'Oh, Richard!' I said. I was surprised to my core, and touched.

Richard ordered the roast beef of merry olde England for himself and I asked for a Dover sole and chips. When the waiter had gone, he leaned forward once more. 'Shall I tell you why Miriam is my favourite grandchild? It is precisely because she can go off the deep end and get things so, well, arse about *tit*.' He said 'tit' with a deliberate intonation, followed by an embarrassed snigger, in order to emphasise that he did not use such a vulgar word unconsciously. 'She's got spark. Do you know what I mean? She's got life. In that she's . . .' there was a pause, while he struggled with notions of loyalty and tact ' . . . she's different to the others, sort of thing. This business about the wild life sanctuary. How many kids give up their weekends to a cause like that? As far as I can see, they're all playing computer games or surfing the thingummyjig, or hanging around shopping malls, gossiping. God knows, it's what Phyllida's seem to do. You mustn't lose heart, you know.'

'I shook her the other night. I was so angry with her. She was being so hurtful, so unreasonable, and I took her by the shoulders and shook her, and you know what she said?' – this had hurt me more than I could admit – 'She said, "Why are you so emotionally retarded, mother?" Withering or what? *You're* a parent. You know how I felt. I saw her watching me. I saw her judging me. And of course, the worst thing was that she was right. I shouldn't have shaken her or lost control like that. I feel so ashamed . . . so *inadequate*.'

'Sounds as if she deserved it to me.'

'Oh, don't, Richard.'

'Tell me, did you hold their mistakes against your parents? Because – hell's bells, Eleanor! – I hope Michael and the girls

147

don't hold mine against me. The absences, the pressures. I never gave them very much. I didn't turn up for their sports days, their prize-givings. When Michael received his A level certificates, neither of us was in the audience. Ann had to be at the girls' school and I was too busy.'

'I'm sure he's forgotten,' I said.

'Well, exactly! Proves my point.'

I smiled.

'I love him, Eleanor,' he said thickly, through his awkwardness, like a mouthful of pins. 'I love my son very much and I have never told him.'

Our meals arrived, and some wine. I go red when I drink wine at lunchtime. I never used to but I do now, something to do with age. I considered ordering water but thought, what the hell . . .

'Erm, I hope you don't mind my asking, but was your childhood happy, as it were?' Richard asked me.

'Happy? Yes, yes, reasonably so. They tried their best. They were not' – I corrected myself – 'are not – completely happy together.'

He cut a slice of beef into a precise, accurate square. Then, a square of Yorkshire pudding. Dab, dab in the gravy. Then he speared a roast potato, but it was too crunchy and skidded away, onto the table cloth. He winced, picked it up between thumb and forefinger, and returned it to the rim of his plate, by the neat pile of salt.

I watched all this listlessly, while I struggled with my own notions of loyalty and tact.

'My father . . . he's not a bad man . . . but he used to suffer from . . . from a weakness, let us say, for wine and women. One of my earliest memories is of being locked in my bedroom while my mother followed him to some poncy hotel bar convinced he was meeting his latest inamorata. I wasn't frightened, not of being left alone, so she must have explained she wouldn't be long. But I remember, I was looking down from my window at her climbing into her car. It was a Triumph Stag . . . that's right, a cream Triumph Stag; a zippy little sports car he'd bought her. Her face was all screwed up.

All this, of course, had followed one of their rows.'

'My dear girl,' Richard said. His face was red; he was half sympathy, half awkwardness. Despite inviting me to talk, he had not really expected such intimacy. Well, for that matter, neither had I.

'It wasn't so bad,' I explained. 'At least, they stuck it out, stuck together, and not just for my sake because they're both still there. It's funny, actually, my sympathies used to lie solely with my mother, but now they've swung round. I'm very fond of my father, now.'

'There, you see,' Richard said, as if I had just explained everything. He leaned forward eagerly. 'You just think back to your own teenage years. Think back to how you were, then, as well as how you feel now. I must say I've been thinking back a great deal over the last few weeks. It's been an interesting process.'

I blew out a breath and my fringe ruffled. I did not think my memories would prove cathartic. Richard had ducked his chin back in again, and was rearranging his knife and fork. We finished the meal in near silence, but at ease. It was the first time a silence between us had been leisurely.

At one point, a waiter passed us. Richard raised his chin, lifted a finger, but the waiter ignored him as conscientiously as only a waiter can.

'Oh,' Richard said. 'Didn't see me.'

He swivelled back in his seat, and fumbling in his pocket for a miniature enamelled case, brought out a couple of round white pills which he took with a gulp of wine.

'Are you supposed to take those things with alcohol?' I said.

'No, I'm being very naughty. But I'm buggered if I'm going to refrain from a drink.'

The waiter passed us again. I caught his eye. Richard jumped. 'Oh, no, it's my shout,' he said. When it came, he checked the bill very carefully, adding the figures up in his head, frowning and running his finger up and down the column, even when the waiter returned and stood enquiring if everything was in order. I was mortified.

'What are the side effects of your interesting little cocktail?' I asked, trying to distract him.

'Who cares? Who gives a damn?' he said, and he shrugged.

I said goodbye to him outside the restaurant. He took me by the shoulders and squeezed me so tightly I thought my bones were crunching against each other.

'Oh, Richard!' I had suddenly remembered Phyllida's message.

'I beg your pardon?'

'Phyllida has read of some miracle cure which doesn't have side effects. She wants Michael and me to talk you into taking it.'

'Miracle cure,' he said, amused. 'I've looked into them all, don't you worry.' He shook his head. 'Tell Phyllida you kept your part of the bargain.'

'I'm glad we did this, Richard,' I told him. I felt choked. He examined my eyes suspiciously.

'Jolly good,' he said, and he carefully smoothed his raincoat over his arm. 'You're a good girl, Eleanor, and you're doing well. I wouldn't fret about it. But having said that, it's so much easier to be a father,' he added with a smile, and I wondered if he really meant this. 'I think you should stop worrying and give yourself a pat on the back,' he said.

As he went, he squeezed my hand in his so fiercely that the wedding ring bit into my flesh. I didn't wince at that, nor, in the end, did I weep. I managed to do this for him, this one tiny act. I caught a taxi back to the office, and on the way I thought of how gracefully we'd avoided the matter most on his mind.

Chapter Eight

So.

When I think of my mother, I see her with her back to me, at the sink, at the cooker, at the washing machine. I see her taking me somewhere in a car – a big, ponderous car, whose leather seats smelt like the gas mask at the dentist's – and I see her dropping me off. She didn't come in and watch the riding lesson or the piano recital. She didn't cheer me on from the sidelines. I was never in any doubt about her love for me. When I was young, she was conscientious about the practical business of caring for me, about regular meals and set bedtimes. But I see her as independent. And curiously, although all of them were housewives, their very existence justified by home and children, my friends' mothers were similarly detached. That was the fabric of motherhood in those times; their love was inexcitable. They thought of you in the third person singular, not as a part of themselves.

But of course, all families are remarkable even in their ordinariness. Children like me develop strategies to enable us to forgive our parents; we blank out whole tracts of family history – months and years crumble and disintegrate. My mind darts among what's left and selects the memories it will feed on with a wary, picky eye. Oh, of course, I told Michael most of it, within a week or two of our first meeting; this was the prime way in which I distinguished between him and everyone else – a singular mark of favouritism, now that I came to consider it. On the whole, however, I say to everyone, including my brother on his very occasional visits – when he sits opposite me at the kitchen table, blows out an expansive sigh, pours another glass of wine, and begins to bleat about our upbringing – I say to him, 'Oh, Philip, it wasn't so bad, really.' Then Michael grows exasperated, because he has loathed my parents since he heard my account of childhood. That's misguided loyalty, in my view; they don't deserve to be loathed. But Michael thinks I am being silly, I'm pretending that what happened, didn't happen.

'They're my parents,' I say, as he walks away to busy himself with some task.

Of course, I can give myself permission to roam among the memories which are normally proscribed. My mother, as she was then, often in white with white boots, was a synthetic beauty much admired by my more impressionable classmates. The slant of her cheekbones, the symmetry and proportions, all united in a flawless and oddly expressionless whole. Her voice was deep, rather masculine, not girly as her exterior suggested.

Astonishing as it may seem, my father rarely saw her barefaced, except in the half light of the bedroom chamber with its drawn curtains. Each morning, she rose at 5.45 and locked herself in the bathroom to begin a process that involved a heap of tools: heated rollers, a metal artist's box of cosmetics, and spidery false eyelashes often still edged with stubborn globules of yellowing glue.

An hour later she would emerge, a groomed, pearly-lipped vision who would take my father a cup of breakfast tea. At night, there was a reverse chronicle. She would go to bed in full maquillage. Half an hour later there would be soft stirrings, the opening and shutting of doors, and she would denude her face, apply Nivea cream, comb out her hair. But when he made love to her, his head poised above hers, he must have looked down upon her artificial self on the pillow, the eyes outlined in black, the lips outlined in mid-brown, infilled with pinky gloss.

I was and never have been jealous of her beauty. In fact, as a child, I enjoyed the reflected glory. My mother materialised in a glittering black cocktail dress by my bed, on her way to some 'do' in their Surrey social life – the neighbours' parties, the Freemasons' ladies nights, the golf club 'functions'. Whenever they went out, she would again lock herself behind her bathroom door, a moment full of mystery and glamour to me. Later, she emerged in chiffon or sequins, always wearing the special earrings my father had once bought for their anniversary, the two fat pale pearls surrounded by a galaxy of diamonds.

I loved my mother in her evening finery. And she loved to show herself off to me. Bathed, pyjamaed, introduced to the baby-sitter, I lay beneath the quilt awaiting her visit. And when she appeared, in a rustle and a halo of hairspray, I jumped up in my bed to get a better view. I wonder if my excitement at these moments meant more to her than the elaborate compliments of the Surrey men who eyed her from behind cut glass, and from the other side of the squared-up furniture in stark drawing rooms.

'Don't bounce, child,' she would say. 'You'll break the bed.' But there was a smile at the edge of her voice, I could tell. In fact, her voice always sounded different when she was primped and coiffed and looking her best.

She worked so hard at it. She was on a perpetual diet, spooning up Special K for breakfast or, for snacks, crunching celery sticks which she dipped in salt (it was not until later that salt joined her list of 'no-nos'), and always, always, refusing puddings with wide-eyed drama.

Every Saturday, however, she allowed herself a treat. She bought herself a little volcano of chocolate known as a Walnut Whirl and, unpeeling the wrapper, crumpling it methodically, she would settle down to eat. This process was always luxurious and unvarying; first, she would bite off the walnut on the top; then, she would nibble down the spiral; finally, she would eat the base, licking her fingers afterwards. This ritual always coincided with Dr Who on television and for a long time I associated the whoa-whoa of the theme music with a deep, mystical act of pleasure.

Now, if I want to remember, every detail returns: my skirted dressing table, the yellow stripy wallpaper with the grey-and-white arrowheads which passed as a discreet pattern. The fake Regency dining furniture (more stripes) rested, its feet in protective cups, on Wilton and Axminster. They bought furniture that would last, and last it has, long after fashion and design have swept on, so that my parents' house is stuck in its time warp, as if it were a room-set recreated for a folk museum.

Ours was a large house, one of the those Surrey minimansions built between the wars. It was a house with shadows in the corners of rooms, dark oak panelling and brick fireplaces, red-brown like ox blood, with a vase of dried pampas plumes sitting in state in the dead centre of the hearth. It was, in fact, far too large for us, especially since my brother, who is more than five years older, had left at the earliest opportunity, shortly before I turned thirteen. He picked a university in Canada which was just about as far away as he could get.

It was on my thirteenth birthday that they bought me the tortoise. Of course, I was too old really to want that kind of a pet and yet – I do remember – on that, the first day of my teenage years, I was so pleased to have it.

I remember waking, that morning, looking in the dressing-table mirror for an age, examining my face for evidence of overnight change. I looked as I always did, too young, too ingenuous – mid-brown hair, long with a fringe, hazel eyes that I already liked to call green, square chin, toothy, cheesy grin. I wore a pink, quilted, shorty dressing gown, and my legs, sticking out beneath the flared hem, resembled chicken bones, thin and pale, with knobbly joints.

I padded down the wide stairs, bare feet sinking into thick carpet. The tick, tock of the long-case clock in the hall was the sound of that house. This clock had belonged to my father's mother and he was inordinately attached to it, winding it, adjusting the weights. He said he found its beat comforting, but I found it disturbing, as if we were living life to a metronome. Besides, it was as large as a coffin and when I was very young I had thought there was something inside it, wanting to crawl out.

As I entered the kitchen my mother was standing at the sink with her back to me; my father was reading the *Telegraph* importantly.

'Morning!' I said brightly.

I was excited.

My mother swivelled and I saw her eyes, red-veined and for once, devoid of make-up. The bulb of her nose was red, too.

Another of their rows.

I believe that for a second the thought fluttered before me, displaying its aggressive markings and lurid colours: why did you have to argue now? Why did you have to spoil my birthday? This of all birthdays? And then self-interest evaporated in the misery of my mother's face, with her nose making her look so childish, so ludicrous.

My father put his newspaper down. There was something about him, with his olive pallor, the shadow of stubble that lay on his chin and cheek, which made him look a worse man than he was.

'Ella,' he said gravely. 'Your mother and I are going to separate. I'm afraid you are going to have to choose. Of course, it's more usual for a girl to live with her mother, but, of course . . . you know . . . I'd be very happy to have you with me.' The image of him and me in a bachelor flat was not credible.

My mother made an odd sound, like a gurgle.

'Oh,' I said.

I had burst into tears the first time they had put this question to me. I'd been eight? Eight or nine. My mother had said – her voice high, plangent – that I was too young to be placed in such a predicament.

I had clung to my father's arm.

'Don't go!'

No reply.

'I'm begging you.'

At this, he unbuckled my fingers from his sleeve and left the room. My heart was racing. I strained to hear. He was in the drawing-room. He had gone no further. I dodged past the open door; he was sitting by the fire.

I wrapped myself into the tightest ball I could, crouched on the swirly Axminster by the long-case clock, forgetting to be scared. Tick, tock. After a while, I heard him call for a coffee. I hung around downstairs for a while, testing the atmosphere. Tick, tock. After half an hour I knew it had blown over.

But I was older now. Thirteen. A teenager, almost an adult. I was past crying. On the other hand, he was older, too, and could not be swayed so easily by my appeals.

'But it's my birthday,' I reminded them. 'And you haven't bought me my present.'

My mother's hands flew to her face, muffling her words. 'Oh my God! How could I? Oh, Ella, what must you think of me?'

My father shot her a look of irritation, pulled out a chair for me and sat me upon it.

'I'll take you to buy something. As we can both see, your mother won't pull herself together to manage it.' (Why did he always have to be so mean? Why did he always have to pick away at the scabs until she began bleeding again?) 'What is it that you want?' he was asking.

I thought carefully. Nothing girly, no clothes, he wouldn't last long in clothes shops, never had. I wanted a transistor radio but that would be too easy, too quickly accomplished.

'A tortoise,' I said. 'I would like a tortoise.'

They were both taken aback. I saw them exchange a glance; a good sign, I felt. It emboldened me.

'I shall call it Archimedes.'

'Archimedes.' My father considered this, seemingly with as much gravity as he had announced that he was leaving. 'That's a good name for a tortoise. Right, first I'm taking Eleanor to buy a tortoise, Maxine. I'll go later instead.'

She didn't respond. When we left she came to the door and buttoned me into my coat. 'Good girl,' she whispered, and she rubbed my arm, and we both knew we were partners in a conspiracy.

'We'll try the local pet shop first,' my father said, almost to himself, as he pondered whether to turn right or left at the end of our road. 'I expect they'll have one.'

156

'It can't be any old one,' I said hurriedly. 'You can't call any old tortoise Archimedes. It's got to live up to the name.'

He frowned and tch-ed his tongue on the roof of his mouth, casting his eyes to the padded plastic ceiling of our Zephyr Zodiac.

'You do understand?' I added quickly.

As luck would have it, there were no tortoises in the first pet shop. We trailed back to the car and my father decided that we would have done better to have gone to Guildford, a larger town, ten miles to the south. There, the pet shop did indeed have a tortoise. It was small, the size of a saucer, endearing as a clockwork toy. I cast it a look of longing, before announcing that it was definitely the owner of a cutesy kind of name.

My father was now more involved in the quest than I was. He considered carefully.

'Kingston,' he said. 'I'm sure there's a pet shop in Kingston.'

Kingston was almost an hour's drive away.

I nodded. 'Let's try,' I agreed.

In this way, we used up the morning. At lunchtime we returned with a sizeable tortoise who would suit his new name.

'But I need a cage for it,' I said. 'Otherwise it will bury itself in the flower beds, or burrow into Mrs Ticknall's.'

My father went off to buy chicken wire and wood, hammering together a nifty structure.

In this way, he used up all the afternoon, and all the leftover anger.

I had a tortoise. We all had a home.

There was a period during which their rows got worse. The house was not big enough to swallow the screams and the yells before they reached me lying in my bed. But as much as the sounds tore at me, the silence that fell afterwards tore at me more. Once I heard his car crunch away angrily, then hers, too. I lay in the darkness while they careered in their mad chase off the motorway bridge or into the path of a lorry, and so left me in the silence forever. It was two hours fourteen minutes before they returned, safely, in convoy, apparently friendly once more. It took me a while longer to get back to sleep. In the morning I had a history test, in which I did badly, and my father said he was disappointed in me.

I was sixteen before I ventured downstairs when the quiet fell. Tick, tock said the clock. Babble, babble, babble said the television. Hum, hum went the freezer. All the familiar household sounds, but to me it was quiet as the grave.

I found her on the drawing-room floor, knocked out cold, her blonde hair spread in a fan across the swirly brown pattern of that Axminster carpet; stupid, the details you remember when you start delving. I fetched a cold flannel and applied it to her forehead, which seemed the right thing to do. She stirred, I helped her to sit up. After a while, she said, 'Oh, Ella, what must you think of me? I feel so humiliated,' and then she added, 'it was an accident. It was my fault.'

The next morning I went to my father and said that he was never to touch her in anger again, and he said it was an accident, she had drunk too much, he had pushed her and she had collapsed, but yes, I was right, he would never lay a finger on her. As far as I know, he kept his word. But the rows, of course, continued.

Not long afterwards, just before my O levels, my parents held a party to celebrate their silver wedding anniversary. Phil returned from Vancouver for the occasion. They picked him up from the airport. When he strolled in, I ran down the stairs. Phil stood in the hall, looking gigantic in a plaid jacket, jeans and brogues. My run petered out of its own accord. My mother was fussing around, so I hung back, hugging close to the wall, grinning and feeling my ears burn red.

Phil turned and saw me.

'Come here,' he said in a tone that conveyed I was being ridiculous, conveyed affection too. He ruffled my hair and pretended to punch me on the shoulder. 'You haven't changed a bit,' he said, which miffed me. He had changed considerably. He had grown a beard, muscles. His lace-up shoes were enormous. During his stay, they sat in the hall by the mat like a living presence, and a sour stench rose from them.

Once, during his visit, he came out to the dining-room table, where I was revising for my exams, and pulled one of the mahogany seats back, leaning his elbows on the back rail. It looked flimsy, as if it would burst apart under his weight.

'How're things with Mum and Dad these days?' he asked me.

'What?' I said, flushing. 'Oh, fine, fine.'

'Good,' he echoed. 'Good. Glad it's simmered down, for your sake.'

I kept my eyes on the rail, waiting for it to buckle. I did not disavow him.

Then his visit was buried in preparations for the party, the planning required for a menu of cheese and pineapple hedge-hogs, asparagus rolls, smoked salmon whirls, mushroom vol au vents. My father and brother went off to order the booze and glasses and returned saying they had bought up half the offy.

The relatives arrived, in droves, and settled into odd nooks and crannies of the house; whole families in each of the spare bedrooms, aunts I had never seen before crouched on camp beds in study and sitting-room, alarming aunts who wore too much make-up and told risqué stories, and pleasant aunts, who carefully concocted an interest in me.

'Hasn't she grown? I'd never have known her,' the nice aunts exclaimed, so that I wanted to hit them. 'And look at Phil! The size of him! Do you think she'll grow as big as her brother?'

On the morning of the anniversary, there was to be a church blessing, but my mother asked me if I would stay behind to lay the buffet table. I was mortified.

'Get someone else to lay the table. Don't you want me there?' I asked her.

'Oh, Ella,' she said, using my pet name, but crossly. 'It's only a blessing. It's not as if it's important.'

Afterwards the swarm descended on the buffet table. Phil put the stereo on and made the aunts dance to Gary Glitter anthems, in a line with their legs akimbo and their right hands punching the air. My father took a photograph of them and I believe my parents have it still.

I was squiffy and laughed till I cried. Rising, I proposed a toast to my parents. 'Shut up! Shut up, everyone!' I cried.

'Here's to Mum and Dad on their silver wedding!'

I raised my glass and around the room everyone shuffled for refills and raised theirs, their rictus grins like disembodied false teeth floating above the champagne flutes.

'Maxine and John!' they chorused. My mother's laugh tinkled like a bell.

About a fortnight later, when the house was our own once more, my parents staged their next argument. It was a fine day and the sun lay in squares on the carpet, stencilled through the leaded light windows. My father was being curt. There was an unrelenting rhythm to his cruelty.

'All I am doing is giving her a lift.'

'Why do you have to? Why can't someone else?'

I drilled my fingers into my ears.

'Well, even if there is nothing in it, how will it look? What will people say?'

'Listen to me, you stupid cow! Nobody will say anything! And what would it matter if they did? You and your appearances!' My father swept into the sitting-room. I removed my hands in case this inflamed him. 'Always appearances.' He cast me a glance.

'Don't you tell her, John. Don't you dare tell her!' my mother said. Somehow I knew that she was not referring to whichever faceless woman they were arguing over.

My father glanced at me. I saw an idea kindle in that dark look from under his dark brows. My mother was always handing him the ammunition to hurl at her. It took me a long time to wonder if this was what she subconsciously wanted.

'Tell me what?' I said foolishly, rising from the sofa.

My mother, emitting a shriek, a wail, rushed from the room; I heard her feet beating a frantic tattoo on the stairs; then, the ceiling, which was her bedroom floor, groaning.

I looked at my father. There was a disagreeable set to his face, the desire which she inflamed in him, with a kind of unerring talent, to hurt her.

'We weren't married,' he said. 'We were living together. I'd been married before you see, and my wife, my first wife, Margaret, she wouldn't give me a divorce. They were much harder to come by back then. And then we had Philip and it didn't seem to matter, and then we had you. Well, that's how it was. We got married the other week, though. That was the party.'

I stared at him, gawping. I finally managed, 'Who knew?'

'Well, urm, everyone. I told Philip when he was eighteen. I was all for telling you, too.'

I went upstairs and found my mother, lying face-down across her bed, weeping. 'He told you, he told you,' she keened. 'I know you won't think the same of me now.'

She seemed small and shrunken, or maybe I had grown.

'Oh, mother,' I said, 'don't be silly.'

Chapter Nine

I climbed out of the office lift to find a small boy in black jeans and baggy sweatshirt standing on the landing. It was Scott, Anthea's son.

'Aren't you at school?' I asked him foolishly. 'Are you ill?'

''spended,' he said, his lip curling. He was a thin-faced child, with a sharp nose that looked even pointier under his crew cut.

What did spended mean?

I looked in at Anthea's office door. She was talking on the telephone, pacing as far as the cord would allow, twiddling a ringlet of hair around and around her finger. Her voice had acquired the momentum that usually indicated that she was talking to her ex-husband. I was on the verge of retreating when she saw me. She opened her eyes wide, a common signal among busy women; it meant, I need your sympathy, please come in.

'Yeah, yeah, well, do it then,' she grumbled at the receiver. 'I don't know! How am I supposed to know? They treat me like I'm nothing to do with this. After all, I'm only the mother . . . Yeah, yeah, OK, ring me back.' Then she put the telephone down and wheeled towards me.

'He's been suspended from school,' she said.

'Suspended?'

'I know, it's incredible, isn't it? They've suspended him and he was only acting in self-defence.'

'Self-defence?'

'Do you have to repeat everything I say, Eleanor? My nerves are stretched to breaking point, as it is.' She strode over to her window, which overlooked the well at the centre of the building, and presented her with a sad little tableau of rusting fire escapes and dripping pipes. 'Who wouldn't kick out if pinned to a wall and ridiculed in front of all his mates?'

'He kicked a boy who pinned him to a wall?'

She looked at me, frowning. 'Of course not. It was a teacher,' she said. 'He kicked a teacher. This teacher had him lined up against the wall for swearing in class. I ask you! Talk about heavy-handed! I mean, I'm not condoning Scott. He shouldn't have used bad language, even though he probably learnt it at school – heaven knows, he didn't pick up a term like that at home . . . They'd had this swimming lesson, see, and this other boy – Bill, his name is, everyone knows he's a bully – he made fun of Scott not being able to swim, called him a wimpo, and then Scott called him a w–, well, a you-know-what, and the teacher only heard that part of the conversation.'

I tried to put a veil over my features so that Anthea would not read a similar message on my face to the one I'd glimpsed on hers, yesterday. Whatever Miriam has done cannot be as bad as this, was what my look would say. But Anthea was preoccupied, firing off her indignation at the dripping pipes.

'Whatever happened to teachers with proper authority? The ones who brought you into line with a look? I had a form mistress who could quell me with one well-chosen phrase. "Anthea Booth," she would boom, "stop doodling on your rough book." And this when she was writing on the blackboard! I swear she had eyes in the back of her head. She didn't have to line me up against a wall, as if I was a criminal awaiting the firing squad. They didn't resort to suspending an eight year old! I mean, you've looked after him. You know. He's a normal, active, mischievous, little eight year old.

'I said to them, "His father won't stand for it, you wait and see. You won't be able to push him around." Sean's going up to the school now.' She wheeled to face me. 'I said to him, "You're his father, do something," and for once, he is. He'll go to his solicitors, if needs be, and he has good solicitors – believe me, I know, he had them when we divorced.'

Her telephone shrilled again and I left her hunched around it, whispering, a hand cupped to her mouth. 'There's no call for it,' she was saying, 'no call at all.' On the landing, Scott was jiggling from one foot to another. As I went past he made a slavering noise, like Hannibal Lecter in *Silence of the Lambs*.

Two large flies were locked in copulation on the kitchen work surface; the air hung with a pestering whine, the beating of minute wings in sun-enriched air. There was a can of spray killer in the cupboard. I wielded it, taking pleasure in its grim, satisfying hiss. One by one, the flies spluttered and went out.

I tried Michael on the kitchen phone but, as was usual now, he was not available. At 5.35, a key turned in the lock; Miriam. I found myself wondering what to say to her.

'Oh, no!' She stood poised in the doorway, her grey eyes blazing in her white face, transfixed, apparently, by the fly spray which I had not yet returned to the cupboard. 'Mum, you haven't! How could you?'

I was flummoxed. 'I was killing flies, 's only fly spray,' I protested, thickly, through a Belgian chocolate. Had she become a Buddhist? Were all pests sacred?

'The crickets!' she wailed. 'You'll kill the crickets!'

'Huh?'

I hadn't thought of that.

'They've been singing,' I said rather wildly. 'I heard them.'

'Well, they're not singing now, are they?' she said, which was incontrovertible.

She froze me with her look. I saw myself from her perspective, a clumsy woman trying to filter excuses through the chocolate gumming her mouth. When had I been transformed from a joky but intelligent, motherly sort of a mother into a self-indulgent, thoughtless dingbat of a mother?

She glowered at a worn patch at the base of the door for a second or two, kicking at it twice with one foot; then she turned and disappeared without another word.

I heaved the cast-ron skillet onto the ring, and made risotto with deliberation, stirring the pan slowly, mindlessly, watching the glutinous rice turn plump and bleed starch. All the while I was straining to hear the crickets, to be alert enough to notice their song, but my attentiveness was repaid only by the refrigerator's hum and by a dishevelled blackbird, which perched in the rowan in our front garden and poured a liquid soprano part into the heedless city street. Beneath the tree, a bold party of sparrows had perched on a low, spreading, blue conifer so that the stems bobbed and quivered, as if loaded with surprisingly drab Christmas baubles.

Miriam took her supper to her room on a tray. She sometimes did this when outfaced by homework. I scraped dark grease from the oven – *great, grey-green, greasy Limpopo oven*, said the nonsensical voice in my head, which was beginning to annoy me – and scrubbed it with a succession of scouring pads. I washed the kitchen floor, using the new super mop – which, with its head of bleached dreadlocks, looked remarkably old-fashioned to me – but it was said to reach into the remotest, finickiest corners. Sure enough, it infiltrated the narrow spaces behind the 'fridge and flushed out the sci-fi body of a cricket, damp, black and lifeless. My heart sank.

I couldn't quite bear to throw the creature that had sung so merrily into the rubbish, or flush it down the lavatory. Instead, I placed it in a matchbox on a folded square of bog roll, and buried it in a border with a trowel, all the while hoping that Miriam would not glance down from her bedroom, and spot me stooped in my furtive funeral rites.

Standing, afterwards, a hand in the small of my back, I looked up at her blank window. A thought struck me. She didn't have homework. She had broken up at noon. It was the summer holidays.

On a shelf in the kitchen was a wooden model of a dog which Miriam had made, aged ten in a design and technology class. It was crude and comical; the legs were thick and clumpy, with square edges, the neck was match-stick skinny (for she had, indeed, used a Swan Vesta) and the head resembled a car. She had glued shavings to the back in an attempt to resemble fur. The whole model was stuck to a piece of plywood, on which, in turquoise felt pen, she had written, Merlin, RIP by Miriam Bányer, Aged 10¾. Then there was a speech bubble with the word, 'Woof!', enclosed in it.

This, then, was all we had left to remind us of the dog we'd owned when she was young, when we employed Debbie, the nanny, and it had seemed like a good idea to give a waif a warm bed and a laden stomach. But Miriam had grown and Debbie had left, we didn't need the services of a full-time nanny once Miriam had started school. We had been so delighted to find the after-hours nursery, which gave school children tea and supervised their reading. And I had been so delighted to get rid of the surrogate mother for whom, from time to time, I had endured such pangs of jealousy. When Debbie appeared in the morning, satisfied, unexceptional Debbie, both the child and the dog had thrown themselves upon her.

So, the last few years of the dog's life had been miserable, insufficient ones, spent snoozing on his bean bag in a corner, emitting killer smells, waking, ridiculously pleased, at our key in the lock, his tail a beating flag. When I sank into the sofa at the end of the day, he would lean against my legs, or lie down with his chin resting on my feet, and I knew, then, how lonely he was. But that sort of thing happens; time picks you up and carries you on, so that suddenly you are not as able to meet all of your responsibilities as you once had been. You are required elsewhere. Your cosy plan has shifted.

After Merlin died, we got a cat whom we called TC, not after the cartoon character, but as shorthand for tabby cat. Purring like a moped, she would knead your leg with her claws. She commandeered my place on the sofa for the six months that we had her, but I didn't mind.

She was run over in the street, just outside, not far at all. The car must have been speeding, it was dusk – you can imagine how it was. I could imagine it; I had been inside, unaware, oblivious, while some motorist squashed my cat and didn't stop to tell me. I found her body in the gutter the next morning. There was no obvious sign of injury, and her fur was still as smooth and soft as air-spun silk. But she didn't look peaceful or merely asleep, for she was cold and heavy, her eyes glassy and unseeing. I wrapped her in my jacket and brought her home.

After that, we gave up, unless you count the escaped crickets, which I don't. We never got round to removing the cat flap though, not even after all this time. Cursing, Michael had installed it in the back door, but his DIY skills did not really stretch to reversing the process. So it continued rattling on windy nights like a ghostly chain, reminding me. Miriam badgered me often about pets, but I couldn't face owning another animal.

'Too much responsibility,' I said to her.

But what I meant was, 'Too much heartbreak.'

If there were any remaining crickets, they did not sing for me that evening, and I knew in my heart they had been hushed forever. Michael came in just after nine, as dusk embraced the city, looking tired. He was wearing his grey suit and a white shirt – he preferred plain white to coloured or striped – and a maroon silk tie with a snazzy abstract pattern which Miriam had bought him for his last birthday. He sank into his kitchen chair with a sigh, dropping his brown leather overnight bag – *clunk!* – next to him.

'I killed the crickets,' I said.

'What? I thought you liked them? Well, the kitchen was sounding like a bloody Greek hillside. Anyway,' he added impatiently, 'I resigned.'

'Huh?'

' . . . They were flatteringly upset. You all right? You look awful. Your face is all red.'

'I went to see Louise Carrington.'

'Oh, God,' he groaned. 'What did you say?'

'And I had lunch with your father.'

'You what?'

'He asked me yesterday.'

'Why?'

'Well, I believe he fancied my company. He also told me what a fine job I've done with Miriam.'

He stared at me. 'Stone me,' he said.

'Thank you very much.'

'That isn't what I meant.'

'Yes, it was. You were peeved that he asked me and not you. Why don't you grow up?'

'Ella-norr,' he said, drawing out the syllables of my name.

'Don't you Eleanor me! I'm fed up of you always patronising me. You're not always the one in the right, you know, you're not always the one who knows best. You accuse me of fussing her and then you go around letting her get away with murder. Who bought her the computer she hardly ever touches? Who insisted on the thousand-pound violin she's lost interest in? "Oh, but she needs a good instrument; she needs the encouragement of producing a decent sound." The fact that the rest of the school got by with violins at a quarter of the price! Oh, no. Not you! And you tell me I spoil her!'

He stuck his legs out and leaned back in his chair. 'Oh, God! Are you really going to regurgitate all my faults as a father, going back to the year dot? You have the memory of a she-elephant. But only when it suits you.'

'You bastard! You're the one who keeps saying I don't need to diet.'

'What's dieting got to do with it? Where's dieting come from?' he asked the ceiling.

'You just said I was an elephant.'

'Not . . . like . . . that,' he said, very deliberately. 'I didn't mean it like that . . . Look,' he sliced his hands outwards, horizontally, 'Let's . . . just . . . get back to the point in hand . . . We've dealt with my father. So,' he took a deep breath. 'What happened between you and the home counties' answer to Dicky Attenborough?'

Against my will, a little sniff of laughter escaped me. 'It's not Dicky. It's the other one – David – he's the one who talks to gorillas . . . Nothing much, if you want to know. Says there's no point arguing because we don't know if Miriam really wants to go through with it. Seems to have this fantasy that we'll let Miriam spend a few weeks with her over the summer holidays. A sort of trial, surrogate daughterhood, I suppose.'

There was a pause as he sat back again, considering this, but not a long one; it all happened very quickly. 'It's not a bad idea,' he said. 'Might bring her to her senses. Get rid of the rose-tinted glasses.'

I think I had my mouth open. 'She's got a dental appointment next week,' I said, as if this was the only reason I could think of for her not going.

He took me at face value. 'Well, can't you rearrange it?' he snapped.

He rose, stalked through to the sitting-room where the clink of glass and an ascending glug, glug, glug, told me he was pouring a whisky. 'Remember that time she went to Normandy?' he called back. 'She got homesick after three days. Do you remember?' He appeared again, smiling as he sipped his whisky. 'Miriam's used to her own company; she doesn't like noisy households.'

'Normandy was camping with a class of thirty eleven year olds,' I said. 'Louise Carrington's is not nearly so noisy.'

'So what?' he said. 'It'll do her good. Make her appreciate her home.'

I could feel my control spiralling upwards, disappearing on a thermal current. 'She is not going to live with Louise and that's final, Michael. Why do you always do this to me? Why?'

'I do not always do anything. I merely try to make you put aside your overemotional reactions and see sense.'

'You patronising pig!'

In the middle of this bellow, Miriam entered. I felt embarrassed. The state of my emotional development came to mind. But we both fell silent as she passed between us en route to the sink for a glass of water.

'I'm going, I'm going,' she said.

'Miriam,' Michael said.

I had this impulse to interrupt him. I may even have moved a step towards them, but then I stopped myself, stopped myself from pleading because I had this image of me begging my father not to go. It seemed to me that the degradation of that moment had forever warped our relationship. I had notched it against him.

'Miriam,' Michael continued. 'Louise Carrington is suggesting you stay at hers for a couple of weeks during these holidays, just to see how it would pan out. What do you think?'

'Oh, Whoa! Coo-well!'

'Just for a fortnight, OK?'

'Sure, Dad, sure. No problemma . . . Thanks, Dad.'

She sped up the stairs and shortly afterwards the noise of imminent departure began, the opening of drawers, the furtive scrabblings as she searched in the bathroom cabinet for spare soaps and toothpastes, and – this caught in my throat – the upstairs extension tinkling, as she informed Louise.

I was standing with my back against the fridge, my arms folded across my chest as if I were physically holding myself together.

Michael said, 'Right. That's that sorted. Is there anything for supper?'

'No,' I said. 'You missed it. Cook for yourself in future,' and I went up to bed.

I lay in the gloom for a long time, the lights out, waiting for true black to seal the window and to blank me out, dissolve me, absorb me. I did not want my face to be visible to Michael when he came up. This had gone on most of my life, all the years we'd been married, and still he had not realised. Oh, tonight there was a reason for my desolation but sometimes there was none. For on certain nights – not all of them, just every now and then – it was as if my soul split open; I would lie in the darkness, the tears coursing down my cheeks, silently. No gasps, no heaving, no involuntary noises or jerks betrayed me, I had grown expert at silent crying. It was an odd skill for a forty-year-old woman to have acquired, and yet I think there are more of us than you might imagine – women like us, who shed tears in the blackness, without our families knowing.

I fell asleep shortly after 11.00 p.m., waking in the small hours with a lurch. In my dream, Michael had been on a business trip to America, returning with a £500 present for Adrian Carrington. In my dream, I yelled, 'Well, that's it. That's the last straw. I'm filing for divorce,' and Michael said mildly, 'But he wanted it so badly, Eleanor.' He really couldn't see my point of view.

Then I had been on the underground, on a down escalator, with Miriam just behind me, but when I reached the bottom and looked for her, she seemed to have got herself separated from me. And somehow now she was a little child again; she was four or five, I had to find her. I ran through the tunnels calling her name. People were staring at me. 'Don't worry, we've got her,' somebody said, but as I pounded towards them, sucking chunks of torn air into my lungs, the group parted and the girl in the centre was not Miriam at all, but Anthea's daughter.

There she was! I saw her grey jumper and red tartan skirt, her old primary school uniform. I set off after her, again, jostling, pushing through the waiting people. She was standing at the very edge of the track. 'Miriam!' I called and my voice was high and desperate. 'Miriam!'

She turned and she really was four. That is, in my dream, I saw her face as it had been then, the bright eyes in plump cheeks, the snub nose, the irregular milk teeth of her smile.

'Miriam!'

It was all on a knife-edge and bound to end with her falling to the track as a train hurtled into the station. But no, all of a sudden, her face lit up as she saw me, and she stepped forward into my arms, her head curled into my neck. And I felt her again as she had been then, the portly little arms and legs, the peach-shaped bum.

My heart was pounding when I woke. I lay there as the dark raced backwards, waiting for my pulse to quieten. I thought, even in my dreams I couldn't let her go. Even in my subconscious I wouldn't let her take that fateful step. For I knew that somehow I'd controlled that dream, stopped it from becoming the nightmare it was shaping up to be.

Michael's back was pressed against mine. I poked him until he rolled further away, beyond the invisible line I had just drawn in the marital bed.

* * *

When I woke again, it was 7.00 and Michael had gone. In the kitchen, Miriam, who was never normally so *compos mentis* at this hour, was gulping back fruit juice from the plastic bottle. As I entered, she stopped, wiped her hand on the back of her mouth, looking self-conscious.

'It's only a fortnight, Mum,' she said. 'It's handy really. There are these kestrels, I couldn't keep them here. They eat mice, frozen mice, dead chicks. You'd freak.'

My eyes felt heavy and swollen. I raised my eyebrows, mimicking a bright mask. 'You'd just better phone me every night,' I said in my best, jolly, rebounding tone. 'Between seven and eight, all right?'

'Thanks, Mum,' she said, and she embraced me much as she had in my dream. But she was angular now, sharp little bones at elbows and knuckles, except for her conical excuse of a bust. Once more I found myself inhaling her smell, a sharp, clean fragrance like pine, which was the tea tree oil gel she used to wash her face, and a gentle childish smell of talcum powder, and something else, indefinable, Miriamish. I stroked her shoulder blade with my thumb. 'You just take care, OK?'

'I'm almost fifteen. I think I've learned to look after myself,' she said, pulling a face, which was supposed to be fierce. 'I am old enough and ugly enough.' Then she clomped off, denim jacket, cotton leggings, Doc Martens, a fright.

I made myself go through the motions of preparing for work, taking unaccustomed care in applying tinted moisturiser and grey-brown shadows, in hot-brushing my hair and wrapping a succession of velvet and silk scarves about my neck, searching for the most complimentary shade. I ran my forefingers from the corners of my mouth up towards my ears, pushing the soft skin upwards, and the apparition of a younger, less careworn me stared back.

Once more, I was reminded of my mother, her recourse to eye lifts, dermabrasion and liposuction – the last the most painful process she had ever undergone, so she said. 'But on the "pro" side, I have a flat stomach,' she told me down the phone. 'I feel like I have a new body, or the old one back, the body that belonged to me before I had Philip and you.' I had found this disconcerting. She had undone the bulge which I had given her, as if she had undone her motherhood. I suppose, under the rules of Nicola's truth game, it was the final proof of her preferring my father. For whatever the reason, I avoided her for something like nine months after that, and she took umbrage with me. The relationship tilted onto a new axis and never recovered.

I should have realised that that can happen.

I rummaged in my grey-and-white spotted make-up bag, searching for the magic pen which brushed out eye bags and the shadows of sagging skin, and I painted over my night of tears.

How nice it would be if I could retouch my life as easily.

The editor of Virus's proposed autobiography called that morning; he was going to deliver an additional chapter which they were certain would increase media interest in the book, which had not been all that we'd hoped.

'It's all about Lucy's battle with bulimia. Wonderful stuff,' she said. She began to titter. 'You know what I mean. She's had it since teenage years, since way before she met him. He only discovered two years ago. I ask you, how can you be married to someone for almost twenty years and not twig something like that? Did he never wonder at the sound of heaving behind the locked bathroom door?'

'Oh, it doesn't surprise me,' I said flatly. 'It was a man who invented the word unobservant. Is she cured?'

'So they say. Telling the story now to help other sufferers, all that crap. I think he thinks he'll come over more sympathetic. Poor Virus, had his nutty wife to deal with, no wonder he didn't keep such a firm hold on his zipper. Wasn't it Diana who called bulimia her secret, shameful friend? Anyway, now we have the "secret, shameful friend" of Lucy angle to help the book along.'

'How about Lucy?'

'She does what he tells her. It's a weird relationship, Eleanor, as I'm sure you've realised.'

'All relationships are weird.'

'This is even more so. He controls her. Poor Lucy.'

'Poor Lucy,' I agreed.

'Ahh, you can't worry about it,' Anthea said soothingly, as we sat on the fashionably sagging sofa in her office. 'It was her decision, she's a big girl.'

'But she isn't,' I protested, 'and it wasn't. He controls her. Even his editor says so.'

'Whoa! Dangerous ground,' Anthea warbled. 'You don't know what makes their marriage tick. I mean, Sean's a control freak, you know that. First of all, when we were newly married, I loved it, thought he was so masterful. After a few years' – she shook her head – 'I grew to hate it. "Anthea, we're going out on Saturday," he would say. "Anthea, I'm going to surprise you for our holidays this year" – which really meant that he got to choose where we went and I didn't get a look in. We ended up at the World Cup!

'But it wasn't the big things that got me so much as the small things, like when it seemed as if nothing was beneath his notice. "Anthea," he said, "do you *have* to leave crisp packets on the floor of my car? I just cleaned it out, Friday." Once he forbade me to buy chicken quarters, can you believe it? Only filleted chicken breast for him. Jeez, I thought, he comes over so manly but really, if you want to look at what lies beneath the surface, I'm married to a selfish, pernickety, domestic overseer.

'And then, yesterday, when he swept into Scott's school and threatened to unleash the lawyers on them, and they quailed and quaked in a corner and surrendered straightaway, well, I thought, you have your good points. I began to fancy him again. I can honestly say that if he'd asked me, I'd have gone to bed with him.'

Robert interrupted us, gingerly carrying between his thumbs and forefingers only, two giant polystyrene cups of cappuccino from the corner café. His face was as expressionless as a poker, so I figured he'd heard Anthea's last statement. She and I exchanged glances. I kicked off my pumps and curled myself up in a corner of the sofa, waiting for him to leave so we could continue.

Oh, I did know what she meant. I'd seen my mother forgive my father a handful of infidelities, but he couldn't forgive her her vacuous moments, her tentative way of saying, 'What would you like for dinner, John?' when he wanted her to serve him something, just once, without a consultation. The way she crunched apples too loudly. The way she said 'Innit?' for 'isn't it?' betraying her uncertain background. No, it was the everydayness of forgiveness that tested your marriage, gave it its bitter flavour, and those who went banded in plain gold to their coffins were heroic, or so it seemed to me.

Once Robert had made a point of closing the door behind him, I filled Anthea in on my recent history.

'And he's really resigned,' she said, referring to Michael. She was looking at me gloomily over a cup-cloud of steam. 'He really means it. Who'd have thought? I'm going to miss you, Eleanor.

''s funny,' she added, 'I wish I could have mastered the art of silent crying. It would have been useful. At the end of our marriage, there was this one particular time, when Sean was making love to me . . .' She paused, debating the confidence. '. . . and it was up and down, breath, breath, in and out in the darkness, and I began to cry. I suddenly realised, you see, how little it meant to either of us. Like it was a polite nothing, like saying "Nice to meet you", to a new client, do you know what I mean? And then, he realised – his cheek must have brushed mine or something – and he was totally furious. You can imagine how he interpreted it! My God!' She threw her head back and clasped her hands together. 'Oh, disaster.'

I smiled at her. Her hair stood up in wild ringlets; her mascara had caught in gungy bobbles on the tips of her lower lashes. She was good at pretending, at making light of things that tore her apart.

We were interrupted, again, by her telephone ringing.

'It's for you,' Anthea said. 'Someone called Ray.'

I made an exaggerated gesture of query.

'Can I say what it's about?' Anthea asked the mouthpiece just as I remembered that Ray was our estate agent. I took the phone.

'Oh, Eleanor. Good news,' he announced. 'The couple I showed round on Saturday called me back. They love the place. They'll pay the asking, subject to survey. We've got a buyer.'

'We have?' I said. My face fell and Anthea made frantic gestures of empathy, assuming I had received bad news.

'*Oh, lawdy, lawdy, lawdy,*' said the voice in my head. Louise Carrington's voice. Perhaps she was taking me over? I definitely wasn't myself any more.

The house became a defined emptiness, a space which normally contained Miriam. Its silence was meant to be filled by her cries for my help or approval, by her comings and goings. It was worse than when she went away for sleepovers at friends' houses. It was worse than that week-long school trip to Normandy. It was worse than when Michael had begun to work late. For this was a prelude to a longer absence. This was the introduction to the rest of my life. My womb was shrivelling, my child was grown. Somehow I became less of a woman.

'You are my sun, moon and stars,' I used to croon above her downy, baby head as I walked her in the small hours when she had colic. She had been at the centre of my thoughts for the last fifteen years. You are supposed to be able to adjust to your children flying the nest, there is supposed to be a time scale. What was I supposed to do in Norfolk, without my daughter, or even my job? Michael wanted more time, and as a consequence, I, too, would acquire it, but for me it would be shapeless and baggy. I saw time engulfing and smothering me.

The telephone on the hall table burbled at 7.12 that evening. I picked it up on the second ring. She had had a pleasant day, there was a vegetarian casserole for supper, then she would take a shower and crash. Oh, and please could I take her black nylon zippered jacket and red scarf to work: Adrian was coming into town and would pick them up mid-morning. She might need them, for in the afternoon, she and Louise were driving out to deliver the squirrels to another centre which was pursuing a captive breeding programme. If she didn't call I was not to worry; they might be delayed.

I will worry, said the voice in my head, which was once more my own.

'OK, bean bag,' was what I actually said.

I changed into a tracksuit as lax and misshapen as my body, collected lemon-scented cleaner, cloths, a bucket of water and set to. I scrubbed every inch of painted woodwork in the house, the doors, the dados, the picture rails, the bannisters, the skirting boards, the window sills. The telephone rang again; I knew it wasn't Miriam so I refused to answer. I washed the door to my bedroom closet, the outside first, then the inside. The contents which I had tidied so carefully at half term lay awry once more; underwear in disorderly piles, shoes lying higgledy piggledy, dresses dangling drunkenly as I had thrust them onto hangers, no longer sorted by length and colour. Miriam had been home, and eager for my company, and I had tidied this closet.

In her room, her diary lay on her desk. Unlike the one I had possessed, at much the same age, this one had no lock. Unlike me, Miriam did not religiously record her days in it. I flicked its gold-edged pages, too betrayed and worn to feel amazed at this prying. It was a catalogue of worthy appointments: history prep due in today; kestrels took six mice, try eight tomorrow; Kate Avery's birthday. Every now and then, though, there was a longer entry, written in her strong, idiosyncratic handwriting, which until the spring of this year had featured ordinary 'e's and standard 'a's, but which later acquired the dash and elan of Greek 'e's and the 'a's you normally only see in print.

'*MD is the best piece of human flesh to walk this earth,*' read one entry. Who was MD? He did not appear again.

'*I don't think I can stand the "in" crowd at school much longer,*' read another.

And then, an entry for May . . . *Mum was going to talk to me about Norfolk, but she didn't. There's never any time for me in this house. No one ever* talks.' I could see Michael interrupting us with his demands for dinner.

I exhaled, a sigh at the injustice of her childish self-regard. I closed the diary, scrubbed the windowsill, the glazing bars, the skirting board. My breathing was heavy and raggedy, but that was only partly from exertion.

In the kitchen, I wrung out the cloths, poured away the filthy water. I washed and brushed my teeth and changed. I lay on the bed in my dressing-gown. The evening had grown grey and grainy. By the yellow pool cast by a lamp, I began to read, but found myself chasing the same sentence again and again. I closed the book and folded my hands, staring at the ceiling. The same cracks traversed it as had been there when we moved in, these were the cracks I had mapped during my bout of 'flu when Miriam made friends with Kim. They had been papered over and painted twice in the interim, and still they broke out anew.

I was thinking like this, my mind aimlessly chasing petty inconsequentials, when Michael's key turned in the lock. I heard him call my name and his footsteps trace a route around the ground floor, and then proceed up the stairs. The bed creaked and sagged as he sat down upon it, and his face, wearing a grave expression, intruded into the ceiling-scape. I continued to stare at the ceiling rose. I had nothing to say to him. To open my mouth would have been pointless.

He looked at me in silence for a while.

'Oh, sweetheart,' he said. He rarely called me that.

His hand hovered above me, then settled gently on my forehead, where I felt it stroke my hair with inexpressible gentleness. I waited a moment, then turned my face to the wall.

I lay there with my back to him, being very careful not to move, and after a while he got up and went quietly away.

Anthea had begged me to accompany her to her health club the next morning; she was signing in Scott, one morning a week, to teach him to swim in the lukewarm luxury of the club pool.

'How did you teach Miriam?' she said. 'How did you get her to put her head under water?'

How had I? I thought back. 'It was a question of giving her confidence. Taking it slowly, in stages. I bought her arm bands,

I remember, and I was very encouraging at the slightest progress. I made a point of never saying anything negative.'

'Arm bands,' Anthea said, jotting a note on her diary. 'Oh, come too. Do. Eight o'clock tomorrow morning and it's on your way to the office.'

Which was how I found myself pushing through two glass doors with long, brushed steel handles, into a marble-floored lobby. There was a curvy-slim receptionist in a white track suit sitting behind a curvy-slim desk, half obscured by potted palms.

'Mrs Booth-Perry has signed you in.' She gestured to more swing doors opposite.

The humidity inside the pool area was sub-tropical, the windows along one side obscured with dripping moisture. At the edge of the pool, a slim woman with a glossy geometric helmet of hair was poised to dive in at the deep end. She was wearing a serious swimming costume, dark and sleek, but with the legs cut very high. There was, I was fascinated to note, not a shadow of hair anywhere on her smooth, golden skin, not so much as a bristle in an arm pit. I passed a woman in the street, once, whom I have never forgotten; she was wearing a simple, yellow, flared dress, with dark pumps, but it was her perfection, not her style, that mesmerised me: there was not a hint of a crease in the fabric, not even at the back from sitting, and her stockings were unwrinkled, sheer, without a snag. The woman by the pool had the same glamour.

Splash! She began to stroke her way in a calm, rhythmic front crawl up and down the pool. Anthea and Scott appeared from another door, presumably leading to the changing rooms. They dodged their way around another potted palm, Scott all knobbly, pale limbs, with the pair of red arm bands forcing his elbows out in a simian fashion. His face looked even sharper, today, with purple shadows streaked below his eyes, like camouflage paint. His lips were almost white. He stared down at the water, deep blue reflecting from the pool tiles, and sniffed loudly.

Anthea was wearing a peach velour tracksuit, spotless trainers, and her glasses on a chain round her neck. She had gathered her hair in a knot at the top of her head from where it cascaded like the contents of a party popper. She was obviously going to change for the office afterwards, and at least she wasn't slithering over the pool surround as I was in my smooth, leather-soled high heels. Gingerly, I picked my way to a plastic tub chair by the wall. As far as I could deduce, Anthea only required moral support, a nudge in the right direction if her patience faltered.

Scott was mincing, a step at a time, down the rail at the side. When he stood on the bottom, the water only came up to his waist. He stood for a few seconds, turned, waded a few steps, lifting his chicken-wing arms high above the water. It took Anthea an age to coax him into dunking his shoulders. I glanced at my watch. At this rate, we'd never get to work.

'Start small,' I'd told her, 'a few strokes of doggy paddle.'

There was another burst of persuasion to prepare him to wade six paces from the side.

'Go on, you can do it,' she declared. 'That's it! Go on. Brilliant! Brilliant!'

Her excitement made me crane to see. Scott's beaky little face, still wearing its woebegone expression, appeared by the side of the pool.

'You did it!' Anthea cried again. 'Three strokes of doggy paddle!'

The sleek form of the female swimmer cut like a shark through the pool, leaving a bow wave rippling in her wake, from which Scott shrank.

'Now let's try four,' Anthea prompted.

There were further trills of enthusiasm from Anthea when he managed this. The whites of his eyes were streaked with pink, and his nose and chin seemed to project even further, like mandibles.

'Yes!' She punched the air. 'Six strokes!'

The dark-haired woman had stopped swimming now, was hanging by her elbows at the side, shifting her back against a jet stream of water. Her dark eyebrows were drawn into an angular glower. She stood up suddenly and ploughed towards the steps.

As she passed near to Anthea, she stopped. 'And what are you going to do when he manages a width?' she said. Her voice was clear and educated, and ricocheted from the bare pool walls. 'Are you going to have an orgasm?'

She hoisted herself out by the step handles and strolled languidly back along the length of the pool, water streaming from her dark bob, the perfect golden globes of her bottom swaying from side to side as she went.

'Well!' Anthea said. She had turned pink. 'Talk about rude! Who got out of the wrong side of bed, this morning? Orgasm, indeed! And talking like that in front of a child, I ask you.'

'Can we go now, Mum?' Scott grizzled from the pool. 'I've learned to swim now. It's easy.'

'Master Confidence!' Anthea sat back on her heels and beamed at him. 'That's the ticket. I've given you some confidence, at last.'

I was at my desk by 9.10 and had cleared my in-tray before Adrian Carrington arrived, later than expected. His lumbering presence, in plaid shirt and torn jeans, threatened the frail stairwell, swelled in the narrow doorways. I offered him a coffee, wrongly anticipating his refusal. He sank into the couch and balanced a boot on the glossy magazines meticulously arranged on the glass table before him. A scattering of mud cylinders, shaped to the tracks of his soles, rained onto the aloof face of the supermodel beneath.

I had forgotten how boneless Adrian's face was. I always liked looking at my family's faces, at Michael's or Miriam's, because of the fine framework beneath the flesh, the plane of cheekbone, the jut of the chin. But the Carrington family faces were compacted globes of cartilage or fat, like the balls of elastic bands which pernickety secretaries make for neat storage. You felt that if you dropped Adrian's head from a height, it would rebound with a thick thud.

He was out of breath from climbing the two flights of stairs and sucked in oxygen greedily, through his mouth, between slurps of coffee.

'Miriam says to tell you she may not call tonight,' he shrilled eventually. I had forgotten how high his voice was: I had the impression of air passing over folds of transparent skin in his throat, causing this adenoidal, bagpipe wail of a voice.

'I know.' I put the carrier with her belongings in front of him, and he leaned forward to inspect its contents with unabashed nosiness.

'They're driving out Essex way,' he said. 'Or is it Kent? Somewhere coastal, anyway.'

'She told me.'

He had a unique ability to make me feel frail yet poised, the sort of woman with unsnaggable tights. I felt an almost irresistible urge to giggle. He was such an unprepossessing boy; had he been at all presentable I would have suspected Miriam of hidden motives in her dogged attachment to the Carringtons and their sanctuary. Firm, bulky Adrian, however, precluded that interpretation. I was struck suddenly by the disparity in the Carringtons' manners and their accents – his estuary, his mother's affectedly American, but educated. But the young are masters of trading class. Miriam has shifting accents which depend on her audience and she uses a fluid tribal jargon.

'Mr Hibbetts is just so-o sad,' she told me earlier in the year of her mathematics teacher. I realised that she did not mean that he was miserable. I had met him at school open days; he was a hunched, ginger-haired man who attempted to ingratiate himself with his pupils by a monologue of facetious comments. I believe this may have worked on the younger forms.

'Mr Hibbetts is a dweeb, is that what you mean?' I asked Miriam.

'Yeah,' she said. 'Sad,' she said.

Adrian Carrington seemed pretty sad to me. 'I've never met your brother,' I said aloud to him, a thought flaring.

'Nah,' said Adrian. 'You wouldn't have. He moved out aeons ago. Works in Spain. Beach bar.'

Louise had made an allusion to trouble with her sons. Suddenly, the prospect of conversing with Adrian presented fresh attractions. I dug half a packet of rather dusty chocolate digestives from beneath the debris in my bottom drawer. I wheeled my chair, which protested squeakily, around the desk and parked it on the other side of the coffee table, then handed the packet to him.

'Thanks, I'm starved,' Adrian said. He ate noisily, ingesting biscuit and air simultaneously through his sagging mouth. 'Yeah, old Pete had enough of Mum and scarpered to Benidorm. She did keep going on. It was after the divorce. She was terrified we'd grow up wild so she rather overdid the discipline angle. "Have you revised? Where're you going? When-you coming home?" Pete said no wonder Dad left. Said he couldn't live under the long arm of the kitchen police.'

'Was your mother upset?'

'Had the screaming ab-dabs. Pete was only sixteen, you see, and first of all he moved in with some mates.'

'And the authorities didn't do much to get him back. She told me, well, she referred to it.'

'Seems to me the filth ought to have better things to do,' Adrian said. 'Anyway, after a bit, he went down to Spain. Me dad's down there, you see.'

'Oh . . . Do you see them much now?'

'Me? Nah. Don't know if I've got much in common with Dad. He moved there after the bust-up with me mother. Got a sun tan, got a bar, got a new Spanish wife. I might get out there next year, when I finish my A levels, before I go up to uni.'

'Oh, where are you hoping to go?'

'Norwich,' he said.

I raised my eyebrows. How ironic. 'University of East Anglia?'

He looked at me blankly. 'It's called Norwich,' he said, and I inferred that it was one of the new ones. 'Got a place to do media studies.'

'I see. What do you want to do afterwards?'

'Dunno, really. Quite fancy film. Directing.'

'Really? That's quite an ambition.'

He didn't bother answering, just breathed in and out. 'Or I fancy travelling the world and writing books and articles about my observations.'

'Are you good at English?'

'Gotta C at GCSE. Could've been worse.'

I was gobsmacked. I ventured, 'It is hard, you know, to get into these fields. Maybe that was why your mother was nagging about homework.' Why was I sticking up for Louise? '. . . Discipline, the right level,' I shrugged and petered out.

'Well, ma never found it,' he chortled. 'Threw her hands up in horror, made the right noises, but when it came down to it, Pete, he run rings round her. That's what's so annoying 'bout her. It's fuss, fuss, nag, nag, niggle, niggle, but you know she's not going to stop you doing anything you want. So why bother? Why cause so much grief?'

I looked at my lap. I wondered if Miriam spoke of me like this.

'Anyway, can't sit here gassing,' he said, unfolding himself, the cushions sighing with relief as he stood. 'Gotta see a bloke about a D-reg. rust bucket,' he added, patting his breast pocket in which a copy of the *Evening Standard* protruded.

'How old are you, Adrian?'

'Me? Seventeen and a half. Just passed my test, see.'

That hadn't been why I'd asked.

'It's good having Miriam hanging out with us,' he said as he edged through the door. 'Be great if you could see your way to letting her come. Takes the pressure off me, don't it? She and Ma sit and gossip so Ma leaves me alone. Anything for an easy life,' he chorused, cheerfully.

Yes, I said to his retreating back, as it squeezed through the lift doors, that's you and your generation all over. I could see Miriam chattering to Louise Carrington at their kitchen table, over bulbous cups of fragrant tea. The image stung me by its intimacy. What was it she had written? *There's never any time for talking in this house*? or words to that effect.

Her callousness took my breath away. Suddenly, the rose-coloured spectacles tumbled to the floor, though it wasn't quite as Michael had anticipated. Her behaviour appalled me. That she was *capable* of doing this. That she had so little imagination or generosity. I, who had always adored her, suddenly found myself confronted with a new possibility: I did not like her. Not at this moment. Not very much. I'd been wrong when comparing her favourably to Anthea's Scott.

Delinquency suddenly seemed preferable to disloyalty.

But who was I to talk? For I had done it. Miriam was all my own work.

Here you are, Louise. Here's one I made earlier. I took a hotch potch of fashionable theories, I preserved them in a vacuum of parental certainty, and this is the result. It is made with the same lack of skill as Merlin's plywood monument and with much the same cheap sentimentality.

But Louise had watched the same programmes, had read the same magazines. She had one – no two – of her own already. Indeed, the only peculiarity was why she wanted my creation as well.

Chapter Ten

Richard died late that night. Ann was wrenched from sleep by a crash, sat up in bed, her heart pounding, for she knew, she knew he had left her. She ventured downstairs in an unreality of hope and fear, but he was dead when she found him. He shouldn't have taken the pills with the alcohol, we did warn him, that was what the doctors would chorus later. She called the authorities, then sat with his body slumped in the middle of the sitting-room floor. She told me later that she laid a picnic rug over him, not because she wanted to hide his face, for she left that uncovered. No, she said, she was trying to keep him warm, trying to keep some life in him, trying to prevent him from turning into a corpse.

Some time later, she called Michael. When the telephone tore me from sleep at 2.00 a.m. I almost had a seizure, thinking it was Miriam; I was out that bed with uncanny speed, like a dark spirit. When it was Ann's voice, I thought, *thank goodness*; that was, until she said, 'Eleanor, I'm sorry.' Her voice broke and it was some moments before she collected herself. 'He died tonight . . . I found him . . .'

'Oh, no . . . oh, Ann, I'm sorry.'

'OK.' She said on a rising note, and put the phone down.

Michael was sitting up now, shaken from the befuddlement of dreams. I switched the light on.

'It's Richard,' I told him, and held my hand out.

He didn't take it. He got up, then sat down, collapsed really, on the wicker chair, a rumpled man in cherry-striped boxer shorts, his head, dark, flecked with silver, in his hand. I went up to him, knelt on the floor by his feet. I didn't feel I had the right to touch him so that the space between us, this carpeted twelve inches or so, was as real as if it pulsed and wriggled. After a while, he said, 'I'm going for a walk,' and began to pull on rumpled items from the pile on the chair. He went downstairs, turned the latch – *click!* – on the front door and was gone. I made hot coffee with a generous dash of brandy, although his must have been lukewarm by the time he reappeared.

He telephoned Ann. From the sitting-room, I heard the low murmur of his voice, the gap while she replied. I took him a fresh coffee and he said, 'Thank you,' in a tight, polite tone. He punched out another number, so I realised that Ann had delegated the business of telling the daughters to him. Of course, she would; she was the sort of woman who would depend on a son.

If he had not invited me to that lunch, I would have had no special memories of Richard, or very few. As it was, I could envisage him across an expanse of white linen, the hang of his head as he searched for words, the stutter of his speech, the mild *niceness* of the man. I might never have missed him had it not been for that lunch, might never have had to wipe away the tears that were suddenly brimming in my eyes, or swallow down the ache in my throat.

I curled myself in an arm chair, waiting. The soft shushing of the shower and a faint whine of pipes snitched on Michael's movements. What was he remembering? He had a pile of years to flick through, searching for the instant which most perfectly encapsulated Richard. I imagined Michael's memories to be like the black-and-white photographs lining Ann's mantelshelf: Richard pitching an underarm cricket ball to a five-year-old Michael. Richard with a grinning whippy boy – Michael at ten – in a row boat, each struggling with an oar. The fragments that made up the complete picture also included Richard's absences, the times he had disappointed his son, all the moments when there was nothing worth pressing a shutter for. These were as much Michael's memory; these were as much kind, dear, flawed Richard.

Birdsong, the whine of milk floats, the shudder of a diesel taxi cab; our patch of London was waking, the sky translucent, as whoever looked down on us from the other side of the bell jar switched the lights on. I went to the window and looked up, as if I might see His eye upon me. The moon was still visible, low in the sky, a silver shadow. How happy if Richard were out there somewhere, how happy if dust did not merely turn to dust.

Why do we make such a muddle of things? Of being a parent, of being a spouse? Why wouldn't the trick of daily forgiveness work always? Why had I been fighting with Michael when his father was dying?

Michael appeared in the doorway, dressed in less rumpled clothes.

'I'm going down to Sussex,' he said. 'I have to sort everything out. Will you call the office and tell them what's happened?'

'And Miriam,' I said, 'I'll call Miriam.'

'Yes, of course,' he said, and he came over, kissed me on the top of my head and left. It was a perfunctory kiss, a polite nothing, like saying 'nice to meet you' to a new client.

That was when Miriam went AWOL. The sanctuary telephone rang off the hook when I tried it, on the hour, every hour. In the evening I discovered her voice preserved on the answer machine, the dear, gurgly pitch, the feeling that there was a laugh caught at the back of her throat, which I'd always loved.

'Mum?' she said, 'Mum? Hiya. I tried you at the office but you'd left. I'll try to cram this into a few nano-seconds. We're popping in at some other centres and then we're going on to see an ecological demo. Staying in B 'n' Bs. Don't worry if I don't phone . . . Ur, be back in a day or two. Or four. By-ye!'

I pressed the button to stop the tape. An invisible hand seemed to swing through the still air and swipe me on the cheek. There was no way of letting her know her grandfather had died. And Richard had thought so highly of her. Louise had certainly stolen our daughter, not just from me, but from all her family. I knew Miriam wouldn't call back.

I telephoned Michael. There was a silence laden with disappointment, before he said, 'Oh, well, maybe it's for the best. She may be a bit young still for the funeral.' He always made excuses for her which he didn't make for me; and doubtless, I did the same.

'How's Ann?' I said. 'How're you?'

'She's . . . bearing up,' he said, which wasn't his sort of remark. It was a nothing comment, the sort you'd make to someone whose concern was faked for appearance's sake, and the truth was, I wasn't worried about Ann. My in-laws aren't on my worry list. That is crowded enough, already.

I had been deputed to pick Daisy up from Heathrow on the morning of the funeral and drive the pair of us down to Sussex. At the barrier, I fretted about whether I would recognise her or not, especially as the minutes ticked by and one by one, the people around me, the families waiting for antipodean relatives, the young singles waiting for sweethearts, squealed, embraced each other, handed over heavy cases, and then peeled off from the line. The taxi drivers holding cardboard notices disappeared, too, though less conspicuously. The board told me that the Frankfurt flight had landed forty minutes previously, and that the passengers were already in the luggage hall. Perhaps Daisy had slipped past me, unseen?

But I need not have worried. When she emerged through the automatic door she was instantly recognisable, her features a plumper, more awkward copy of Michael's. His face is linear, you could plot it with rulers and protractors and learn some Da Vinci-ish lesson about correct proportion. But in his sisters the family features have sagged or diminished, their noses bobbled with cartilage, the bones of their cheeks padded by little bolsters of fat. The maybe-grey, maybe-blue eyes which crinkle with laughter, or threaten to in Michael, are turned down in Daisy, making her appear woebegone and distracted, under her mop of mouse brown curls. Today, she was wearing jeans, deck shoes and a capacious grey cardigan.

'Daisy!' I called, and waved an arm.

Her face fell microscopically. She had expected some member of her immediate family to collect her, one of the siblings at least, if not her mother.

'Eleanor,' she said. 'How kind of you to meet me,' and put an arm around me. We wheeled the trolley through the concourse, into the lift, bumping along the uneven concrete ridges of the car park, both of us a little tongue-tied. We hadn't seen each other in . . . five years it must have been . . . and we had forgotten the contours of each other's personalities.

'How was the flight?' That was a safe one.

'Oh, fine, a little turbulent,' she replied, and another silence fell.

In the car, we occupied ourselves navigating our escape from the airport and onto the motorway, but once we hit the ring road it seemed insensitive not to broach the subject of Richard. So I told her about his decision to turn down the chemo, which she did not seem to have been told by her sisters, and his refusal to abstain from alcohol, which had apparently contributed to his abrupt death. He had, I surmised, probably gone just as he intended, cutting short the pain and indignity. There had been a point behind his anecdote about Flora.

She didn't turn weepy. She simply stared out of the passenger window of my hatchback as I talked, fidgeting with the strap of her pouchy, black leather handbag, twisting it around and around into a tight spiral.

Suddenly, a comment burst out of her: 'Bloody selfish bugger,' she exclaimed. She stabbed the cigarette lighter, fumbling in the pouch for her packet.

It was a coolish day and the car windows were closed. I wound mine down and the wind flooded us in a torrent, sweeping our hair behind us, then whipping it in our eyes. I inched the handle upwards, leaving a slit at the top. The rumble of lorries diminished.

'So bloody selfish,' she muttered. '*I* can't face the pain. *I* don't want to fight. *I* want to go quickly. He was always completely self-centred.'

Self-centred? Surely not, – well, that was what I wanted to exclaim. It certainly wasn't how I had figured him. I pictured him again, sitting opposite me at our lunch; I could hear the inflexions of his voice, his funny qualifying idioms, see him gaze at his lap, his hesitant smile. Always, with Richard, there was this balance between awkwardness and gruffness, a mix of perplexity and tetchy convictions. 'He was . . . very *English*,' I said. I decided I would risk telling Daisy about our lunch, our first and last lunch alone. After all, I reasoned, she at least was unlikely to be offended by his preferring Miriam to his other grandchildren.

She listened, puffing away on her German cigarette, the yolky yellow packet on her lap at the ready. The fug expanded inside the car, clogging up my nostrils and throat. I coughed as discreetly as I could.

I described his regret at not having told Michael that he loved him, hoping that she would infer a parallel emotion for herself. But she exclaimed vehemently, 'There! You see! Bloody self-indulgent! That was the whole point of it, wasn't it?'

'Excuse me?'

'You were supposed to deliver the message, Eleanor,' she said impatiently. 'You were delegated the task. Tell Michael his father loves him.'

'Oh.' She was right of course. 'Only I didn't.'

'You didn't say anything?'

'No,' I said. 'I was angry.'

'With my Dad?' she said, and for some reason I didn't contradict her. Her voice had softened, as if she had suddenly found she approved of me more than she had expected to. 'Will you tell Michael now?'

I considered. 'No, not now,' I said. 'If Michael doesn't know anyway, what's the point?'

She snorted and sat back. For some reason I had flown upwards in her estimation. 'So typical, isn't it? The English middle classes attempt to communicate. I'm well out of it.'

'Do you think so? Don't you miss anything?'

She shot me a withering glance and I felt myself descending, rapidly.

'Oh, I know I sound bitter,' she said curtly. The tears welled in her eyes and vibrated in her throat. 'I'm angry. Shall I tell you why? Shall I tell you what really, really bugs me about them? I mean, it's been all these years. Maybe I should have spoken to them? But what's the point?' she answered her own question. 'They wouldn't listen. All these years,' she continued, 'and they've never come to stay with me; only the once, when they couldn't avoid it any longer.'

I shifted self-consciously; we hadn't been to see her either, not since Miriam was tiny. But she didn't seem to intend any veiled barb. She lit another cigarette, inhaling deeply, desperate for the nicotine to hit her brain and calm her furious emotions.

'You remember when Jane and Adam moved to Scotland? Two years they were up there, two or three. My parents went up to stay four times. Christmas. Easter. Half terms. You name it. And I've been in Frankfurt for fifteen fucking years and they've only been once. There are always excuses. "We don't want to put you out," they say. "We don't want to inconvenience you", like I'm a bloody stranger or something. It hurts, you know? The truth of the matter is that they don't want to come and see me. They're making their feelings known. They're placing me under the small but ominous black cloud of their disapproval.

'I'm the daughter who hasn't got some man to support her. I'm the daughter who didn't produce two point four children. I'm the daughter who dared to live differently from them. I've been waiting for them to eject me from the family group for years, but they've been amazingly subtle about it; they've kind of edged me out to the side. Daisy, the black sheep. The child who isn't quite one of us. Oh, I'm in no doubt how unimportant I am in their scheme of things.'

The tears were streaming down her cheeks. She blew her nose robustly, examined the handkerchief, folded it.

'I had no idea,' I said lamely. I tried to think of something reassuring to tell her, some fond comment one of the Banyers had made when her name cropped up in conversation – I was aware that Michael was fonder of her than of the other two – but nothing came to mind, just that time Michael had steered Miriam away from learning German. This was because a plausible scenario had presented itself to him, in which Miriam proposed staying with Daisy to buff up her German accent and Daisy exerted some nefarious lesbian influence upon an impressionable Miriam. I had gleaned all that by osmosis, without Michael needing to say a word. Not that I had challenged him; I, who had always thought I had no prejudices when it came to the sexual peccadilloes of consenting adults. It was interesting, really, to see how superficial your tolerance was. I saw Michael and me swimming through a sea of moral relativism, and doing no better than Scott in his arm bands.

'Shoot!' Daisy made me jump. 'We're almost here, and I look a fright.' She rummaged in her bag with unnatural concentration, and began dabbing at her face with cosmetic sponges, squinting up at the vanity mirror in the sunshade. Somehow, I got the distinct impression she regretted blurting out her resentment to me.

The car bowled down the motorway. I was driving without seeing, internally examining Daisy's view of Richard, which was so different from the one I had recently constructed for myself. As far as I could see, it was all a matter of angles. Viewed from the perspective of his daughter living in Germany, or from that of his daughter-in-law living at arm's length, Richard was bound to emerge differently. Even from my single point of view, the light could play tricks. I could view Michael at one moment and see him as selfish; view him at another and believe he was kind. But it wasn't the light, was it? It was the truth. He was both: selfish and kind, thoughtful and thoughtless. I had looked at Miriam for years and seen only the princess, but now, the trick had revealed itself and the witchy hag had appeared, just like that trompe l'oeil picture in my childhood puzzle books. People were relative. People were complicated like those pictures. You saw an aspect of them that seemed solid, but really it was a layer, hiding another reality.

The signposts to the village steered me left, then right. Daisy and I didn't speak much for the rest of the journey, and she never mentioned how rejected she felt during her brief stay, not to my knowledge – not to any of them – and I didn't tell them, either. But that's a family for you. You never know when the truth is going to burst out or a hush descend, behind which, if you listen carefully enough, you can hear the feelings churning. I had always assumed that Daisy's exile was a proud, independent act, but I, of all people, should have recognised her childish strategies: if I go away, but not too far, they might miss me; if I don't flaunt my sexuality, they might accept me. Yes, I should have recognised Daisy, a fellow negotiator, loud, detectable, *inept*.

I never could imagine how Ann and Richard had raised four children in this miniature house, the bedrooms were tiny, the kitchen a cell. It wasn't the management of it, the beating on the bathroom door, the squeezing around each other on the stairs, which puzzled me. It was the idea of all those overlapping emotions. But walking in with Daisy to find it bursting with children and grandchildren, all being scrupulously polite, it was obvious how they had done it.

Ann was upstairs but when we arrived she came down. She was dry-eyed but vague and dazed. She kissed Daisy; she kissed me. There was no differentiation in the greeting. I gave Michael a peck on the cheek and the suit I had brought him, on its hanger, in a plastic coverall. He was standing in the tiny kitchen, leaning against the battered units, looking too big and grown for the room certainly, but also as if he belonged. I felt my differentness from the rest of them, united by their shared grief for Richard. Because while I was sad, I hadn't lost a part of my history, I hadn't lost flesh and blood.

Phyllida, of course, had taken charge. She bustled into the kitchen, looking unnaturally contained within a black bouclé suit with brassy buttons, her stomach bulging in the slim-line skirt. She was wearing inappropriate boots – pixie boots, I believe they are called – which made her legs look as stout as fat hams. She had even applied blue eye shadow.

She was consulting a list in her hand. 'Right,' she said, 'the precedence for the limousines.' And she looked up to make sure she had Daisy's and my attention.

Precedence? I wanted to say. There's a strict social etiquette for funerals?

'Mummy and Michael in the first; me, Jane, and our respectives in the second. Daisy? You and Eleanor and two of the grandchildren in the third. The other grandchildren in with the aunts. Mummy, Michael, Jane and I will sit in the front pew. Daisy and Eleanor and the grandchildren in the second.' I glanced at Daisy; I could see the sandpaper abrade another bit of her heart. Second best, even at your father's funeral. I was so concerned for her I managed not to be offended at my separation from Michael. He had disappeared to change; not that when he reappeared he raised any objections. I shrunk into the shoulders of my navy suit, feeling rather small.

'I've ordered a nice bright bunch of flowers from all the grandchildren,' Phyllida said to me. 'Miriam included. Her name's on the card.' There was a tsking noise at the back of her throat, a sort of silent censure at Miriam's not being here.

'Oh, good,' I said.

'You can settle up with me later,' she added, and I realised I should immediately cough up my fifth.

I fumbled in my bag. 'How much?'

'Oh,' she said, 'Call it a tenner,' and she took the bill from my hand, folding it and secreting it in her black suit's breast pocket, patting her bosom, as if she had heartburn.

Daisy took her case to her old room and came down in drooping black. We all looked so sinister. The door bell shrilled, the first of the various relatives arriving from various parts of the country. The Banyer family's aunts looked alarmingly like those who had attended my parents' silver togetherness party all those years ago, the same grey perms, the same scent of lavender water, the same netted hats, the same thick stockings and stout lace-up shoes. It occurred to me that they were, indeed, the self-same people, members of a roaming band of rent-an-aunts, on hire for every family occasion. At our wedding, they could have masqueraded as both his side and mine; no one would have been any the wiser.

In the third limousine on the slow, dignified passage to the church, I whispered to Daisy about the true origin of the aunts. We both began to snuffle with laughter. One of Phyllida's boys, Josh, shot us a sly look from under his long, Disney lashes. He appeared so uncomfortable and buttoned up, somehow, in his blazer and tie; he was longing to behave badly, or to flee at the slightest excuse. We were pulling up at the church, a stout, grey-stone building behind a lych gate. A path, framed by a double row of exclamation mark yews, led to a lop-sided porch. Gravestones leaned at irreverent angles. As he alighted from the car, Josh was already craning to see if he recognised the lie of the land, if he could escape and make his way home without anyone noticing.

I saw him in the queue as we preceded the coffin into the church. Michael had his arm around Ann's shoulders, although she remained upright and composed. Phyllida was holding her handkerchief, although she was not crying. Jane was fussing over Eddie, her beanpole son, dabbing at some spot on his tie with a licked corner of her glove, and he, mortified in front of his cousins, was swatting her away.

There was an absence of sound until we were through the dark, heavy door, whereupon a muted organ met us. I felt very conscious of every step I took, every squeak of someone's pair of new shoes, and the pressure of Daisy's hand in mine, as she tightened her grip on me. We filed into our allotted pews, family at the front, extended family in the middle, friends and villagers already seated at the rear. I recognised certain members of the cricket team. To the chords of 'Abide With Me', the casket, with its family flowers, was borne in by the undertakers. Josh, I noticed, had disappeared.

I didn't blame him. I hate funerals. I'd only been to two before, my grandmother's and Michael's grandmother's. My grandmother was cremated. When the miniature doors slid open with a flimsy whirring and the casket skimmed silently away, I was paralysed with the terror that they would not close before the jets of fire spurted. So perhaps it is not surprising that I cannot recall any detail whatsoever of Richard's service:

not the hymns, not the address, not a single phrase from a tribute. Daisy remained hunched in hysterics, on my shoulder, throughout, and everyone but me thought she was weeping. I saw Michael, from the front pew, where he was supporting his mother, direct a concerned glance at Daisy's hiccuping form; the vicar, too. Phyllida whispered something to Jane, but something disapproving, I felt sure.

I took Daisy's elbow and steered as we retraced our steps down the aisle to the little graveyard, where the hole in the earth lay ready. It appalled me, that hole; the green turf sliced from the rectangle, draped in fake grass mats, the pit dug deep, the orange clay gleaming except where it gave way to the dark pin-prick mouths of tunnels. It was squirming with life, that hole.

One of the aunts had her gloved hands clasped before her, her eyes raised to the horizon beatifically. I tried to glue my thoughts to her and the associations she conjured for me: the chorus line of aunts at my parents' party, tipsy on sherry, as Philip tipped the crackling stylus into the groove. So, when they lowered the coffin into the ground, it seemed to me that Gary Glitter and the Glitterband were chanting, '*Come on, come on, come on, come on*', like rubber-suited demons of hell, arms aloft in an anthem of greeting.

Daisy gripped my hand like a vice, her nails biting into my palm; a noise escaped her, a hee-haw which she almost blotted up by blowing her nose loudly. *Don't laugh*, I said to myself. *Don't laugh.* Such an inappropriate response, but, in our fevered state, such an understandable one.

The earth splattered like hail and brimstone on to the coffin, making a hollow noise, as if it were empty after Richard had crept out in stealth, and made his way elsewhere.

Rather than staying overnight, as they had for my parents' phoney anniversary, the rent-an-aunts dispersed during the course of the afternoon, taking trains and ancient shooting brakes back to the leafy, Miss Marple-ish counties from whence they came. Michael ferried several of them to the station. One by one, the locals repaired to the pub. Finally, thankfully, it was only the family who sat around the dining-table, sipping wine or tea.

It was too cramped for all of us in that room, but we congregated there nevertheless, the young ones sitting on the floor, their backs glued to the walls, the rest of us perched on the oak chairs, threading between knees and elbows and jutting arm rests when required to fetch something from the kitchen or answer the telephone. I knew why we were there, though, and not spreading out into the sitting-room; it was because we did not want casually to invade the place where Richard had lain. Each of us was conscious that he had died next door, as surely as if there were a chalk outline of his body marking the carpet. And I don't think any of us wanted to walk over the spot, just as we wouldn't have wanted to march unheedful over a grave set in a church aisle, not through superstition but out of reverence.

I say this, but I suspect that Phyllida's emotions, at least, were slightly different. She seemed to wish to remove or avoid all reminders of Richard. I had seen her, that morning, pausing on her way through the hall on some busy errand of hers. There was a checked wool rug hanging on the bannister and it had occurred to me earlier that this was the rug Ann had used to cover Richard. It seemed likely that she had placed it there, meaning to take it upstairs. I was on the landing, on my way back from the bathroom, when I saw Phyllida pause, and the same notions run through her head. Quietly, she snatched up the rug, then drummed up the stairs.

'Oh, Eleanor!' she said. She looked shocked when she saw me.

I stood aside as she passed. She halted by the airing cupboard door, in which Ann stored her linen and spare blankets. Phyllida folded the rug roughly and bundled it onto the top shelf.

'Mummy! Honestly!' she said; I'm not sure whether to me or to herself.

That afternoon, Ann wandered in and out of the dining-room, as if she couldn't settle, eventually disappearing upstairs, perhaps to lie down and collect her feelings on her own.

Phyllida was going to follow her, but Michael shook his head wordlessly. Looking pensive, he sat in a corner, astride a back-to-front dining chair, his chin resting on the back of his hands. His tie hung loose round his neck, a black tie. He didn't own a black tie, so he must have borrowed it, or perhaps it was one of Richard's.

Adam, Jane's husband, was going on and on about certain aspects of the service which had irritated him; a muddle over Richard's middle names, the organist fumbling rather badly, none of which I had registered. 'Sounded like he was playing in bloody boxing gloves,' he said. 'And if you ask me . . .'

'Nobody did,' Daisy interjected, tartly.

Adam had had too much wine. 'Oh,' he said, putting his hands up with a wide smile, pretending he was joking, 'The *Obergrüppen Führer* has spoken,' he said.

'Shut up Adam.' This was Max, Phyllida's husband.

'Of course,' Phyllida interrupted hurriedly. 'We must close up the house.' Michael sat up slightly, frowning.

'Why? What do you mean?'

'Well, Mummy can't stay here, can she? One of us – at least – had better stay overnight and then help her pack up in the morning. She can come to me for a bit. Jane, you'll have her, won't you?'

Jane, who had a mouthful of shortcake, nodded quickly, widening her eyes. 'Mmm. 'Course,' she mumbled.

'But naturally, she won't be coming to *me*,' Daisy said.

The other two swivelled, astonished. I watched the family dynamics stretch and condense, like elastic. Pinging, dangerous stuff, elastic; you never know when it will lash you and leave you smarting.

'After all, I'm staying the night, too,' Daisy said.

'Well, she won't feel like *flying*,' Phyllida explained in a tone which meant, 'Really, you ought to have thought of that yourself.'

'Later,' Jane, the more conciliatory one, added. 'Later would be better, don't you think?'

Daisy shrugged and let it go.

'What makes you think she wants to leave here?' This was

Michael, roused from his reverie, and sitting upright now. 'How long do you envisage this proposed visit to you lasting?'

'Well, a month or two. You surely can't think she can stay here?' Phyllida was getting irritated. Having subdued Daisy, she had not expected Michael to put in his 'two pennies' worth', as I knew she would call it. 'Just leave it to me, all right?' Her tone now seemed to say, you may be the son and organise the reading of the will, the death certificate, the funeral arrangements, but as the eldest daughter, I shall handle the emotional consequences of the death.

'Why can't she stay here?' Michael said stubbornly. Next to me, Daisy leaned forward and put her elbows on the table.

'You know nothing,' Phyllida said. 'What do you know about it? Why do you always try to undermine me?' Her voice rose and quavered.

'Everyone's very fraught,' Max said, holding a hand up so that the reddish hairs glinted in the light of the chandelier. 'Let's wait and discuss this some other time.'

'What other time?' Phyllida asked, still an octave higher than normal. 'It's got to be sorted out now. We can't leave her alone here.'

'I agree,' Jane said. 'My neighbour shut herself in her house after her husband died and it wasn't until we saw the milk bottles piled outside that we realised something was amiss. We had to break in. I was the first to find her. Oh, my God, the smell! I can't tell you. She'd been dead *two* weeks. Died of a broken heart, just couldn't go on living without him; I don't know why, though, I'm sure he beat her.'

A little silence greeted this announcement. Then Phyllida picked up the conversation as if Jane hadn't spoken. 'What you don't understand,' she said, shaking her head, tucking her hair behind her ears in that way she had when she was getting fussed, 'is how happy they were. They are . . . they were, an exceptionally happy couple. Rare enough nowadays.' She glared at Michael as if he were personally responsible for the trend in the divorce statistics. 'It was a very unusual marriage, you know.'

'No, it wasn't.' Much to my own surprise, I spoke up. A

plump blue vein in Phyllida's forehead throbbed as if it might burst. I could sense Daisy egging me on. 'It was a completely ordinary marriage. A real standard issue marriage. Not this unrealistic honeybunch togetherness that you're conjuring up. It was ordinary happiness, ordinary irritations and disappointments. And that's fine; it's good. It's made up of day to-day forgiveness, which is . . . *heroic, I* think. To be able to forgive someone for the sum total of pettiness, that's what marriage is all about.'

Nobody said anything to this, but Michael caught my eye; the corner of his mouth moved upwards, a gesture imperceptible to anyone but me. It was a moment of perfect, silent understanding, invisible to all but ourselves. In that instant, we had wiped our slate clean. For there comes a time in a marriage when somehow, somewhere, you realise you have lost the will to match your mood to your partner's. Once upon a time, if Michael was indignant about an injustice at work, I would create an answering rage. If he was elated, so was I. But now we played Snap! with our emotions. He turned up irritation; I turned up contempt. He turned up sex; I turned up worry. It was purely a matter of chance if the cards came out the same; but there, across that room, we looked up from the matched pair that said 'forgiveness' and felt comforted. And I suppose it is in anticipation of those random moments that the married carry on, knowing that by the law of averages, they will be a match again, for a moment.

'Phyllida.' It was Ann. She was standing in the doorway, and we all lurched guiltily. None of us knew how long she had been listening. She had changed from her funereal black suit into a grey A-line skirt, baggy at the seat, and a fudgy, nothingy, soft cotton shirt. She looked composed, if tired.

'Phyl, dear, I don't want to go with you, or, Jane, my dear, with you either.' She did not mention Daisy, as if that would have been stating the obvious. I noticed that and I'm sure Daisy did, too. 'I want to be *here.* In my own home. With my own memories,' Ann was continuing.

'But it's going to *depress* you,' Phyllida exclaimed.

'Well, of course,' said Ann in her most reasonable tone of

voice. 'Of course, it is. But I can't avoid that, can I? It would only be waiting for me when I came back. Or would you have me sell this house, trying to escape it?'

'Oh, mother!' Phyllida's face was contorting into tears.

'Don't blub, Phyllida. I want to be here,' Ann repeated, enunciating each word fiercely. 'I *want* to be depressed. I am going to mourn my husband. It's the right thing to do. And none of you can stop me.'

She turned on her heel. It was quite a stylish intervention. All eyes now swivelled towards Phyllida, half-expecting her to crumple, but she sniffed, took a deep breath, and announced, 'She is not in a fit state to decide. You,' she said, looking at Jane, 'and you,' she turned to Daisy, 'had better come with me and talk some sense into her.'

'Oh, Lord! Give me strength!' Daisy threw her head back and beseeched the ceiling light,

I got up and inched my way through the forest of chairs, into the kitchen. Ann was crouched by the table, one hand on its edge for balance. She saw me but didn't speak, instead patting the side of her knee rapidly three times so that the spaniel, which had been dozing in its smelly bed underneath, stumbled forth to greet her. It had been dreadfully subdued all day, as if depressed at Richard's absence; now its tail wagged three times, but slowly, a sure sign that it was merely humouring her. Ann held the lead in her hand, one of the extending sort, she clipped it to the collar. I followed her to the hall where she wrestled with the pile of visiting family coats clumped on the pegs, removing a batch. Richard's old tweed cap fell to the floor.

She picked it up and replaced it, shot another glance at me. 'I'm not going to tidy him away,' she said defensively. And then she softened, as if remembering whose side Michael and I were on. I held the lead and helped her into her worn, green bodywarmer, which looked as if it belonged in the dog's bed, the quilting stitches unravelling in long, trailing threads. As she opened the front door, she stood for a moment, chewing her bottom lip thoughtfully, looking out across the cricket pitch. The spaniel twitched its nose at the expectation of a walk, then gazed up at her with its bulbous, brown eyes, dropping its chestnut haunches onto the doormat when it realised she was not moving.

'He was seventy-three,' Ann said to me, very quietly, her voice cracking. 'A good age to reach. No one is going to read his obituary in the local paper and say, "How tragic, he died so young." We were married for almost fifty years. It sounds a long time, doesn't it? That's what Phyllida's worried about. All that time together, we've become a habit. But what you don't realise, none of you, not really, is that it wasn't long enough. Fifty years passes too *quickly*, Eleanor. And I don't know where the time went.' She had swung to look at me, as if appealing to me for an answer.

I just stared at her, dumbly. I didn't know what to say. She dropped her chin, fumbled with her zip, did it up with a fierce tug; *brrrp*.

'I'm going for a walk,' she announced.

I went from the hall to the sitting-room. Jane's voice at its most placatory floated into the room: 'She'll change her mind, come this evening. We'll talk to her quietly.'

From the bay window I could see Ann stride, quickly, brusquely, her head down against the wind, across the angle of the cricket pitch, the spaniel pulling the expanding lead out to its full length, as he struggled towards the enticing under-growth.

I knew what she was saying. My last fifteen years had gone by too quickly, too. It was wicked the way time accelerated. I have often thought how much kinder it would be if life were like a video cassette, so that you could press the rewind button, or fast forward over some tricky bit, or sometimes freeze the frame. But no, time is a single line and you don't travel the track at an even pace: your gimcrack wagon jolts, then whisks you forward, and you find that while you have been looking astonished, over your shoulder, at the tableau of you cradling a new-born baby in your arms, the carriage has speeded forward, and already the baby is a teenager.

'I love you forty Wembley Stadiums full,' Miriam told me once, when she was six or seven. It was the biggest volume she could conceive. That is my Miriam, but that is also the Miriam of my imagination. I hadn't been paying attention, and no more had Ann. To her, too, life was happening at some previous stop on the track, when she and Richard were bringing up their family together, full of hope. So when she took her nose out of her everyday reverie and glanced out of the window, it was a terrible shock, because the scenery had changed so dramatically, and was so *bleak*.

Of course, she needed to be alone. She needed to press her nose to the glass and examine it all, every fold of rock and barren outcrop, the sinister monolith, the space that stretched, empty and grey, towards the horizon.

I drove myself home in the hatchback shortly afterwards. Michael walked me up the potholed road to where I had been forced, by the sheer number of family cars, to park.

'You must stay tonight,' I said. 'Stop Phyllida and Jane bugging your mother. And talk to Daisy, will you? She feels left out.'

He didn't reply, but he clasped me, fiercely, his fingers clamped to my shoulders, his arms shaking with the effort of holding me as tightly as he possibly could, so that my breath came shakily when he released me and tears were starting in my eyes. He felt as strong as a tree, bristly, male, *alive*. And he reminded me of Richard, when he had said goodbye to me, because that is what he had done, too.

'It's true what they say,' Michael's voice loomed in my ear. 'You may be expecting it, but that doesn't lessen the shock. It's the removal, the . . . extraction from your life.' I pulled out of his embrace and looked at him, smoothing his hair. His face had that tight, restrained look, which meant he was struggling with emotion. 'I went to see him, you see, at the funeral parlour. I wish I hadn't. It wasn't him.' He shook his head and looked at the pothole by his foot, sighed, kissed me once more and trudged back towards the house. I watched him go, a tall, lean figure with his head bowed.

Back in town, the house was dusty with quiet and lack of use. I lay on Miriam's bed, holding the soft, crumpled, cotton T-shirt she used as nightwear which I found under her pillow and which smelled of her. But I could not sleep. Instead, I mourned the changing of families, the dogs who died and were no longer to be found in their corner, the parents who aged and went on ahead of you, the children who grew and no longer loved you best.

Chapter Eleven

A postcard arrived in an unfamiliar hand.

'Just a note,' Louise Carrington wrote, for it was she, 'to reassure you that we are alive and well. We were staying in bed and breakfasts but now we are camping, and having a marvellous time. Miriam is such good company, you must be so proud of her.'

It was ironic that everyone but me seemed to like my daughter.

There was a power failure on the tube and I was stuck in a carriage in a tunnel for half an hour, next to a small, sallow man who picked at the gaps in his teeth with his fingernails and sniffed loudly and continuously. Ah, the men on the tube! I decided that they are a band of especially unprepossessing individuals who are hired secretly, like the rent-an-aunts; but the job of these men is to travel the Northern Line, pressing their bellies against working women. *Go back to the kitchen!* Their message is clear. *Look at the nasty things that can happen to you when you're out in the world, earning a crust.*

Thank goodness I had a seat! People were packed upright, in rows, as if they were toy soldiers which had been crammed into too small a box. For a while they were silent, but then they began to rustle and whimper, and an odour leaked from their pores, like dissatisfaction.

I discovered that if I twizzled my head, I could avoid looking at every single individual pressed against my knees, but could gaze, instead, through a six-inch patch of smeary window at a six-inch patch of tunnel and pipe, all of it lying under a thick, soft powdering of soot. My daydreaming skills had deserted me, however. I tried out my favourites, one after another, like someone flicking through the frontispieces of much-thumbed novels, but none of them fitted my mood.

So I ended up gazing through the sooty gap at Louise Carrington's postcard. What were the reasons for my dislike of Louise and her influence over Miriam? Were they based on anything sound? Perhaps not. Louise had sown these doubts in me, with her questions about possessiveness and her references to boarding school; it was not difficult. There was no black and white in my life, only shades of grey.

The tube jerked, stopped, yanked itself forward once again, to the accompaniment of an odd popping noise from the brakes. The people around me rustled once more, but hopefully. We changed tracks with a squeal, and ground our way into the station.

I sipped coffee at my desk, browsing the thick pile of newspapers which arrived each morning for me, scanning an opinion piece in one of the broadsheets. My eyes skimmed an interview, an obituary, a small photograph; the black-and-white grainy image of a grimacing face in the foreground, behind it, riot police and crash barriers. All at once, the mug slipped from my hand, spilling a dirty, brown puddle upon the page.

I held the newspaper up by a corner, so that it dripped from the opposite end onto my desk . . . the carpet . . . into the wastepaper bin in turn. Louise Carrington's face, taut with anguish or fury, splatter-stained with coffee, lay on the lip of the bin. Beneath it was a caption about a demonstration against the live export of farm animals to the continent. I suddenly understood Miriam's answer machine message, her subterfuge, her suppressed excitement.

My heels made satisfying, resolute clicks over the battered

linoleum and down the stairs. I caught a taxi home, changed into jeans, checked the map, climbed into my car. On the trunk road out of London, passing petrol stations and superstores, their Matterhorns of red tile topped by Bavarian clock towers, it struck me first, that my unexplained absences were going to exhaust Nicola's patience, and secondly, that Michael had a right to know where I was going and why. But I didn't do anything about either scruple, though it would have been easy to pull into a lay-by and dig out my mobile telephone. For some reason, some compulsion much stronger than logic, my hands steered straight and my right foot remained depressed on the accelerator with exactly the pressure required to maintain an even sixty miles an hour. Indeed, it was only when I reached the port, with its unmistakable reek of wide water, its unmistakable music of the shrieks of wind-blown gulls, that I began to consider very much at all.

I parked the car in a small municipal car park, and even remembered to buy a ticket at the pay-and-display machine, pushing in a clanking £2, which was the maximum charge. I stuck the ticket firmly to a corner of the windscreen; then methodically checked each of the doors was locked, which was very unlike me. I was here; now what was I going to do?

The car park was bordered on two of its sides by a high, grimy, red brick wall, the backs of terraced houses visible beyond it. A narrow, quiet road and the blank concrete back of a supermarket stood opposite.

An elderly man carrying two sagging carrier bags was returning to the car park as I left. I made in the direction he had come from, figuring it would be busier, but as I neared him, he smiled, and in that disarming way that rural people still have of greeting strangers, he smiled and said good day to me.

I stopped – 'Excuse me' – and so did he. 'I wonder, do you happen to know where the livestock demonstration is?'

He put down his bags, which slumped as the contents spread themselves on the pavement. I studied him; his skin, which was the colour of parchment and stretching into complex folds, his yellowing eyes, watery, benign. His voice was husky, suggesting he was a heavy smoker. I wondered, afterwards, what would have happened had I not bumped into him, had he not been so homely looking, so welcoming. But, 'The demo?' he said. 'Going to join up with the anarchists, are you?'

'I'm trying to round up my teenage daughter, actually.'

'Oh,' he said, in a way that implied sudden understanding. 'Oh, well,' he said, 'don't you fret yourself, now. I was joking about the anarchists. There are some very respectable types up there – most of this town's middle-class ladies; you wouldn't have dreamt of them joining anything more vigorous than the WI. But they're all up there, now, waving their placards.'

'Really?' I found this comforting, as if I would find the barricades manned by old acquaintances from my Surrey childhood; my mother's friends from the golf club, for example.

'Can't say I blame them. I can't abide cruelty to animals, cruelty to animals and children.' He shook his head before remembering my question. 'How to get there, you said. Your best bet is to go down the pub, I reckon; The Bull, on the corner of Market Street.'

'Market Street,' I repeated.

'That's it. Go through the lane – that one, there – you can't miss it. A load of them gather in there, about now, 'fore they set off for the front.'

I thanked him. As he bent to retrieve his bags, he shot me a look from his milky eyes that was brimful of sympathy.

The Bull was one of those unprepossessing pubs which are normally inhabited at lunchtime only by whiskery, beery pensioners, and in the evenings, by leather-clad, fearsome youths playing beeping, interactive games. The outside had been painted white and the street grime had collected in the furrows of the pebble-dash render. The doors and windows were outlined in black. Inside, the carpet was red, patterned in greenish brown swirls and in years of dirt, and the air was heavy with stale tobacco.

There were two glazed doors which led from the corridor; the one on the right said, 'Saloon', and through the pane I could see the group that I wanted. They looked so out of place,

the women with what could only be called hair-dos, one of
them powdering her nose in a compact, the men in Barbours
with checked wool scarves. And their accents! So crystalline,
so confident, pitched to ring across their half-acres of green
lawn. I felt immediately emboldened.

'Excuse me? Are you the animal rights group?'

'What? That's us. A new recruit?' one of the men exclaimed.
'Splendid! Splendid!'

'Well, only by default,' I said, and I explained that I had come
to find my daughter, whom I considered too young for violent
confrontation, and as I did so, I felt giddy for some reason. It
struck me that this sudden mission was deranged, my reasons
just excuses, but then the woman next to me tsk'ed to herself
and muttered, 'Fourteen? Much too young!' She sat me down
at a small, polished table, dotted with beer mats and centred
with an ashtray.

She was a sixtyish woman, with dark, arched eyebrows
which looked odd and dramatic when juxtaposed with her
back-combed busby of silver hair. Her lipstick, a bright carmine
colour, had bled into the creases feathering her mouth and
smeared itself on her teeth. She pulled a wagon wheel chair up
close, balancing her bag between her ankles. 'My children are
worried sick about me,' she said. ' "Oh, mother," they say,
"you'll be bowled over, you'll break a bone." Honestly, they act
as if I've got galloping osteoporosis already. Don't worry! I say.
I'm on HRT.

'But that's as it should be. At my age, it's all swopped around;
my children worry about me and I, freed of all my responsibilities, can rush off on wildly irresponsible sorties,' she
chuckled. 'I'm Joan,' she added.

'Eleanor.'

'Jenny! Come and meet Eleanor!' Joan called.

Jenny had her back to us, so that at first all I could see was
her white T-shirt, baggy grey tracksuit pants, topped by a frizz
of faded salt and pepper hair. But when she finally responded
to Joan's patting on her arm, she revealed a plump, ingenuous
face with an eager smile. She was in her late forties, I guessed.

'We've none of us done anything like this, have we? I'm

Jenny,' she said, and offered me her smooth, chubby hand, placing her half of lager carefully on a beer mat as she sat down.

Jenny was saying, 'There are some young people who they say are anarchists, which is a bit worrying, not our sort of thing at all. But the rest of us are normal, middle-class, law-abiding citizens. We just want to make a peaceful protest. We're worried it's getting a bit out of hand now, but we can't give up. It's an odd feeling.'

She had started out addressing her remarks to me, but really she was talking to Joan. They had reached that stage where they were both so discombobulated by events that they could only believe them if they ran over them one more time.

'You see,' Joan said, ostensibly to me, 'I had never expected to be head to head with the law. I used to be a magistrate, for heaven's sakes! I'd always thought that the law would be behind *me*.'

'One day, out of the blue, they turned up in riot gear. They'd been in normal uniform till then,' Jenny said. 'But now it was shiny black helmets with visors, like something out of Star Wars. It was transparent shields. It was truncheons at the ready. The atmosphere changed overnight. And you thought to yourself, this is ridiculous. Look at me!' She held her hands out inviting inspection of her spherical stomach, her slouching bust, the lazy figure of a woman who for years had picked at leftover chips and the hunks of fish fingers growing cold on her children's plates. 'Do I look like a dangerous insurrectionist?'

Joan was smiling and nodding, not in answer to the last question, but in general agreement with Jenny's sentiments. 'My neighbour was punched in the stomach by a policeman yesterday. She was in agony, up at the hospital for hours. Would you credit it? The British police! I feel as if . . . as if everything I believed in has turned topsy-turvy. As if we're in a sort of Lewis Carroll nightmare.' Then she saw my face and pinched her lips together, clapping her hands to her mouth. Her eyes, under their heavy eyebrows, were comic-book circles. 'Oh, damn and blast! I've worried you.'

Jenny waved a negating hand at me, and said, as she

swallowed a mouthful of lager, a foam moustache forming on her upper lip, 'Don't, don't, don't. Put it out of your mind. We'll be making a move in a minute and we'll find your daughter very first thing. For sure, we will. Very first thing.'

I walked with them down to the seafront, past the desultory rows of shops, the newsagent's with its national lottery posters, the butcher's with their trays of chops and pale, pimply chicken legs, the fish and chip shop into which one of the men dived, emerging with two newspaper-wrapped portions of chips, into which we were all invited to dip. The smell of sea, the smell of a working port, oily and unclean, blew the cooking smells away.

The wind whisked my hair into wild formations. The sea wall marched along on our right, so that I could hear the water slap heavily on stone and on the hollow metal side of a ferry. Crowd control barriers, some with their metal rails buckled, as if pulled apart by giant hands, were piled on the pavement. A line at the kerb, neatly interlocked, channelled us onwards. Ahead, there seemed to be a wider space where a group of a hundred or so were already gathered. A low cheer rose when they spotted us.

I was glad of Jenny and Joan's company. I had never been to a demonstration before, not one. The furthest my youthful politics had taken me was to speak for the motion – this house believes Britain should be a republic – in my grammar school debating society. We were defeated. Oh, and once I wrote a letter to a right-wing broadsheet protesting against the war in Vietnam. I had an American pen-pal and she had written to me about her brother who had been drafted. '*We received a letter,*' she wrote. '*He was in action again. He said he threw a grenade and a gook's head was blown off and rolled right up to where he was lying, in a bush or a trench or something. He put, Ha, Ha! The only good gook is a dead gook. This is a boy who cried from sympathy when I had to have my routine shots. What will he come back like? Not as my brother, is a sure thing.*'

My parents' Sunday newspaper was lying on the fake Regency coffee table. I fired off a letter to the Editor. 'Your coverage of the war is a travesty. Do you know what's happening out there? To young people not much older than me?' They didn't print it.

I was here only to find Miriam. It was odd that I had to remind myself of that.

'Have a good look, dear,' Joan urged.

My pulse had quickened. I searched the unfamiliar faces; the middle-aged citizens who were smiling and chatting to each other just a little too self-consciously, the younger element in denim and drab colours. I was struck overall by their ordinariness, their unremarkability, as if a Pied Piper from a polling organisation had danced through the town ensuring that only an absolutely representative cross section of the populace had followed him here.

'Sometimes,' said Joan, who was holding my hand now, 'sometimes even I wonder what I'm doing here. How did I get to be here, protesting about animals, when there are so many other injustices in this world? How come I'm not out on the street protesting about the homeless? Or outside the local hospital protesting against its closure? How come animals? Am I just a sentimental old biddy? And then, there's my daughter! A five-month-old baby and her husband walks out. She hasn't even regained her figure, she's still breast-feeding! Turns out he's been having an affair with the woman down the street for simply ages. And Lorrie didn't have a clue. He's living there now, shacked up three doors down, his car parked on her drive.

'Well, Lorrie needs my support, she needs my help right now, and I am trying to give it. But it isn't easy when I'm down here all afternoon, sometimes all night, when they try to get a shipment away under cover of darkness. But you know what? I said to her, "Do you think I should give it up, Lorrie? Would I be more help to you if I did?" And she said, "No, Mama, I don't want you to. Not in my heart of hearts. I think it's important." That's what she said to me. Don't you think that was nice?'

'I do,' I said. 'Oh, Joan, I do.' A surprising rush of emotion flooded me, and I squeezed her hand in both of mine.

There was no sign of Miriam. Perhaps I had been mistaken. Perhaps they had been here yesterday and left already. Everything was hushed and watchful, but the only really discomforting thing, now that I came to think about it, was the silence of the police who stood on the other side of the barrier, in their black helmets and their visors, watching us. I had this suspicion that they relished the menace the riot gear lent them, that they were actually enjoying this on some deep, unconscious level, that it lent them importance after the nights spent fruitlessly patrolling through darkened streets, pulling up a kid here, only to discover he was under the age of criminal responsibility, stopping a motorist there, only to find the breathalyser negative; and especially, that this was welcome after the reams and reams of forms they had filled.

This was so easy for them. No, my instincts were all with the demonstrators: I wanted to take my chances in the front line, facing the indiscriminate force of under- educated police. I still knew the recipe for Molotov cocktails. Looking round, I caught Jenny's eye and I thought, 'Why! she isn't much older than me after all! She'd have been in her teens in the sixties, I'd bet. This is the natural place for her to be; it's not such a surprise at all.' I wished I could tell her that I, too, would have liked to have made a stand, small though it may have been – a tiny grunt of outrage – at what had been lost from the broad range of dreams of our youth, because somehow people like us didn't quite catch the changes when they had happened. We were not awake when factory farming took over, just as we were not aware that our idealism had altered into rampant materialism. We had let everything slip to live in stripped pine splendour.

'Lorries due at two,' someone said, and the message spread, like Chinese whispers.

Jenny appeared at my side. 'Do you have a picture on you that we could pass round?'

I shook my head. The only photograph I carried on me was several years out of date: it showed Miriam in her school uniform, aged eleven, her first day at her new school. She was still a child in that photo, with a child's guileless grin; and I suddenly realised why I had never swopped it for a more recent example.

How pathetic I was! And Michael was no better, trying to recapture a simpler time by moving to a simpler place. He wanted to metamorphose into a younger version of himself, the idealistic one, who was going to make such a difference.

There was a grinding rumble of heavy engines. The convoy had arrived, throbbing, in low gear, towards us. The crowd must have surged forward; my hips and stomach were pressed against the barrier, my arms pinned to my side. No one heard my cry of pain above the crescendo. A young woman next to me, with wild corkscrew curls cascading around her shoulders, was ululating fiercely. I thought I could hear the bleat of frightened animals. There were gaps in the metal sides of the lorries, through which I could glimpse the soft, dun-coloured flanks of the animals. I had drawn a study of a cow for my art A level; forever after, I was entranced by their wide wet noses, their warm hay breath, their bulbous, brown eyes on opposite sides of their skulls.

Joan, next to me, was huffing and groaning, as she was pushed against the barrier. She was winded, I thought, and in pain. The policeman on the other side of the barrier had a hand on her shoulder; he was pushing her back blindly, his head turned in the direction of the convoy as it inched towards and behind him.

Something hit him, I believe. Something thrown from the crowd. He turned suddenly, and knocked Joan backwards, his forearm striking her chin. I fastened onto his arm with both my hands, and pushed it away, so that he staggered and almost fell. This was done wordlessly. It seemed as if I had crept inside a newspaper photograph, an item on the television news, as if I were acting a part.

Then I saw her: Louise Carrington first – twenty, maybe thirty feet to my right, where the road curved, waving a placard which said, in badly scrawled felt pen: Stop This Trade in Blood!!! Those three exclamation marks were so childish that I knew instantly that Miriam had written out the slogan. I sensed her youthful indignation, which could only be expressed in punctuation.

Miriam was in front of her. The edge of her nostrils had gone red as they always did when she was trying not to cry. There were deep purple shadows under her eyes, a muddy splodge on the front of her jacket, as if she'd been sleeping rough or something. She looked thin and pale and unkempt. *My* daughter. That almost concave stomach of hers was pressed against the barrier, where the crush of the crowd impelled her. Her mouth was open in a jagged shape. I knew she was in pain.

I gained that superhuman strength that mothers find in an emergency and pushed my way, against the tide, through the pressing mass of elbows, shoulders, backs, chests. Each time I looked up, they loomed closer.

I fell once, lost my balance, tumbled onto hands and knees. A boot thwacked my jaw. I managed to struggle up; the heels of my hands were grazed, my jeans torn.

'Miriam!' I was nearer; she might hear me. 'Miriam!' My voice was lost in the general babble.

She was crying now, tears spilling over her pink-rimmed eyes. Louise Carrington was yelling at the tail end of the convoy, she hadn't noticed.

I hurled myself through bodies, struggling back the way we had come. Then I was through in an eerie rush, as if a force of nature had parted the crowds for me, and I was standing in front of Louise. It was funny; the battle-cry died in her throat; she gaped at me, slack-jawed. But had she said in her oleaginous, deceptive way, 'Eleanor, well, it's nice to see you,' I would not have been surprised.

Like Miriam, I could not express my fury and my relief in mere words. I felt my hand on its trajectory, jerked like a puppet's, like a mother's. ('Mum?' Miriam said.) I snatched the placard from Louise. She released it instantly as if it were red hot. ('Mu-um?') I brought the placard down on Louise Carrington's head.

It wasn't very solid. It cracked and splintered so that Louise Carrington's face poked through the centre, her hair awry and her lower lip torn, gory. She put a hand up, through the centre of the placard, felt the cut, stared at the blood on her fingers.

I had torn one of my fingernails, badly, near the quick. I remember looking at the red line and thinking, Oh, shit! because they'd taken me an age to grow to the right length and file to the right curve.

'Shit!' I said, looking at my nail.

'God! Mum!'

Before I could respond, somebody grabbed my arm, twisted it behind my back, so that a new pain, a burning sensation in my shoulder, was added to the smarting of my finger.

I was hoisted somehow over the barrier. I struggled, twisted, kicked out. There was a muffled curse. I found myself propelled, accompanied by a stream of invective from my captor, who I now realised was a policeman. I seemed to be under arrest. He half threw, half pushed me through the doors of the van, and the crowd nearby cheered me, as a heroine.

I sat in the van.

This sounds daft, but I was examining my fingernail. I was concerned about it.

The cell sobered me up. The horror of the door opening onto this grim space and its locking behind you; that experience makes you small and frightened on the instant. The cell itself seems so foreign, so totally, so thoroughly not of your experience, despite the succession of police series you have caught, over the years, on television. You know the door will be metal, you know the bolts will clang, but you are still unprepared. Nothing in your middle-class life has brought you close to a police cell before.

Some previous occupant of the cell had been a smoker; the bare concrete floor was littered with butts and the air had that tired, bitter, wrinkled after-scent to it. I stood for a moment, my arms folded across my chest, like a corpse's. To tell the truth, I was frightened to move, because at that stage, I would become a part of this scene, I would truly inhabit this cell.

In front of me was a wooden bed topped with a thin plastic mattress; above this a reinforced window constructed of those thick, wavy glass blocks. An insect, transparent, segmented, with many legs, scurried confidently from the drain on the floor, and circled once, twice. By this stage I was so totally lacking my own will – I was *squashed* somehow, after the elation of the demonstration – that it didn't cross my mind to grind it beneath my heel. Instead, I hopped on my tiptoes to the bed, and perched on its edge, trying to draw myself together, so that as little of me as possible should come into contact with anything in the room.

I looked around. The cell was maybe twelve feet by eight, painted a cold, institutional grey, upon which graffiti jeered at me, strong swear words in a multi-coloured crowd. '*Fuck the pigs*', said one entry, and I was surprised that the insult remained in use, I would have thought the young of today should have managed some new invective. Someone had turned the buzzer into the nipple of a pencil breast. Above this, '*I was here 2/4/96*', was written in a free, extravagant hand; '*I'm innocent*' in a tiny, cramped script. '*So am I*', someone else had daubed adjacently, and the voice in my mind was piping up to agree when it struck me that I probably wasn't. I had, after all, assaulted Louise Carrington, and only she and I knew how much she had provoked me. A ripple of awareness disturbed the placid surface of my mind; I was still partially in a state of unreality, when the truth of what has happened is skittering somewhere outside full comprehension. It was better to remain disconnected.

After a while, I realised that in my hand, somewhat crumpled, were the leaflets explaining my rights which I had been given by the officer when I'd arrived. I arranged them in a fan shape on the mattress. I didn't want to read them. I hadn't paid attention when, after I'd answered his questions – name, address, age, next of kin, medical conditions, for heaven's sake – he'd run through my rights verbally. He was very efficient, imperceptibly condescending. His eyebrow rose faintly at some of my answers: he did not want me to reconstruct my bourgeois exterior.

A draught plucked at my ankles. Bending down, elbows tucked in, remaining as small as possible, I spied, beneath the bed, an air vent. I had left my cardigan in the car, thinking I would return for it if it turned blowy.

'Behave yourself now and I'll bring you a cup of coffee,' said a male voice, presumably the sergeant, to someone unseen nearby.

'Fuck off,' said the unseen one.

A chant rose nearby. *'Pigs eat veal! Pigs eat veal! Pigs eat veal!'* The livestock protestors. A shrill young voice shouted something. A telephone. A siren starting its spiralling vortex of sound: *whoo . . . whoo . . . whoo.*

The strip light wavered. My watch hands continued their impassive rotation. I was waiting for Michael and I blamed him for the passing of the hours. I had called him at work.

'He's busy, he'll call you back,' the new temp said.

'Tell him I'm under arrest and he'll talk to me now,' I said.

There was silence from the temp at that point, and a silence from Michael, too, as he listened to me, except that his breath echoed with a gaspy, hurried sound. Then, he said, 'I'll be right down.' He was exasperated; his device for making me feel inept and over-emotional. He was concerned; he was a rock on which to lean. Could have been either, could have been both.

There were only two places Miriam could be. Either she was waiting for me here, or she was with Louise Carrington, had accompanied her to the hospital, presuming that Louise had needed to be checked over. Michael would find Miriam, I told myself But, of course, I was worrying for her safety, the old familiar worry mixed in with the new ones. And somewhere, underneath all this, I was also sick with nerves as to which of us, her two mothers, the real and the assumed, Miriam had chosen at this moment.

You always see everything as a competition, I told myself. You are so possessive. You are so insecure. But of course I was; I was preprogrammed to be. I suddenly felt so alone, so marooned and abandoned, as if all the links that connected me to other people, the casual links of good will and common concerns which I shared with this motley band of demonstrators, the serious, family links of blood and vows, it was as if they had all snapped in a flash of truth, of growing up, of

knowing, finally – *really* – that we are each of us on our own.
I had known that as a teenager, with a teenager's ruthless clear
sight, and Miriam knew it, too, which was why she was here.
But somewhere along the road, I had forgotten, or pretended
to.

'Shall I get you some Frizz Ease,' I once offered Miriam, the
morning before a party.

'No,' she said. 'Why?' And she looked at me with something
like impatience pulling at the edges of her mouth. 'I wouldn't
look like *me.*'

'You're right,' I said, and felt stupid.

'You should have some confidence, mother,' she added
pointedly. When was it that she had first begun assessing me?

But she had no idea of how dearly I had wanted that gift for
myself. To be confident! How miraculous! How transforming!
It would change everything, like being born again. But unable
to acquire it for myself I had determined that she should have
it in my stead. All the attention, the praise, the willing her
forward and upward and on, had been to that end. It was a
shock to see how well I had succeeded.

Now she stood on her own two feet. How easy it was for
a child to be rid of her parents; you read about American
children divorcing their parents and you envisaged a whole
legal formality, a process from A to Z, through courtrooms and
learned judges. There was a satisfying drama to the notion. But
here, it was a simple unremarked matter, a little omission, that
the courts and the police did not feel it worth their while
recovering a teenager who'd moved away from home, or that a
parent wasn't quite sure what to do.

I hadn't wee-ed since the morning and the lager I had drunk
at the Bull at lunchtime – cold through the froth, tasting bitter,
reminiscent of student unions – was pressing on my bladder.
There was a lavatory bowl to the right of the bed, but no paper,
no wash basin to wash your hands, and on the wall directly
opposite was a spy-hole. I didn't put peering at a woman on
the loo past the policemen I had encountered.

A whole parade of unrelated incidents returned, out of the
blue. Eating hot porridge with cold top of the milk and

crunchy brown sugar on winter mornings before school. Getting drunk at college and waking in the night with the room spinning round; taking a glass of water and waking in the morning feeling fit as a fiddle. A dog capering in front of me as we walked across a field. Miriam, on a gravel drive, shortly after she had learned to walk, clinging to my hand, and me having to lean, to walk lopsided, because she was so small. I remembered waking one Sunday to a clatter from the kitchen, the soft thud of cupboard and fridge doors, which told that Miriam was making us breakfast in bed; and we lay on and on, though we were longing to get up, until there was an almighty clatter, a storm of sudden tears, because she had dropped the tray on the stairs.

I saw her jumping bamboo canes balanced on milk bottles in the garden, pretending to be a horse. Her crying, 'Mum? Is that you?' eagerly, before I'd got the door fully open. When had that petered out? I saw a present-day Miriam saying, 'I can take care of myself. I'm old enough and ugly enough,' though she was a skinny whippet of a girl, with wrist bones so frail it seemed as if you could snap them with your bare hands, a hobbledehoy kind of a girl, impulsive and too young to be afraid.

I crossed my legs. A chant began in the next cell once more, loud and insolent. I jumped up and paced the floor, five paces, that was all you could squeeze in before you had to turn.

I was on my sixth lap and it was three and a half hours, near as damn it, since my arrest, when the door opened and the sergeant told me we were all being released without charge. 'Softly, softly, says the powers that be. Bridges to build with the local community.' He seemed to doubt the wisdom of this.

In the corridor, the other doors swung back. Some spiky, punky girls from the quayside sauntered out, chewing gum and brandishing clenched fists at each other, followed by an elderly lady, tearfully nursing her wrist. She fastened on to me immediately. I lent her my arm.

'I'd never have believed it,' she said. 'Police acting like Fascists. They pushed me to the ground. I'm going to make a complaint, I am, I don't care what they say.'

I patted her elbow and uttered soothing words. Her name was Elsie, she said. I led her towards the room where we had had to surrender our handbags. We collected our belongings and filed out. In the corridor, a handful of people waited on benches; two of them jumped up at the sight of Elsie, an elderly man with a pinched, angry, frightened expression, and a woman in her thirties in a blouse with an incongruous pie crust frill.

'Here's your mother,' said the man.

The woman rose. 'Mother! Oh, mother, how could you? I knew it would end like this.'

'I hope we've heard the last of this nonsense, now, Elsie,' the man rumbled. 'This is the giddy limit, it really is.'

But I forgot her then, because Michael was rising from the end of the bench.

He enfolded me in his arms. 'How's my gaol bird, then?' he said. Then he stepped back, took my shoulders, examining me. 'You've paid your debt to society; now, Mrs Banyer, you're coming home,' he said.

I looked behind him. No one. No Miriam.

He knew what I was doing by husbandly ESP. 'She's quite safe. She went to the hospital with Louise Carrington.'

'Oh,' I said in a small voice. 'I thought she might.'

Michael steered me out of the station, buckled me into my seat in the Jeep. We found the car park where I had left the hatchback. The low breeze-block building hunching to one side was a public lavatory and I hurtled in, ignoring the stench, the pools on the floor, the absence of paper or hot water. When I came out, Michael was waiting right by the entrance. He hadn't uttered a word of recrimination; it seemed that suddenly he understood how I felt, probably was ashamed for having entrusted Miriam's safety to a harum-scarum, scatty piece like Louise Carrington. And I hadn't uttered a word of recrimination either. I felt proud of myself

I thought I'd lost the key to the hatchback. It was sitting in the side pocket of my handbag all along, where I always keep it, but I hunted right through every section, balancing purse and cheque books and telephone upon the bonnet before I located it. I promised Michael I was OK, I was fine, I would follow him home.

It seemed to me for the first twenty minutes of our journey, as we negotiated the one-way system, swinging west onto the trunk road, that my car was playing up. It jerked and shuddered. I thought of signalling to Michael to pull over, so he might check my tyres, but as we stopped at traffic lights, I realised that it was me causing the car to jiggle. Tears were coursing down my cheeks and I was shivering compulsively, even my foot, so that it jogged on the accelerator.

In this erratic way, I lurched home.

Once there, I went straight to bed. I had had enough.

I awoke to the burble of the fax machine. I lay listening to its tickety, clickety dots of noise competing with a soft thrumming which told me it was raining, quite heavily. My jaw ached. My finger throbbed. Whatever time it was, it was so dingy outside that the bedroom was choked with gloom. I flicked on the bedside light, and the fax beeped and went quiet. When she was eleven, Miriam's party turn was a very amusing imitation of a fax machine receiving a complicated diagram. Miriam! I sat up, too quickly, so that the room span slowly, then I inched my way across the carpet, onto the landing, down the stairs.

A long pale tongue of paper lapped from the slit of the sleek, black machine, spilled over the edge of the table and lay on the floor quietly. I bumped on my bottom down the last steps and examined it. The typing said it was some kind of official letter from the estate agents. I dropped it and swayed into the kitchen.

There was a note from Michael on the kitchen table.

Sorting everything out. I know I have handled Miriam badly. Country life can wait.
                    Love Michael.

And after this, there was a kiss and smiley face.

I smiled back at the face, but sadly. Michael had never found

224

it easy to tell me how he felt about me. That was as near as he ever nudged. A kiddish doodle. I'd felt so bold and liberated about proposing to him, but now I realised it had been the only way to get matters resolved between us.

The door bell shrilled. I peered round the jamb. Two female figures were visible, in blurred, indistinct patterns, through the stained glass. I rushed forwards. The figures resolved themselves. It was Phyllida and Jane. I backed away but there was a squawk, 'Ah! Eleanor, you are there. Hurry up! It's pouring cats and dogs out here.'

'Hello, lovey, we're just bringing Michael some keepsakes,' Jane said as I opened the door onto a blast of damp air. She was holding a brown carrier bag. They clomped into the hall and stood dripping onto the tiles. Jane registered my pyjamas. 'You ill?' she said. 'Maybe you've the bug. I've been feeling so poorly, I can't tell you.'

Phyllida dumped her carrier on the floor, where a puddle spread from it slowly, and marched into the kitchen. 'I could slaughter a coffee,' she called back at me. 'Thought one of you might be in. Saw the light on upstairs.'

I got out the cafetiere, coffee; I boiled water. Phyllida was wearing a tracksuit, and Jane, jeans. Jane's hair was tied up and her long, pale face looked spectral without the habitual framing frizz. Plainly, they were in the middle of an almighty clear-out of Ann's house.

'How is your mother bearing up?' I asked them.

'She's being awfully stubborn about coming,' Jane said.

I plonked the coffee mugs on the table and subsided onto the chair between them. Phyllida was pretending she wasn't reading Michael's note upside down in front of her, but then she blurted out, 'Where's Miriam? What does this mean?' poking at it with her stubby forefinger, so I was forced to fill her in, which I wanted to do as briefly as possible, with no reference to the events of yesterday. I couldn't quite face Phyllida's commentary on yesterday.

'She's staying with this woman she works for,' I said. 'And it's all rather complicated because Michael wants to move to Norfolk and Miriam doesn't want to go.'

'Oh,' Phyllida said. It was a gloating kind of an oh, I thought. 'And you're not happy about it?'

'No,' I said.

'She can live with us, if you like,' Jane offered. 'We're commutable to London.'

'So that's why she wasn't at the funeral,' Phyllida said. 'Has there been some sort of row?'

I took a gulp of coffee and the steam stung my cheeks and my eyes while the liquid scalded my mouth.

'Do you remember,' said Jane, 'when I wanted to go to boarding school? The tears! The tantrums I staged!'

Phyllida gave her a distracted glance.

'Boarding school?' I said. 'Did Ann mind?'

'Said she didn't. But she did underneath, wondering what was wrong with the home she'd created for us. My father said he couldn't afford to send me, that was the official reason for the parental refusal. I'd probably have hated it. I thought it was going to be Mallory Towers.'

'So tell me about Miriam,' Phyllida said. 'Maybe I can help.'

'Has Daisy gone?' I said.

'This morning. Don't change the subject.' Phyllida fetched the milk bottle, topping up all three mugs without asking, scooping sugar into her own. 'You've got to put your foot down, Eleanor.'

'Oh, I agree,' Jane said. 'You read about this sort of thing in the papers. Teenagers are all at it nowadays, you know, especially the girls. They get fed up with their parents. Get themselves taken into care, then go on the rampage. It happened to someone I know.'

'But . . .'

'That's what she'll do. Children's rights, you see. Everyone bends over backwards to accommodate them.'

' . . . it's not as easy . . .'

'Oh, it is, believe me,' Phyllida said. 'Look what happened to Jane's friend.'

'Huh?'

'Lucky you didn't hit her,' Jane said. 'My friend's daughter claimed assault, claimed she was in danger. She was bored, that was all.'

I didn't hit her but I did shake her, said the voice in my head. A panic stirred within me.

Phyllida was nodding sagely. I looked across the table at the two sisters with their wide grey eyes and the freckles across their noses, the one face plump and apple- cheeked, the other pale, straight and thin. They looked so plausible. 'Before they knew it, she was ruined. Social workers just let her run amok. Boyfriends. Under-age sex. Drugs.'

I put my head in my hands and felt the hot tears course onto my palms. My nose was running.

'No wonder she's upset,' Jane said to Phyllida. 'I was so upset that time Eddie stormed out the house and I thought he'd gone for good. Found him dodging behind the ladders in the garage four hours later. Do you remember, Phyl?'

Phyllida chooked her tongue and put her arm around me. 'There, there,' she said. 'First things first. I'll make us all some more coffee, then we can lay a plan of action. Do you think Michael's hunting out a good solicitor?'

But all I could do was gulp down salt tears and chunks of air. I seemed to be having trouble breathing, as if Phyllida and Jane had sucked all the oxygen from the air.

Chapter Twelve

It was midday by the time the sisters left and my spirits were low. They hung around, hoping to catch Michael and discover what he had been up to, but in the end they had to go; they had promised Ann they'd be back by lunchtime and they had to drop various boxes and bags at Phyllida's on their way. When they'd gone I opened the serrated lips of the paper bag; inside, there was an extraordinary collection; an old watch which appeared to be broken – certainly, I did not remember ever having seen Richard wearing it – a pile of school reports dating back to the thirties, a dusty cummerbund and bow tie.

I went upstairs, showered, changed. As I opened the curtains, the Jeep drew up outside, Miriam in the passenger seat, her cheek, in profile, white and bloodless, her hair looking matted and uncombed. She did not glance up at the house, not as Michael parked, not when he opened her door and took her bag, not when they walked up the path. It was an omission I found significant, and a little tide of dismay lapped through me. I remained in the room for a moment. I didn't want to gambol towards her if she was going to be begrudging and resentful. It would start everything over on the wrong foot.

I smoothed my tunic in the mirror, ruffled my hair with my fingers, and by the time I opened the door, she had reached the top step, and was across the landing from me. She froze for a second, her eyes with that blank stare that looked almost frightened and almost contemptuous, and which I never quite knew how to take. Her mouth opened and closed.

'Mum,' she said, as a greeting.

'Miriam.' I was unsure what to say.

She dropped her eyes to the floor and edged into her room, closing the door. She felt remorseful – that was it – but by then it was too late to react.

The ripple started up again. I felt . . . forlorn, is the word. I'd got it all wrong. She probably thought I was acting cold and offended. I went down to talk to Michael.

He was in the kitchen, unpacking the carrier bags, and it wasn't the time to ask him questions, either. The contents of the bags told their own story. He laid the items on the kitchen table, each in a neat, little square of space, then stood back and examined the still life he had composed. Phyllida's carrier had contained a King James version of the bible, black with a flicker of gold to the leaves; a silver cigarette case, very old and dented, Richard's tweed cap.

Richard's tweed cap! I stared at it, the inside discoloured from many years of wear, from the hair oil he used, I supposed. I picked it up. It still retained its Richard smell.

'I wonder if your mother knows this is gone?'

Michael clamped his lips, raised his eyebrows. He was fighting down emotion. 'We can take it back,' he said.

I laid the cap on the table and Michael sat down in that very male way, legs apart, taking up so much space in a confined area, with that throwaway assurance I had always loved. I put my arms round his shoulders; my chin on the top of his dark head. He placed his hand on top of mine.

We remained like that for some moments, and then, just as my back was beginning to ache, Miriam appeared at the door, having descended from her room more quietly than ever before in living memory. We sprang apart.

Michael brought himself back from his reverie. 'We'd better fill your mother in on what we've agreed,' he said.

Miriam sidled into the kitchen, stopping as she caught sight of the items on the table. Her face crumpled, ugly with grief,

and Michael rose and took her in his arms. She said something
to him; it was muffled by Michael's shoulder, but it sounded
like 'Sorry, Dad'.

I turned my face away. At that moment there was nothing
else for me to do.

In the books I read as a teenager, the characters I liked best
were expansive and generous – they overlooked things. They
were people, in short, who seemed as far removed as possible
from my parents, with their endless totting up of private scores
and their habitual niggling at each other. It doesn't work
like that, though, does it? Before a sentence is finished, true
emotions swing from love and gratitude to irritation and
resentment. At least, that's how it is with me, and that's how it
was when Michael perched at the edge of a chair in the sitting-
room, with Miriam lounging against it, kicking one trainer
rhythmically against the other, and he told me how he had
resolved our dilemma.

Michael's hands hung between his knees, as he fiddled with
something – the broken watch and its leather strap – while he
talked. He had withdrawn his resignation, he told the watch,
revolving it. He had given up his pipe dream of Norwich, then.
It was a sacrifice. A surge of gratitude flooded me. The firm
had offered him more money to stay on in any case, he continued. Well, he'd never told me *that.* The warmth was
replaced by a chafing of indignation. Would no doubt have
never told me, had events not taken this twist. I did not keep
important matters secret from *him* . . .

But my misfortune is to always see the other point of view.
I was back in the car with Daisy.

'*Will you tell him?*'

'*Not now.*'

I interrupted him. 'Michael?'

He looked at me, with a querying eyebrow.

'I forgot to tell you. We've sold the house.'

'We have?'

'Apparently, the estate agent showed a couple around while
we were out and they put in an offer. I think there's a fax.'

Miriam looked at me for the first time.

'Well, we're withdrawing the house from sale,' Michael said.

A horrible idea was niggling at me. 'But can't the agent demand his percentage anyway?' I said. 'What's one and a half per cent of almost three hundred thousand, for heaven's sake?'

Michael did the sum in his head. 'Four and a half thousand, near as damn it.'

My stomach whirled.

'We'll work it out,' Michael said, so implacably calm I wanted to hit him, but I let it go. He placed the watch, its strap laid flat, on the arm of the chair, and stood up suddenly. 'Let me make some phone calls,' he said, and went off.

When he left, Miriam's lounging took on an awkward air.

'What have you eaten recently?' I asked her with a passable imitation of my habitual mock-severity.

She stood a touch more upright and flashed me a glance. It was as if a light had come on, and I suddenly realised that she was pleased. She wanted me to mother her. It's funny, isn't it, you think you know your family so well, especially your child, you think you can read them like a book, but half the time you're so blocked in by your own inadequacies, your past and your flaws, that you can't spot anyone else over the obstructions.

I went to the kitchen and pulled bread and butter and some cheese from the fridge, and found a packet of vegetable soup at the back of the cupboard. Miriam edged in after me, and stood watching.

'I'm not going to work there any more,' she ventured.

I paused, the knife with a slab of butter poised above the slice of bread. 'You're not,' I said, in as neutral a tone as I could muster.

'See, I had to check she was all right yesterday, so I went to the hospital, and then I called Adrian and he came down on the train and drove us all back. And then, I was going to leave this morning, early, but Dad preempted me, drove up breathing fire from his nostrils. What got me, you see, was when she tried to reassure me at the hospital. She grabbed my hand, and I suddenly thought, "Leave me alone." She's always so touchy-feely and it gets on your nerves after a while. Anyway, she said, "I don't want you worrying and all, Mirry. She's your mother, I won't press charges," and it hadn't crossed my mind, of course, that she would do that, but I knew then that it had certainly crossed hers.'

Sometimes, she was so much more astute than I was. I turned and looked at her, her face in profile, Michael's nose, the expressionless tone, the teenager's pout which didn't actually mean anything malign.

'Anyway,' Miriam continued – she was holding out her left foot, wiggling it from side to side, as if admiring the trainer's design afresh – 'I don't want to be a vet any more. There was a vet at the port, helping the exporters, and I suddenly realised half the time I'd be working for farmers, for some agri-business with cesspit principles. Or I'd be trying to persuade some stupid, middle-aged woman not to keep stuffing her obese poodle full of chocolate. I'd probably spend about a nano-second on indigenous wildlife, or on anything that really mattered. It was like, "Durr!" ' – she slapped the side of her forehead with the heel of her hand and cast her eyes to the ceiling – 'I'm such a durr brain.'

'Oh, no,' I said.

'And I hate doing dissection. Puke, puke. And I've always preferred English.'

'That's true.'

I put a plate of sandwiches in her hand and she tucked in as if she hadn't eaten in days. We could hear Michael, still on the telephone, in the background. Miriam began to wander around the kitchen table, stopping every now and then as if examining the tablescape of Richard's belongings from every angle. She picked up the topmost of the report books, in a faded green, stained cover, and leafed through it. There was a little sniff of amusement. She turned the page towards me, her finger underlining an entry.

'*Games*,' she read aloud. '*Richard is a cautious boy and seems extremely nervous of physical risk. We have spent the summer term swimming once a week but he has yet to get his face wet . . .*

'That's Grandpa all right. Remember at the Isle of Wight? Grandpa's head up above the water like a tortoise while he did breast stroke . . .' Her voice tailed off 'Mum? Mum, I'm sorry about not being here when . . . you know, for Grandpa's funeral.'

'You should tell your father that.'

'I did already.'

'Good girl,' I said and smiled. And suddenly, as if it were a cue in a play, she was hugging me. She was still holding the plate, I felt the rim sticking into my ribs; when we disentangled ourselves there were crumbs down my tunic and a crust on the floor.

'Durr brain strikes again,' Miriam said.

She handed me a cloth from the work surface. While I was wiping the floor, she thundered upstairs, and soon I heard the pipes keening as she showered.

When I first met Michael I loved him blindly. I remember now. I returned from that first weekend at his parents' house, and cornered my best girlfriend in the bar. We drank lager and nattered for hours, bellowing to be heard above the hubbub. I could see Michael through a crowd of people, talking intently with two friends, and while I talked I would check on him, check that he was still there, admiring him, this near stranger whose body was already so familiar. I knew the hard muscle on his shoulder, the rangy, lean stretch of his leg, lightly speckled with dark hair, I knew the intimate parts of him, the soft pouch between his legs and the sudden hardness of a rod of flesh beneath smooth skin. So I kept glancing across, through the reek of spilt beer, the fug of cigarettes, the pulse of a juke box, to his tall, dark head bent in conversation.

I told my girlfriend! – I can see her, now, the mass of wavy mousy hair, the apple-pink cheeks, although her name has faded away – about my visit. I told her of his mother's charm and breeding, of his father's affability, and I added, 'Oh, and he's not spoilt. That is, according to his mother, and who should know better? In fact, she says he's used to taking orders from women.'

234

'Oh, Eleanor,' my friend said, 'Anyone can see he's never taken an order in his life.'

Well, I couldn't see it, though heaven knows, it was plain as the wide, thin set to his mouth at certain moments, and the flicker of stubborn pride in his eye.

When did I first see that there was another side to his mother, of haughty self-approval, another side to his father, of bone-crushing shyness, another side to Michael? But afterwards, when I did see this clearly, I was no more circumspect, for otherwise why had I performed the same trick with Miriam? Apparently, I was bewitched.

I had expected her adolescence to bring disillusionment, but only hers with me. I feared the ready verdicts that a callous teenage judge might pass. Like Anthea, I had been frightened of my child not liking me. It had never crossed my mind that there would be an echoing disappointment – mine in her. Now my eyes were open and I saw her as she really was, stripped of her childish charms. Finally, I saw my daughter's flaws. And that was the hardest part of growing older. In fact, it was the moment that withered me. Truly, I had stopped living in my dream world.

But actually, it didn't matter.

Like the one in my wallet, the photographs of Miriam on my bedside table were years old, and needed replacing. A beam from the street lamp caught them, so that I could make out the outlines of heads, silhouettes; the pale half-moon of smiles. The green numbers on the clock radio pulsed and winked from 2.43 to 2.44. My silent clock meant that the only sound to break the sleeping night was the low rumble of the water heater and the tinkling hum of the refrigerator. Those were the noises of our house.

I sat up and edged my way into the blackness, like a blind woman. Michael stirred as I hitched up the covers, and he rolled onto my side of the bed, seeking my warmth. The street lamp shone on his features, the straight nose, the straight dark slash of eyebrows. His snuffly breathing quickened, then he sighed, and fell silent, and he buried deep into my pillow and into deep sleep.

I went to Miriam's bedroom, sensing she was awake. There was a gentle, padded movement of air, suggesting that she had either sat up or flicked the duvet back.

'Mum?' she said.

'Can't you sleep?'

'Not really. Cover your eyes.'

She switched on her bedside lamp and I reeled for a moment. Blinking, I saw her, drowsy and comfortable and younger than during the day, more my Miriam again, more the Miriam of the past. Sitting up, her legs scissoring beneath the duvet, she leaned her head to her knees and yawned, stretching an arm out. Her wrist, thin and pale, with its fine tracery of blue veins on the underside, poked out of the brushed cotton sleeve. She needed new pyjamas. She was still growing.

Her bedroom faced onto the garden and I sat on the cushioned chest by her window and pressed my nose to the glass. It was funny, even at night you could make out most of the back gardens; the residual light of the city, the security lights which the neighbours had installed, the landing lights left on for nervous children, it gave enough illumination. I could see each neat rectangle enclosed by its high wall or fence.

The blind backs of workaday houses, many of them sprouting a conservatory, concealed dozens of lives like ours. Reduced lives, I suppose you might say. Dozens of people of our age, whose dreams had fallen away. Dozens of people who – if you wanted to be ruthlessly honest – didn't have the smallest vision. Dozens of people who weren't going to make much of a difference, bringing up children to be just as they were.

There was so much mounting inside of me, so much that I had to tell Miriam.

'When I was eighteen,' I said to the window pane, 'I discovered that my parents had only just got married. I will never forget it. I will never forget how *alone* I felt, how excluded from the magic circle of knowledge. And I made a sort of promise to myself you know how you do, through clenched teeth – that I would never have – secrets from my children, in my turn.'

Right, I thought. How to continue? I knew what I wanted to

tell her, about how fractured and weedy I had been at her age, how fragmented after the years of being buffeted by my swaying, tottering family. About how little I had known myself.

But would it be wise to tell her where it had led me? To tell her of the back of an estate car and a twist of paper with its instant, chilling promises? To tell her why I had wanted so badly for her to be the strong, self-willed, adamantine creature she so clearly was?

I swivelled on the seat to look at her. Her chin was resting on her tucked-up knees. I thought she had been looking at me, while I stared out into the city half-night, but now her glance flashed quickly down to the mound of her feet. Frowning, she picked at one of the poppers on the duvet cover, clicking it open, pressing it shut. And I saw that she was holding her breath. She didn't want confidences from me, any more than I had truly wanted my father's. She really didn't want time to talk.

A family's silences are important, I saw. Like locked doors. They are a vital part of its structure. They help it keep its shape to the end.

'Anyway,' I said, rather lamely. 'That was a long time ago.'

Her head turned back to me and she smiled. Her relief was almost radiant. She shrugged.

I bunched my dressing-gown around me and stood up. 'When you're young, you think that you'll grow up and you'll somehow *feel* grown-up. But it doesn't work like that. You're still about ten years old inside. You could look down this street at random, pluck just about any adult from behind the identical façades, and what you would find is somebody who inside feels pretty klutzy.' In the doorway, I stopped. 'Do you want some hot milk?'

She was frowning again. I could see her considering my penultimate sentence with a mixture of relief and dismay. But all she said was, 'Oh! No, no thanks.'

She leaned out and fiddled with the light switch. Dark swallowed up the room.

'Mum?' said her voice. I lingered. 'Mum, there is one thing I want to go back to do.'

I said nothing.

'The kestrels are ready for release,' she said. 'I'd like to let them go.'

I nodded.

She knew I had nodded.

'Thanks, Mum,' was all that she said.

During the next few days, we picked up our lives. It felt rather as if we were plaiting trailing ribbons back together again, at least, that it is how I felt, although Michael was the person with the most to do.

Nicola said, 'Well, it's nice to have your mind back on the job. I suppose we're all allowed one walkabout in the course of our careers,' so that I was left in no doubt that I had used up all my chances and would always work now with a question mark displayed behind my head, rather in the way that Nicola's most prestigious invitations were lined up on the shelf right behind her desk.

Michael said, 'When Miriam's gone to university, that's when we'll downshift.'

I put the pictures of East Anglian cottages in the rubbish bag, tied it up, dumped it in the wheelie bin. 'Yes,' I said.

One Saturday evening soon afterwards, Miriam asked me to accompany her to the sanctuary. Reassurances tumbled from her lips and landed in a jumble before me. Louise wasn't there, or if she was she didn't mind, Adrian had said. She'd spoken to Adrian not to Louise, but Adrian was sure to be right. Anyway, she wanted me to go with her.

We strapped ourselves into my dented old five-door. She twiddled with the radio knobs until a loud, beating rendition of an Oasis song rocked the car. She bounced up and down in her seat and warbled to the chorus. The roads were jostling with aggressive Saturday evening traffic.

'You went awfully close to that bike, Mum,' Miriam said at one point. And, 'You will keep this car until I'm seventeen, won't you? I couldn't learn in Dad's car, could I? And you wouldn't insure me for that middle-aged woman's excuse of a sports car you're always on about . . . The light's red, Mum.

'And I was wondering, do you think that Dad has to do vivisection in his line of work?'

I shifted the gear stick into neutral and yanked on the protesting brake. It was hard to elevate my mind into the plane of her stream of consciousness. 'You know that after he insisted we switch to organic meat, and then the government slapped a secrecy order on his work, I've never asked him any questions whatsoever.'

'I bet he does,' she said. 'It's worrying me. Maybe he should have taken the Norwich job, after all.'

'You are very close to death, Miriam,' I told her as I drew away from the lights.

'Yeah,' she said, 'I can see. Flattened in a road accident.'

Louise was standing by the booth when we pulled up outside the sanctuary. When she saw us in the car, she checked her appearance in the darkened window, furtively finger-combing a layer of hair by her ear, then she stood with her head to one side, and a hand restraining her fluttering scarf.

'Miriam. Eleanor,' she said, in what seemed to me like a tight, forced tone.

'Louise,' I said.

'Well, as you can see,' she said, 'there's no harm done.' Her voice was not as lyrical, it seemed to me, or maybe it was just that she had lost her siren-like power over my daughter, and therefore over me.

'Well, I'm glad you're all right.'

Miriam wandered off, casual as could be, taking up a station under a tree.

'Adrian will be glad to see you,' Louise said. She managed a wry smile. 'He says he wants to congratulate you on braining me. Says I'm always steamrollering everybody. The thing is,' she snatched a look at me, 'I never meant to. I don't seem to know when I'm doing it. It's not like I look power-crazed, is it? I don't think of myself as formidable, I don't think, well, Louise, girl, there you are flattening everybody in your path. I kind of think of me as reasonable, looking for compromises, like my Pops taught me.

'I really like Miriam, you know, but I didn't mean any harm. I wasn't trying to make you jealous. If you come right down to it, I think I was trying to make Adrian jealous. And Peter, out in Spain.'

That caught me by surprise. I let out a sigh, an exhalation. I understood her, at long last. What a durr brain, I was! Louise was one of us.

'You know where the kestrels are,' she called to Miriam. I think she was going to follow us along the track, but she was stopped by a young mother with a toddler in a pushchair, wanting to know if she could have her donation back.

'We only came to see the owls.' Her whine followed us. 'My Luke's mad about owls. But we didn't catch a glimpse. They're all asleep or summin' in their boxes . . .'

'Well, they are nocturnal,' Miriam said to the air as she pounded down the track in front of me. How did anyone so slight always manage to shake the ground when she walked?

Adrian, bulky and cumbersome Adrian, was waiting by a garden shed.

'Yo!' he cried, when he saw Miriam. 'And Mrs B! Wicked! How's your pulverising bionic arm? How's your right hook?'

'It's in perfect working action, Adrian,' I told him levelly and he wheezed with laughter, belly jiggling, shoulders hunching, so that his round, goggly spectacles slipped down his nose. He pushed them back to the bridge with his fore-finger.

The middle pane of glass in the shed window had been removed and replaced by chicken wire. I peered in, my nose brushing the wire strands. I could see greenery inside; also, resting in the crook of a thick branch, the downy yellow body of a young chick, its neck pathetically scrawny and limp. A couple of large bluebottles buzzed upon it. I took a step back, made a nauseated face at Miriam. I couldn't see the kestrels.

Adrian was fiddling with a padlock on the handle. When he had undone it, he handed it to Miriam, opened the door and, ducking, went in. I walked to Miriam's side, took her arm. The kestrels were sitting on a branch at the far end of the shed, huddled together. They stared across at him with those alarming pale eyes above the hooked beaks.

'Oh, my beauties,' Miriam cried, under her breath.

Adrian walked very slowly and carefully towards them, but the shed creaked and tilted with every laboured footstep. Finally, as he neared them, he stretched out an arm and clicked his tongue. There was a flurry. One, then the other, dived into greenery on Adrian's right. They were frightened. Miriam swayed, straining to see, holding her breath.

Suddenly, there was a rush of beating brown, as one, then the other, streaked out of the door, past us, up, up, gaining height, into the sky. It was one of those glorious summer evenings, with clouds splattered, like over-enthusiastic kisses, onto a soft blue sky. The two small, fighter-plane shapes hung for a suspended moment above the suburban roof-tops. Then, as we watched, they spiralled upwards on some thermal current, up and round and up, until they dwindled into two specks in a vast blue freedom. I strained, my eyes screwed up, until the last possible moment, but finally they disappeared, risen beyond human sight, somewhere high, near the underside of the bell jar.

Miriam's face was screwed up, trying to hold the tears within her lashes. 'I did that,' she said. Her voice wobbled. 'I did that.'

Adrian was still watching the sky, a hand shielding his eyes behind their pebbly glasses. He let out a sigh.

'Awesome,' he said finally. 'Miriam, that was awesome.'

Miriam told Ann about the kestrels when we went to see her. It was the weekend before term started again and everybody had descended. Phyllida and Jane had been unable to winkle Ann from her house, so they had taken to spending alternate weekends with her, instead.

When had Phyllida and Jane metamorphosed from the plaited, horsey, wholesome girls of the photographs on Ann's mantelshelf into their meddlesome, offensive selves? But perhaps I was projecting my own irritations onto Ann; she didn't say anything, but there was a certain set to her jaw when

Phyllida started ordering us about which made me wonder,

When Phyllida and her family arrived, I was in the kitchen, which was why I saw her stop in the hall in a comical double-take, doubting her eyes. She took in Richard's cap, triumphantly returned to its peg, and frowned. She pushed out her lips, peeling a strand of skin from the lower one with her teeth. Then, she blew out a puff and continued into the sitting-room.

'Michael?' I heard her say.

'What?'

'Oh, never mind.'

Miriam was saying, 'It was so moving, Grandma.'

I went into the room, did my duty kisses. Ann was bent over a piece of needlepoint, pretending to listen to Miriam. She had rearranged the furniture. The sofa was now in the bay window; the blue Victorian chair was at an angle to the fireplace. I knew why she had done it, and she knew I knew.

'Had to blot the space out,' she had said to us when we first arrived, her eyes lingering on the base of the chair.

'Oh,' I said. I hadn't wanted to know where he had died.

'I want everything about me, but I don't want it all un-altered,' she said. 'Does that make sense?'

'Perfect sense,' I said.

Miriam was continuing with her story. 'I can't describe how I felt, happy and sad and proud, all mixed together.'

'That's quite an accomplishment, dear,' Ann murmured. It wasn't really the sort of story that fired her imagination. She wasn't particularly interested in wild life. Richard, on the other hand, would have loved this story.

Jane, who had caught the tail end, said, 'Oh! Oh! We used to go to a wild life sanctuary quite often when Eddie was small, didn't we, dear? Where is Adam? It was lovely. All these little furry, rabbity things. What were they called? Prairie dogs, that's it. Prairie dogs. You should go there, lovey, if you're interested in that kind of thing. They had a goat which butted me in the back and sent me flying into a cow pat. I laughed till I cried. Now, what was the name?'

Miriam gave her a withering glance and stood up. 'Where're

the boys?' she said, rudely. But she had spotted them, through
the front bay window, and she made off.

'Eleanor,' Phyllida said from the kitchen door. 'Do you make
your turkey gravy with ginger? I see a knob of ginger, in with
the giblets.'

'Er, yes, as you can see, I do.'

There was sharp little intake of breath. 'Tck! Max hates
ginger. Can't abide it. I suppose we could disguise the
flavour . . .'

Adam handed me a sherry. When I looked again I could see
Phyllida manoeuvring the ginger out of the stock pot with a
pickle spoon.

I took a deep breath, and took my sherry to the other side of
the room, stepping over Michael's lanky legs, stuck out straight
in front of him, while he read the newspapers. I plonked
myself in the sofa in the bay window and fumed.

Why did we always have to come here to see his poxy
relatives? And talking of poxy, look at him! He made about as
much effort as a comatose slug, hiding behind the newspapers,
not a word out of him all day. Proposing to him was the
stupidest move I'd ever made . . .

I blinked back tears of frustration and swigged a long, sweet
draught of sherry. Through the soft, undulating glass of the
window, Miriam was racing across the cricket pitch, jêté-ing
into the air from time to time, like some madcap ballerina.
Phyllida's boys were running after her, laughing, all
admiration.

Well, said my equable inner voice; his father has just died so
we have to come here. Also, my parents are in Canada for the
summer, visiting Phil, so we could hardly see them at the
moment.

Miriam was prancing along a bench on the other side of the
cricket pitch now, playing air guitar with great panache. She
looked as pliable and whippy-strong as the silver birch trunks
behind her. It was better to see her as she really was, beautiful
but pitted, whole but marked, qualities and faults. It made her
somehow unobtainable, like one of those semi-precious gem
stones that you stared into and saw flecks of colour far away.

And it was better to be seen as clearly, too.

When I'd first met Michael, I had tried always to look my best, make-up applied, hair washed and swinging shinily, the jeans that showed off my legs. The first couple of times we'd tumbled into bed, I'd slept in my make-up. But then we got past that stage, we got to the stage where we knew we'd be spending the night together, might even simply sleep together, arm linked with companionable arm, flank against warm flank, with no sexual stirrings.

I can still recall how awkward I'd felt, with my cold cream and my pad of cotton wool, in front of his bathroom mirror. I'd wiped all my make-up away and a plainer me stared back. Now I understood how my mother's routine had started: I could see her looking in her mirror, one night long ago, ready for bed with my father, and shivering at the ordinary, accustomed image reflected back at her. So she put down her cotton wool, she pulled out her make-up bag, and carefully, quickly, she re-applied her face.

But I was determined to break the pattern. I walked back into the bedroom, where Michael was hunched over his desk, under the light of an angle-poise, mugging up on something urgently. I climbed into his bed, under the cold sheet and heavy blankets.

He glanced across. 'You get some rest,' he said. 'I'll join you later.'

And I'd realised then that he hadn't noticed, or rather, that he had, but it didn't matter. It seemed natural to him. He wasn't looking for perfection. That was probably when I'd decided to marry him. For even then, I'd seen that at their best marriages are a retreat from the image adopted for the world, the one place your hourly faults are likely to meet with hourly forgiveness. Where it is accepted that love diminishes and that it swells again, to its own pattern, many times in the course of a day, a month, a lifetime.

I smiled to myself over my sherry and suddenly I felt eyes on me. I looked up. Michael was watching me, concerned, his newspaper angled to one side, as a sort of shield against the prying room.

'What's the matter?' he mouthed silently.

'Nothing,' I mouthed back.

He regarded me for another moment, then rustled his papers and returned to reading.

There are ways and ways of saying nothing.

He knew he had heard my great affirmation.